PRAISE FOR M.

C000253734

Tom Clancy fans open to a strong female lead will clamor for more.

— *DRONE*, PUBLISHERS WEEKLY

Superb!

— *DRONE*, BOOKLIST STARRED REVIEW

The best military thriller I've read in a very long time. Love the female characters.

— *DRONE*, SHELDON MCARTHUR,
FOUNDER OF THE MYSTERY BOOKSTORE,
LA

A fabulous soaring thriller.

— *TAKE OVER AT MIDNIGHT*, MIDWEST
BOOK REVIEW

Meticulously researched, hard-hitting, and suspenseful.

— *PURE HEAT*, PUBLISHERS WEEKLY,
STARRED REVIEW

Expert technical details abound, as do realistic military missions with superb imagery that will have readers feeling as if they are right there in the midst and on the edges of their seats.

— *LIGHT UP THE NIGHT,* RT REVIEWS, 4 1/2 STARS

Buchman has catapulted his way to the top tier of my favorite authors.

— FRESH FICTION

Nonstop action that will keep readers on the edge of their seats.

— *TAKE OVER AT MIDNIGHT,* LIBRARY JOURNAL

M L. Buchman's ability to keep the reader right in the middle of the action is amazing.

— LONG AND SHORT REVIEWS

The only thing you'll ask yourself is, "When does the next one come out?"

— *WAIT UNTIL MIDNIGHT,* RT REVIEWS, 4 STARS

The first...of (a) stellar, long-running (military) romantic suspense series.

— *THE NIGHT IS MINE,* BOOKLIST, "THE 20 BEST ROMANTIC SUSPENSE NOVELS: MODERN MASTERPIECES"

I knew the books would be good, but I didn't realize how good.

— NIGHT STALKERS SERIES, KIRKUS REVIEWS

Buchman mixes adrenalin-spiking battles and brusque military jargon with a sensitive approach.

— PUBLISHERS WEEKLY

13 times "Top Pick of the Month"

— NIGHT OWL REVIEWS

GHOSTRIDER

A MIRANDA CHASE THRILLER

M. L. BUCHMAN

Buchman Bookworks

Copyright 2020 Matthew Lieber Buchman

Published by Buchman Bookworks, Inc.

All rights reserved.

This book, or parts thereof, may not be reproduced in any form without permission from the author.

Receive a free book and discover more by this author at: www. mlbuchman.com

Cover images:

Hercules with flares © Senior Airman Julianne Show

SIGN UP FOR M. L. BUCHMAN'S NEWSLETTER TODAY

and receive:
Release News
Free Short Stories
a Free book

Get your free book today. Do it now.
free-book.mlbuchman.com

Other works by M. L. Buchman: *(* - also in audio)*

Action-Adventure Thrillers

Dead Chef
One Chef!
Two Chef!

Miranda Chase
Drone*
Thunderbolt*
Condor*
Ghostrider*
Raider*
Chinook*
Havoc*
White Top*
Start the Chase*
Lightning*
Skibird*
Nightwatch*
Osprey*
Gryphon*

Science Fiction / Fantasy

Deities Anonymous
Cookbook from Hell: Reheated
Saviors 101

Contemporary Romance

Eagle Cove
Return to Eagle Cove
Recipe for Eagle Cove
Longing for Eagle Cove
Keepsake for Eagle Cove

Love Abroad
Heart of the Cotswolds: England
Path of Love: Cinque Terre, Italy

Where Dreams
Where Dreams are Born
Where Dreams Reside
Where Dreams Are of Christmas*
Where Dreams Unfold
Where Dreams Are Written
Where Dreams Continue

Non-Fiction

Strategies for Success
Managing Your Inner Artist/Writer
Estate Planning for Authors*
Character Voice
Narrate and Record Your Own
Audiobook*

Short Story Series by M. L. Buchman:

Action-Adventure Thrillers

Dead Chef

Miranda Chase Stories

Romantic Suspense

Antarctic Ice Fliers

US Coast Guard

Contemporary Romance

Eagle Cove

Other

Deities Anonymous (fantasy)

Single Titles

The Emily Beale Universe
(military romantic suspense)

The Night Stalkers
MAIN FLIGHT
The Night Is Mine
I Own the Dawn
Wait Until Dark
Take Over at Midnight
Light Up the Night
Bring On the Dusk
By Break of Day
Target of the Heart
Target Lock on Love
Target of Mine
Target of One's Own
NIGHT STALKERS HOLIDAYS
*Daniel's Christmas**
*Frank's Independence Day**
*Peter's Christmas**
Christmas at Steel Beach
*Zachary's Christmas**
*Roy's Independence Day**
*Damien's Christmas**
Christmas at Peleliu Cove

Henderson's Ranch
*Nathan's Big Sky**
*Big Sky, Loyal Heart**
*Big Sky Dog Whisperer**
*Tales of Henderson's Ranch**

Shadow Force: Psi
*At the Slightest Sound**
*At the Quietest Word**
*At the Merest Glance**
*At the Clearest Sensation**

White House Protection Force
*Off the Leash**
*On Your Mark**
*In the Weeds**

Firehawks
Pure Heat
Full Blaze
*Hot Point**
*Flash of Fire**
Wild Fire
SMOKEJUMPERS
*Wildfire at Dawn**
*Wildfire at Larch Creek**
*Wildfire on the Skagit**

Delta Force
*Target Engaged**
*Heart Strike**
*Wild Justice**
*Midnight Trust**

Emily Beale Universe Short Story Series

The Night Stalkers
The Night Stalkers Stories
The Night Stalkers CSAR
The Night Stalkers Wedding Stories
The Future Night Stalkers

Delta Force
Th Delta Force Shooters
The Delta Force Warriors

Firehawks
The Firehawks Lookouts
The Firehawks Hotshots
The Firebirds

White House Protection Force
Stories

Future Night Stalkers
Stories (Science Fiction)

ABOUT THIS BOOK

When sabotage threatens the US Air Force's newest gunship, there's only one woman to call.

An AC-130J "Ghostrider"—the latest variant of America's most lethal aerial gunship—goes down hard in the Colorado Rockies. Except the flight data doesn't match the airframe. Air-crash genius, and high-functioning autistic, **Miranda Chase** leads her NTSB team of sleuths in to investigate.

But what they uncover reveals a far greater threat—sabotage.

If she can't solve the crash in time, a new type of war will erupt. One far too close to home which threatens to shatter her team.

A list of characters and aircraft may be found at:
https://mlbuchman.com/people-places-planes

PROLOGUE

Tacoma Narrows Airport, Gig Harbor, Washington
Elevation: 295 feet
(1900 hours Pacific Daylight Time)

Miranda's laptop barely fit on the end of the plywood workbench in her airplane hangar. One of Jeremy's ever-expanding projects was squeezing her aside, but she managed to hang on long enough to deliver her latest report.

She selected Upload on the NTSB's secure server. Her report "Airbus A320neo excursion from runway and collision with taxiing 737 at SFO" was complete and ready for final peer review.

It had led to a large number of jokes about Boeing versus Airbus that had seemed irrelevant to the destructive mechanical interactions of the two aircraft or the fatal error to the pilot who had caused them.

She had to blink twice at the following screen because it didn't make any sense.

"It's blank."

"What is?" Jeremy didn't look up from where he'd taken over most of *her* workbench. He'd scavenged a full set of cockpit instruments from a mothballed military C-5A Galaxy jet transport on his last trip to Davis-Monthan Air Force Base's boneyard. He was meticulously dissecting, studying, then restoring each one. She appreciated that his thoroughness matched her own, even though they would never be used again. The faint scent of lightweight machine oil permeated the immediate area.

She and her site investigation team—Team Chase they were now called, for reasons that continued to strike her as unfair to the others—were gathered in her hangar at Tacoma Narrows Airport. It was a warm summer day and the main doors were slid back to let the sun in.

Her two planes were parked to the sides of the cozy hangar. There was room for a third. But her team used the Mooney, and she'd never found another plane she wanted more than her Sabrejet. Two planes were sufficient. Their "office" in the back corner was functional and smelled of a Pacific Northwest summer: all ocean, pine, and fresh mown grass...with just a hint of familiar avgas and Jet A fuel.

Through the back wall, the sound of small aircraft taking off to the south occasionally filled the hangar with a cheery buzz. At the brief roar of a twin jet on the nearby runway, she looked up from her screen. She just couldn't break the habit even though there were no windows facing in that direction. It was the sound of Williams FJ44-1 engines, but was it the -1A or -1AP—she couldn't tell without seeing the plane.

Aside from the occasional aircraft, the hangar was far quieter than her agency office at the National Transportation

Safety Board just twenty miles away across the Tacoma Narrows Bridge.

She focused back on her screen, but nothing had changed.

"Our queue is blank."

Mike laughed from where he sat opposite Holly.

The two of them were playing Backgammon. Mike was playing as if he were reading a good book. Holly clearly felt that Backgammon was a blood sport. She didn't roll her dice out of the cup and onto the board—she slammed it down with a crash that threatened to dislodge the wooden slats from the stout spare-parts crate that they were using as a table.

"Why is that an issue? I could do with a break." Mike eased back on the sagging sofa to look at her. "We've been busy campers of late."

"Just play, goddamn it." Holly snarled at him.

Miranda considered pointing out that the more anxious Holly became, the more casual Mike became. She didn't understand it herself, but she'd observed the dynamic before.

It was still unclear if having an intimate relationship was somehow at the core of their verbal swordsmanship, or perhaps their lack of one. Her attempts at studying human emotions as interacting dynamic systems were still providing erratic results long after any merely mechanical systems would have been clearly delineated.

She returned to the queue, which was far more comprehensible, however unlikely.

"I've been investigating accidents for the NTSB for eighteen years. My queue of open tasks has never been empty. There's always been returning metallurgy, additional witness interviews, drafts in need of editing, and so on." And now there was nothing. "The lack is...disconcerting." With Mike's assistance, she was trying to be better about labeling her emotions.

Holly seemed to shift modes between one heartbeat and the next; the cheery Australian appeared in a flash. "Well, goodonya, Miranda. It means we're so awesome that we've gone and solved everything. Let's declare a national holiday. Won't last longer'n a roo hop, so better do it fast. Call your pal Roy and have him declare it right now."

Miranda had actually picked up her phone before she spotted Mike's amused smile. It was interesting that they always seemed to be ready to go three rounds in the verbal boxing ring, yet Mike was Miranda's best gauge of Holly's intentions.

"Ah, a joke." Which she also should have noted based on Holly's abruptly thick Australian accent—Strine, Holly always insisted on correcting her. As spoken in Oz, *not Australia*. Miranda set her phone back down without calling the President. Besides, it was early evening here in Tacoma, Washington.

"I don't want to disturb him as it's almost bedtime in DC. I also note that it's dinnertime and you haven't yet mentioned food, Holly. Are you feeling okay?"

Now that she'd thought of it, she could smell the burgers grilling at the midfield restaurant wafting into the hangar. Simple conclusion that the smell had made her think of dinner and then thoughts of dinner had made that awareness conscious. What other unconscious triggers was she responding to? Were the triggers short-term or across a longer framework of experience?

This time there was a bright screech of tires striking pavement and suddenly spinning from zero to eighty or a hundred miles an hour. It was hard to identify a small plane just by the sounds it made landing. The lack of a rear window in the hangar was more irritating the more time they spent here.

"I'd be good-o if Mike played this game faster that a sloth on Xanax. Food, Jeremy."

"Oh, okay. You know, the 1983 version of the artificial horizon instrument was dependent on a gyro mount that should never have lasted as long as they did. The lack of wear is simply amazing considering the number of hours that were logged on that airframe. I was hoping to create a calibration of wear versus time for identifying instrument usage, but I'm having little luck." He moved to a bench microscope.

"We'll have to tell the Air Force that they need shoddier workmanship in the future." Mike turned back to the board, rattled his dice briefly, and rolled a perfect three-five.

"Yank bastard," Holly's Australian drawl was thick, which Miranda reminded herself indicated Holly was enjoying herself no matter what her expression and tone said to the contrary.

He sealed up the home board, knocking one of Holly's pieces back to the bar. Another three rolls allowed him to get all of his pieces safe, and still her lone piece was trapped on the bar.

"Hope you roll snake eyes."

He rolled double fives and cleared the point.

Holly managed to escape and avoid being gammoned by getting off a single one of her pieces before Mike finished clearing the board.

Holly glared at the half empty board—his half. "Are you sure there aren't any crashes, Miranda? Maybe if I dropped a plane on Mike's head we could investigate the death of an American weasel."

"Love you too, Harper." Mike began stowing Holly's pieces.

"Not even a little, Munroe." She helped him.

"It wouldn't work anyway." He snapped the case shut and stowed it on top of the rolling tool case.

"Why's that?" She kicked the upside-down wastebasket she'd been using as a seat. She hit it just right so that it flipped with a loud clang of metal, then a ringing wobble that echoed back and forth across the hangar before it settled upright.

Loud noises were so alarming. Miranda held her cringe for several moments longer.

Sure enough, Holly then slapped it sideways like a soccer ball, sending it skidding loudly over the concrete floor before finally settling beside Miranda's feet.

"Only planes here are both Miranda's. I know you wouldn't risk damaging one of hers," Mike explained.

"Not on your thick head," Holly declared particularly emphatically.

Miranda's Mooney M20V Ultra was the fastest single-propeller piston-engine production airplane there was. And her 1958 F-86 Sabrejet fighter plane was one of the last dozen still flying anywhere, out of over ten thousand built for the Korean War and the decade following.

She didn't believe that either would be damaged by an impact with Mike's head, especially since his skull was unlikely to be significantly thicker than the average human's no matter what Holly said. But dropping one of her planes in such a way that it would impact Mike would imply that it would then hit the ground—and she'd rather not have that happen, notwithstanding the damage to her personnel specialist.

During her moment of inattention, Jeremy's reconstruction project had consumed the last of the workbench; a line of engine gauges (N1 and N2 stage RPMs, exhaust gas temperature, fuel flow, and oil pressure) now separated her from her laptop.

She supposed that it was fortunate that there *wasn't* an accident investigation going on at the moment as she'd have nowhere to work. Over the last eight months, her team had slowly shifted most of their work from the NTSB's Western Pacific Region office into her private hangar at Tacoma Narrows Airport.

Miranda had initially insisted that they use the National Transportation Safety Board's agency office as it seemed both proper and convenient. But as her team had become more and more specialized, particularly in highly classified military mishaps, the isolation of the hangar at TNA had become a better fit than the main office where all of the west coast investigators assumed that everything was open to their inspection.

"Food it is," Holly stepped up behind Jeremy and lifted him physically off his stool. He managed to drop his tools with a clatter before she began walking toward the hangar door with him dangling under her arm. Mike stepped up and grabbed his legs as Jeremy broke out laughing.

It was fortunate for them that Jeremy was little bigger than Miranda herself. She was five-four and Jeremy was an equally slender five-seven. Holly still worked out hard. Perhaps not as hard as when she'd been a Special Operations warrior for the Australian SASR, but she did spend time every day at the weight set beside her and Jeremy's workbench.

Apparently, Jeremy was an easy load.

Miranda picked up her phone and computer, without knocking aside any of Jeremy's instruments, and followed behind them.

Above Aspen, Colorado
Elevation: 39,000 feet
(0300 Mountain Daylight Time)

"DENVER CENTER, THIS IS SHADOW SIX-FOUR."

"Roger, Six-four. Go ahead."

"Declaring an emergency. Depressurization event. Current altitude three-niner-thousand. Request clearance emergency descent to one-five-thousand."

Missy Collins had only been on the Denver Air Route Traffic Control Center desk for six weeks, and she'd never handled an emergency before. She pulled up the checklist on a side screen. Suddenly the hot coffee smell that permeated all Traffic Control Centers tasted stale on the air and her stomach roiled in protest.

"Please confirm Shadow Six-four is declaring an emergency? Squawk seventy-seven hundred." Seven-seven-zero-zero was the official transponder code for an emergency.

"Confirm emergency."

And right away the pilot changed the codes. It flashed brightly on her flight-tracking screen. The four-digit transponder squawk code immediately identified the plane's position if not its type or other status.

She checked the status of all other flights in the area.

Nothing intersecting in the next five minutes. The air routes were generally very quiet at three in the morning—too late for the redeyes and too early for their intercontinental arrivals.

"Shadow Six-four. You are cleared to initiate immediate descent at your discretion. Number aboard?" Next question on the checklist.

"Full crew. Thirteen."

As she watched, the altitude readout dropped to thirty-eight, then thirty-seven. Their rate of descent was dangerously fast, even in an emergency situation. In fact...

Kenneth, the head of her section, had been both kind and relentless in training their team. ARTCC wasn't a job that allowed for inattention, yet he'd found moments to squeeze in additional training at every opportunity. He'd also showed special interest in her, but she still wasn't sure how she felt about that.

Now the training paid off. She slapped the supervisor-call switch. Then, pulling up the plane's filed flight plan, Missy began studying the sector chart.

Kenneth hurried over and patched in his headset beside

hers, "What are we looking at, Missy?" As always at work, his tone was completely professional. They'd had dinner together after last night's shift—the third in as many weeks. He'd been charmingly roundabout with how he'd propositioned her over dessert of brandied chocolate mousse and herbal tea.

She'd turned him down; he was her boss after all. She also had a boyfriend, technically. Vic was very unhappy that she'd left LA, even for the nice promotion offer from Denver Center, and they weren't on speaking terms at the moment. It was becoming clear that he was more upset about having to pay all of the apartment's rent than about her actual departure.

"We have a depressurization emergency on military flight Shadow Six-four. Which is listed as..." she inspected the record, "...an AC-130H. Is that the C-130 Hercules?" She didn't typically interact much with the military planes and was still learning them.

Kenneth whistled softly. "A for attack, C-130 for Hercules airframe, but the H isn't for Hercules. It's actually for the Spectre variant. It means that it's a very nasty gunship with side-firing guns, big ones—like a 105 millimeter howitzer," he held up a clenched fist to demonstrate the bore of the latter, as if she didn't know that 105 mm was over four inches across. He couldn't help himself but to include the extra information.

She'd heard him do that with everyone. And it helped calm her down. Still, she pushed her coffee cup to the very edge of her station.

"Do you know its V-max airspeed? They're descending at two-eight...two-nine...now three-zero-zero knots."

"V-max on the standard C-130 is three-twenty. But on the H variant, I think it's just two-sixty."

"They're in major trouble." She mumbled out as she searched for any problems along their flight path. There was... "Holy shit!"

Crap! Now that would be on the tape forever if there was a future investigation. And if she couldn't help them soon, there would be.

She keyed the radio right away.

"Shadow Six-four, this is Denver Center. Be aware your current airspeed is very high. Also your direct line of descent includes seven of the fourteeners." They stood in a tight cluster barely southwest of Aspen, Colorado.

"Fourteeners?" Was the plane's radio operator's voice more strained? She couldn't tell. The military pilots were even more resolute than the airline pilots. It was the private pilots of general aviation who panicked all the time.

She hadn't known the word fourteeners either until Kenneth had told her about them over last night's dinner. Out-of-state pilots weren't used to mountains reaching that elevation, or the weather systems the mountain peaks generated for thousands of feet higher.

"Mountains over fourteen thousand feet tall. What's your status?" She checked her map for the nearest airports. She needed one big enough. Oh. Maybe... "Kenneth, the Hercules is designed for short-field landings, right?"

He shot a thumbs up into her peripheral vision without interrupting. Kenneth wasn't giving her any corrections, so she must be on track. She appreciated his oversight though. This was escalating too fast in many ways.

She keyed her mike. "Shadow Six-four, can you divert to

Aspen or Glenwood Springs Airport? Each are roughly twelve miles from your current location."

"Total LOC. Negative divert."

Total Loss of Control.

They were falling through twenty-five thousand feet at over three hundred and fifty knots, four hundred miles an hour.

"Roger, Six-four." She looked away from the radar to Kenneth. What could she say from the ground to help the pilots? They'd know they were doomed. This was a cargo plane, not a fighter jet—it wouldn't even have ejection seats.

Kenneth cricked his neck to the side for a moment, then shrugged a little helplessly.

"Denver Center. Status, Six-four?"

"Negative control. Negative recovery." His voice was dead calm. There was a pause, a sound she'd never be able to identify, then he said, "Aw, fuck." He sounded more ticked off than scared.

She hailed him again, but there was no response.

Eleven seconds later, two new radar images appeared alongside the plane.

"That's the wings," Kenneth whispered softly. "Ripped off the plane."

Nine seconds after that it impacted Snowmass Mountain, a fourteener, at twelve thousand five hundred feet, the very top of the ski area.

Missy looked down at the checklist. She managed to get her finger on the phone number for Mountain Rescue, but she couldn't make out the numbers.

"I can't see to call them. I can't, Kenneth. I—"

He rested a hand on her shoulder and picked up the

phone himself. Brushing aside where her tears had blurred the number on the call sheet, he dialed and called out the search teams.

They pulled her off the console and sat her in a small conference room. One of the assistant supervisors conducted the post-incident interview, recording and noting down everything she could recall. When they gave her a fresh mug of coffee, the scent actually made her puke into the wastebasket until she was a weeping, shivering mess.

The assistant super was nice enough to say that it happened all the time after a bad one. He was also nice enough to not mention her weakness when Kenneth checked in on her during breaks in his own round of interviews. Though she could see from his extra sympathy that Kenneth knew.

Fifty-three seconds.

First-call to crash was just fifty-three seconds. That fast—thirteen people lost their lives. She couldn't get around the fact. How could life suddenly be so short?

When they were done, when *all* of this was done and the investigation was over, Missy knew one thing. She was so done with Vic.

She also knew the pilot's final comment, that one final moment when his humanity had slipped past all of his military training, would haunt her for the rest of her life.

Aboard Shadow Six-four
Elevation: 27,000 feet
(23 seconds before impact)

As soon as Lieutenant Colonel Luis Hernandez broadcast the final report from aboard the diving plane— "Negative recovery. Negative control."—he released his seat harness.

The plane wasn't quite in freefall, so he fell into the yoke and flight console. "Aw, fuck." Like it was going to hurt anything now other than his ego. The plane was safely past recovery and no one was left aboard to see anyway.

He pulled off his headset and began climbing uphill through the Hercules' cockpit. He moved fast in the near freefall. Two of the thirteen bodies scattered strategically through the plane had ended up in the aisle and he was forced to crawl over them. They were wearing his and Danny's dog tags. They were also close to their build and coloring just in case anything survived the crash. Hopefully not, they weren't that close because no way did he look like the fake Luis. Homely bugger.

He continued aft quickly, having to struggle to shake off the memory of the last time he'd done this. He'd crawled over the bodies of his own crew when his C-130 Hercules had been shot down in Afghanistan due to insufficient fighter support in a war they never should have been in. He'd fought the plane all the way down—been one of the few to make it. He came to, crawling from body to body looking for other survivors.

At least this time, neither the iron stench of hot blood nor the stinging kerosene of burning Jet A fuel permeated the air. Everyone except he and Danny had been dead before they boarded this flight.

The ladder down to the main cargo deck was easier to

navigate. They were in true freefall now and he could just pull himself along it.

Major Danny Gonzalez had left the forward passenger door open after popping it at thirty-nine thousand feet. Though, Luis supposed, his copilot was just Danny now. Their military rank was one more thing they'd all agreed to leave behind along with the dead.

Luis shrugged into the parachute rig.

He took a moment to ensure that he was oriented properly and then grabbed the bottom edge of the door. It wouldn't do to fling himself out of the plane and straight into the massive four-blade propeller of the Number Two engine spinning at a thousand RPM.

The fuselage twisted sharply and he almost lost his grip as it began to tumble.

Looking out into the darkness once more, he saw that the propeller was no longer an issue—the entire wing had ripped off.

The temperature was a bitch though.

Even on a warm June evening, ten thousand feet above Aspen was damn cold. Be lucky if he didn't have frostbite by the time he got down. But no time to pull on a balaclava—the ground was coming up fast.

He still made a point of flinging himself downward as he exited, just in case the tail was still attached.

As soon as he'd ejected, he opened his black tactical ram-air chute. It was for night insertions deep behind enemy lines, and, like his specialized clothing, had the radar signature of a bird—a small one.

He watched the plane continue down. Less than five seconds after he had his chute deployed and stable, the

Hercules impacted at twelve thousand feet atop a high peak. It was supposed to plunge into the back-country wilderness beyond, but it didn't really matter. At almost five hundred knots, the destruction was more than sufficient.

As rigged beforehand, one of the rounds of 105 mm ammunition for the big howitzer—the main weapon of the AC-130 series of gunships—ignited on impact.

In a single moment, the other eighty rounds lit off.

The combination of all of the forty-two-inch-long, thirty-three-pound rounds igniting simultaneously unleashed sixteen hundred pounds of high explosives in the heart of the plane.

If there had been anything left of the fuselage, it was now shattered. Probably the top of the mountain as well by the scale of the blinding fireball that lit the surrounding mountains like daylight. He hoped that no one was looking in his direction for the one moment he was starkly lit against the night sky.

The wings landed farther down the slope, bursting into flame when the fuel tanks breached. The conflagration spread rapidly upslope. In minutes, any remains of the plane would be engulfed as well.

Perfect.

Then the shock wave caught up with him.

Shit!

"Didn't think of that one, did you, Luis?"

For a thousand feet of descent, he could do nothing but curse and flail as the shock wave dragged him wherever it wanted to.

Once it cleared, he was amazed to still be holding the control toggles. *The wonders of stark terror.*

He hadn't jumped much since Basic, just enough to stay qualified. But the loud roar of the wind had to be a bad sign. Yanking on the toggles didn't seem to do much either.

Not daring to let go in case he couldn't find the handles again, he almost snapped his own neck from nodding hard enough to flip down his night vision goggles. He managed it just in time to see what was happening above him.

"Shit!" He didn't have a parachute. He had a ripped-up mess of tangled nylon. It looked as if half the chute was missing and the rest was snarled.

He yanked the cutaway. The general was going to be pissed if someone spotted the errant chute, but Luis was out of options.

One side of the risers released, but not the other.

Falling sideways.

Dragging the main chute along off his right shoulder.

Glance down.

Out of time.

Deploy the reserve and pray it didn't snarl in the crippled main. It came out clean and almost gutted him with hard deceleration.

He was well past Snowmass, but nowhere near the Aspen car racing track where Danny and their motorcycles would be waiting.

Down below there was no sign of anything except sharp peaks and deep valleys.

The wind still seemed too loud. Up above, two-thirds of the reserve was drawing clean, the last third was fighting with the trailing main—and losing.

"Two thirds has gotta be better than nothing, right?"

A massive edifice loomed up in front of him.

COLONEL HERNANDEZ CLEARED THE SHARP CRAGS OF Willoughby Mountain with feet to spare.

Down the backside, the colonel wasn't in freefall, but his training had taught him that any attempt to slow the chute would only make the entanglement worse.

He hit the scree slope at a forty-five-degree angle. Luckily for him, the head-sized boulders gave way rather than his legs.

But it didn't stop there.

The whole slip face let go. The field of a million rocks began to slide and tumble.

For a brief few seconds, with the support of the collapsing chute, Luis Hernandez managed to dance along the top of the stone avalanche.

He fell.

Rolled once.

Made it back to his feet.

But that single roll was his undoing. The three sets of parachute risers, two from the reserve and one from the main, had wrapped around his upper body like the old cartoon of tying a villain to a chair with a hundred feet of rope.

Unable to move his arms, his balance didn't last another full second.

He remained conscious for the next two hundred feet of descent as eleven and a half thousand tons of rock swept him toward the valley floor. As he tumbled and rolled, his body acted like a fisherman's reel, winding the parachute's riser lines tighter and tighter around him.

At three hundred feet below his initial point of landing, one of the risers sliced off his head. It was all that saved him from being killed by the rocks.

At the base of the scree slope, the mountain built a burial mound—wider than four school buses parked end to end, and over three stories high.

Lieutenant Colonel Luis Hernandez's head, body, and parachutes were near enough the bottom of the pile that the general wouldn't have to worry. No one would ever spot the errant chutes or the man it had killed.

1

Gig Harbor, Washington
Elevation: 37 feet
(0300 hours Pacific Daylight Time)

MIRANDA'S PHONE VIBRATED VIOLENTLY UNDER HER PILLOW. IT slipped into her dream of a single-element plane.

No engines.

No separate fuselage.

Somehow all one, single, unified machine of perfect flight.

Nothing to break.

It flew clean.

Pure white.

Transonic but with no boom to echo across the pastoral land below.

Untouchable by fault or error.

Perfectly silent and safe for—

The phone's second vibration shattered the plane. Not

merely broke it apart but shattered it into a hundred thousand pieces from within.

Her breath caught and she could taste the panic of every soul on board. Somehow they all survived, only to die in the long fall to—

The end of the nightmare was familiar enough, if not the white plane, that her hand only shook a little as she slid it under her pillow to silence the call.

Across the room, Holly mumbled something in her sleep but didn't appear to wake. On the rare occasions when Miranda stayed in town rather than flying back to her island home, she had taken to staying in Holly's spare bed. Holly, Mike, and Jeremy had rented a three-bedroom house in Gig Harbor.

It was a quiet little community just ten minutes from the airport. The cozy harbor was thick with pleasure boats, ringed by houses and then tall conifers atop the surrounding ridge to three sides. To the fourth side, beyond the harbor mouth, was a splendid view of the icy peak of Mt. Rainier; the quiescent volcano soared fourteen thousand feet above all of the surrounding area. The tickling smell of roses blooming outside the just-cracked window floated on the damply cool June air.

Miranda had woken hours ago. Actually, she'd finally given up after a few hours of not really sleeping at all.

Even leaning sideways close toward her parents' picture —the only way she used to be able to tolerate a hug was one-armed and sideways—didn't help.

Normally it did, because the image was so familiar. Her parents in their garden by the house on Spieden Island. Behind them the one-third-sized replica of the enigmatic

Kryptos sculpture at the CIA she'd spent so many hours trying to decrypt with her father. Her mother in her big gardening hat. And herself, carefully not in any photograph, safe behind the camera.

Tonight, all it did was make her miss them all the more.

Twenty-four years ago next month they'd gone down when TWA 800 had exploded over the Atlantic Ocean. Through all the Kübler-Ross phases of grieving, even the anger phase, she'd never stopped missing them.

Unable to sleep, she had sat up in bed and fired up her laptop.

The discussion at dinner had circled around a variety of topics. But one had kept coming back. Once during the fried chicken taquitos appetizer, twice during the main course—two bean enchiladas for her, a monstrous plate of shrimp-and-steak fajitas for Holly, and carne asada burritos for the boys—and yet again over flan and deep-fried ice cream.

Their workspace.

Her personal airplane hangar at the south end of Tacoma Narrows Airport wasn't really up to the task of high-security military plane-crash investigations any more than their Western Pacific Region offices at the NTSB.

After two hours of lying awake and organizing her thoughts, she'd decided it was time to make some changes. Windows, with one-way glass, cut into the walls.

A bigger workbench for Jeremy and a small desk for herself that he would be forbidden to encroach on. But she wasn't comfortable having to say that to him, or to the others. Then she spotted the answer. A lovely, hand-carved teak rolltop desk that she could lock "for security's sake" without having to tell the others not to use it. It was only a little underhanded and she decided that she was okay with that.

When she was done with the furniture and fittings, she focused on ordering interior walls, heating, high security... It had taken her much of the night, but she was pleased with the results.

She'd finally lain down and gone to sleep at three. The house at Gig Harbor was even quieter than her own island residence. It was rare to not hear the waves at home, and the gulls here apparently slept very soundly.

Now it was four a.m. and the stars were just dimming in the east beyond Holly's big bay windows. Miranda's phone vibrated again with a re-call rather than a message. She slipped out of bed and raced into the bathroom to avoid disturbing Holly, then closed the door on herself before answering.

"Miranda, we've got a bad crash in Colorado. Are you available for a launch?"

"Good morning, Jill." Miranda had been practicing what Mike called "appropriate human interaction." It was supposed to make things easier, or so he said. She wasn't convinced yet.

Jill sighed. "It's too early in the morning for this; I haven't had my coffee yet."

"It's four a.m. here. It is seven a.m. in Washington, DC, where you are."

"Oh, right. Sorry. Still haven't had my coffee. Are you available for a launch?"

And for all her efforts in appropriate human interaction, they'd ended up exactly where they'd started. "Yes," seemed to be the simplest way forward. Holly had, as usual, been right: their empty queue hadn't lasted for long.

"The military has put a high priority on it. They've asked me to forward you through to the military liaison for transport." Jill's mumble of "I really need some coff—" was cut off by the military liaison clicking in and Jill hanging up.

Miranda liked this version of Jill much better. Normally her conversations were rife with incomplete sentences and laughter when Miranda asked for the rest of the thought. Barely awake, Jill was just business.

"This is Major Swift." She hadn't expected him as the liaison, though perhaps she should have. He was an officer of the Air Force's Accident Investigation Bureau and she'd known he was returning from his overseas assignment. They'd also been lovers briefly before he'd left, which had been nice.

"Good morning, Jonathan."

"Miranda!" The enthusiasm in his voice said that *he* was not struggling to wake up. "I was hoping it would be you they called in. It's wonderful to hear your voice. Where are you?"

"Sitting on the edge of the tub in Holly's bathroom. It's still just four a.m. here."

"Are you wearing that white flannel nightgown?" His voice shifted to a low and soft tone that probably implied something, but tone of voice was often deceptive. It didn't sound like sarcasm or irritation...

"Yes, why?"

His laughter seemed friendly. "Just like picturing you in that."

"I would have thought that you liked picturing me out of

it. Or is that some way of saying you don't want to have sex again?" She really hoped it wasn't. Jon had been the first man she'd really enjoyed spending time with that way.

"I also like picturing you out of it, and no, I'm not saying that at all."

"Then why did you say that you liked picturing me more clothed rather than less clothed?"

"You look lovely both ways, Miranda. Different, but lovely."

"How different?"

"Would it be okay if we tabled this discussion until after we talked about the crash? How you look in your full NTSB gear versus that flannel nightgown versus completely unclothed is something I'm happy to discuss—at length. But not at the moment."

She was getting better about when to set aside a topic. Her system was to note it down in her personal notebook that she reviewed each evening for Incomplete Issues. But the notebook wasn't here; it was in her vest out in Holly's bedroom. She'd have to wait to write it down and only hoped that not too many other conversational threads had to be set aside before she had a chance to access her notebook and record them.

"Yes, it would be okay."

"Based on the call sign, we just lost an AC-130J Ghostrider gunship. It's—"

She cut him off. "You know I don't like to *hear* about the crash. I prefer to witness it for myself and reach my own conclusions."

"Right. Okay. Where are you now?"

"Sitting on the edge of the tub in Holly's bathroom." She

didn't like repeating things, but this time it helped to ground her as she remembered the last time she'd been able to meet up with Jon.

It had been right after a Black Hawk helicopter crash in Hawaii. She'd been called out because it had collided with a Cessna Citation Sovereign 680 business jet. Hawaii was part of the NTSB's Western Pacific Region, which was based out of the "Seattle Office" incongruously located *thirty miles* south of Seattle in Federal Way—a fact that continued to bother her but upper management had remained unwilling to rectify.

After the investigation, they'd had three particularly enjoyable days together, touring the air bases of all five branches of the service. Jon's rank had granted them access to study many types of planes she'd never before been aboard.

Jon had explained the various crew chiefs' curious reactions to her.

"You're famous now, Miranda. Every crew chief is spooked by what you might find that they've done wrong, but they're also crew chiefs who love their aircraft and are desperate to learn how to do their jobs better. You kind of freak them out both ways."

She really didn't understand the former sentiment; only the results mattered. On the latter sentiment, she and the crew chiefs had aligned perfectly.

She and Jon had also spent two equally enjoyable nights together, then he'd been posted to the Middle East for a three-month assignment shortly afterward.

Ninety-seven days since he'd left. So, it was reasonable to assume that he was back in the States again. He'd called several times, but talking on the phone had never particularly worked for her. Their e-mails had gone better and she'd looked forward to hearing from him.

But now was a perfect example of the problems with phone conversations.

Jon's continued silence told her she was being too literal again.

She never seemed to get that particular question regarding her location right. Her answer of her position on Holly's bathtub was the most valid and descriptive but, she was learning, not the most useful to the situation.

"We're all ten minutes from the Tacoma Narrows Airport in Washington State."

"I'll have a C-21A Learjet there in fifteen."

"I haven't even woken the oth—"

Holly threw open the bathroom door. She was dressed in her full gear. "What are you still doing in your nightgown? There's a crash, isn't there?"

Miranda could only nod.

"I already rousted the boys. Mike is doing his fancy-coffee-machine thing." Sure enough, there was the soft sound of grinding echoing from the distant kitchen.

She noticed coffee was the one habit of Mike's, perhaps the only habit, that Holly didn't roll her eyes about. Mike always made sure that Holly received a monstrous thermal mug full each morning.

"And he's making his espresso and your hot cocoa," and there was the missing eye roll. "So, let's get going, Miranda. Not like you to be so slow off the mark."

She always left Miranda a little breathless when she was

in this mode. Actually, from what she'd seen, she left *everyone* a little breathless most of the time.

"I'm still on the phone to—"

Holly pulled the phone from her fingers. "I'll flirt with whatever yobbo is on the mobile. You, go! Get dressed." She put the phone to her ear. "Is this Drake, ye old bastard, or Jon sniffin' round our Miranda?... Jon! How ya garn? Guess what? Miranda's about to get as naked as a James Bond girl in the next room, and you aren't here to see it, you poor sod. She's hot, you know."

Miranda opened her mouth to protest but, as Holly burst out laughing over some reply, she decided that escape was her best option.

2

MIRANDA HAD NEVER BEEN TO ASPEN. IT WAS A SMALL, municipal airport known to her primarily for its general aviation crashes. She had specialized in commercial aviation early in her career, but the military investigations had become her team's most common callout.

"Colorado has the third highest number of small planes per capita of any state in the US after Alaska and Montana. Though their pilot fatality rate is lower than seventeen other states, it's still a lot of crashes." Miranda was glad that the statistic did not carry into commercial air crashes in the state; the countryside beyond the plane's window looked to be very rugged.

"You know..." Mike leaned back in his leather airplane seat. The little eight-passenger C-21A VIP transport Learjet was a very comfortable way to travel, even if it did belong to the Air Force.

Aside from the pair of military pilots, there were just the

four of them aboard. They sat in pairs of facing seats on either side of a narrow aisle.

"There's a saying about Aspen. 'The millionaires ruined it for the hippies, and the billionaires ruined it for the millionaires.' So, don't forget about all the out-of-state jetsetters flitting in and out of here in the worst of conditions for your crash tally."

"It's late June," Miranda looked out the window as they began their descent into Aspen. "Presently sunny. On the high lakes I can see only a little ice, so I would project that it is warm with a decreased chance of low-altitude icing on the plane's surfaces. As there are no clear reflections off the water, there must be wind-rippling. However, the lack of buffeting aboard our flight would indicate that this wind is not of sufficient velocity to turbulate the air significantly despite the close proximity of numerous high mountain peaks."

Jeremy had a Bluetooth earpiece and was listening to something intently. "Aspen ATIS currently reports barometer steady at thirty even, winds at fifteen out of the west, humidity forty-seven percent, and temperature is sixty-eight." She hadn't realized that he carried a broadband receiver that covered the FAA frequencies. The Automated Terminal Information Service frequency would have all of the weather and pertinent airport information regularly updated on a broadcast loop.

"This does not appear to be the 'worst of conditions'," Miranda concluded. "We'll need to verify, of course, but it seems unlikely that last night's conditions were significantly different."

Mike just shrugged. "Not quite what I was saying, but

one point to you, Miranda."

"I didn't realize we were keeping score. Are we keeping score?" If so, was she doing well? She'd never understood competitive sports and if they were now—

"No, Miranda," Mike leaned forward. "Not a competition. We're not keeping score." He waited until she nodded that she understood, even though she didn't totally, before he settled back.

"So, you've been to Aspen, Mikey?" Holly's tone was derisive. "Chasing some hot snow bunny?"

"If by that you mean Stephanie Garr, the country singer, yes." Mike sipped at his sparkling water again.

Miranda didn't know her, but then she rarely listened to music composed after Mozart.

Jeremy began humming some tune that sounded just like every other tune on country radio.

"As you know, it's not just her singing that's so lovely." Mike appeared to be very pleased at another chance to tease Holly. "What you may not know is she also has the exceptional legs of a top skier. She was born and raised here, even if all of her 'country credentials' are thought to be Tennessee. Anyway, we skied all of these areas, though she was especially fond of the expert trails atop Snowmass."

"Is that Snowmass?" Miranda pointed at a feature she'd noticed on their approach. It lay ahead and below but it was hard to miss as there were still some areas of it on fire— bright flames with billows of black smoke above. Several helicopters were flying between the mountaintop and a clear lake in a valley just five miles to the south, fetching loads of water to dump on the last of the flames. It must have been a massive torch in the night when it was first burning.

Below the fire's location, the top of the mountain had a black ring where fire had begun five hundred feet or so below the top, then spread upward.

Mike turned and glanced out the window.

Then he jolted as if Holly had punched him, and pressed his face to the window.

"That's Snowmass Ski Area all right. The entire summit is gone. I can't see what's—"

Jeremy handed him a pair of binoculars.

Mike grabbed them and stared out the window. Their angle of view slowly shifted as the plane continued toward its landing.

As they continued toward the airport, Miranda could see a long weave of wide trails traced through the pines that she presumed were for skiing in the winter season. They weren't close enough to see the details, but there were several long straight lines that crossed all the twisting trails that might be the paths of the ski lifts.

"The Cirque Poma lift is gone," Mike groaned. "Oh man, are the owners ever going to be pissed. They spent at least a hundred thousand extra to *not* impact the summertime environment when they installed that lift. Winter work, helicopters for all of the steel and concrete. There's also a whole May to June wildlife breeding area at altitude up there they were trying to protect. I guess that was just wiped out."

Miranda didn't like to see crashes before she was ready to, but it seemed to be okay this time. Perhaps it was the angle but she didn't think so.

This was the first crash site she'd ever seen from above where she couldn't see any sign of the plane.

3

The HeliSki/HeliSee helicopter awaiting them at the Aspen airport was an AgustaWestland A109 Trekker. But while they were allowed to load their gear in the side cage that hung along one side of the helo—where skiers would normally place their skis and poles—they weren't allowed to board the helicopter.

Miranda wasn't sure what to do as that was the obvious next step of the process.

"What's going on?"

In answer, the pilot pointed aloft before walking back into the terminal building.

She looked up, but didn't see anything except for a flight of crows.

"Well, if that's how he treats his tourists, I'm amazed he's still in business," Mike scowled after him.

Miranda inspected the quality of both the helicopter here and the three more she could see in the hangar. Externally, they were all in immaculate condition. She sniffed the air for traces of spilled hydraulic fluid or avgas, but detected none. A glance inside revealed that the waiting helo had been upgraded to a very high-end set of avionics. That would have been a very costly retrofit. This operation was clearly successful and well run despite Mike's assessment.

The Aspen airport sat in a narrow valley among the highest peaks in the Rockies, none of which were visible from the field. Any snow that had fallen during the drought year had already melted off all of the lower, visible peaks.

White-barked aspen trees bearing bright green leaves covered some of the lower areas. And scrub oak.

It was all a little...disappointing. She'd barely had a glimpse of the highest peaks due to her attention to the Snowmass fire. Dark green conifers didn't take over until the higher elevations. They were generally softer woods of spruce and larch that would interact less catastrophically with a plane crashing through them than the far stronger Douglas fir so prevalent in the Pacific Northwest. A two-hundred-foot Douglas fir sometimes seemed as if it could swat a plane from the sky. A thirty-foot aspen or fifty-foot larch would just snap or perhaps even be flexible enough to bend against a plane's onslaught, barely retarding its demise.

Miranda made a note in the back of her investigations notebook to consider a paper studying the effects of differing pre-grounding flora on the final crash zone.

The air was so dry that it was nearly odorless. It was also cool, shadowed down here at the base of the valley. The sun wouldn't climb clear of the peaks for another hour.

The taciturn HeliSee pilot—after all, it was the wrong

season for the HeliSki portion of their name to be relevant—returned from the hangar.

He handed each of them a quart-sized water bottle, then a ridiculous hat with a five-inch brim all the way around. Even after Miranda got it adjusted so that it didn't keep sliding down over her eyes and ears, it was still wide enough to extend out to her shoulders.

"Once the sun clears the mountains, those yellow ball caps of yours aren't going to be enough protection, even down here. Get you up on top of Snowmass and the sun'll cook ya. Coming up from sea level, you're going to get heavy-duty headaches from the altitude change. Your best fix is lots of water and move slow. Don't even think about running while you're up there or you'll get a wicked migraine, even if you don't get migraines."

While he might be less than friendly, Miranda appreciated his clarity of communication.

Mike donned his hat.

Holly was refusing to give up wearing her beloved Matildas soccer team hat until Mike teased her about not wanting to be a team player. That seemed to be a rather unfair assessment in Miranda's opinion, but it worked and Holly changed hats—only after she punched Mike's arm.

Jeremy had simply reached into his big field pack and pulled out his own hat very similar to the ones from HeliSee, though without their mountain peak logo plastered around the crown in garish tie-dye colors.

Holly yanked it off his head. "I have to wear one of these ridiculous things? Then so do you." And she slapped a HeliSee hat onto his head. Then she turned and spun Jeremy's hat away like a Frisbee. Mike sprinted about ten steps, jumped up gracefully, and snagged it from high in the air. Even as he was landing, he twisted and spun the hat through the air back to Jeremy, who caught it and tucked it away.

The pilot was shaking his head. "That. That's the kind of thing you don't want to be doing."

"Used to live in Denver. Skied up here plenty of times," Mike looked unworried as he rejoined them.

"And where do you live now?" the pilot shot back.

"About thirty feet above sea level with the rest of us," Holly answered for him.

The guy just shook his head, then shaded his eyes despite the silvered aviators and looked up.

Miranda had already noted the bright spark of an incoming flight.

"That'll be the rest of your crew."

"But my team is already here."

The pilot shrugged at her response and then began his preflight inspection of the helicopter. Again, the professionalism showed in his care with each detail. She wasn't familiar with the exact procedures of the AgustaWestland Trekker's preflight and caught up with him.

"Does the preflight checklist include a torque check of the swash plate bolts?" As that's what the pilot was doing.

"No, lady. But it's my company and I do a lot of my own mechanicking. What do you care as long as it's right?"

"I'm considering whether or not that would be a good addition to recommend. Should the FAA mandate that the procedure be included for all rotorcraft preflight checklists?"

"And you have that kind of power?" He moved to the tail

rotor and actually ran a hand along the front and back edge of each blade rather than merely inspecting it visually.

"I do."

He turned to look directly at her for the first time, raising his eyebrows above his mirrored aviators.

She never understood why the truth always seemed so surprising to people.

Even though she couldn't see his eyes—all she saw was the twinned reflection of herself with the rather garish hat—she found it disconcerting. So instead she looked up at the approaching airplane above his right shoulder.

"Does it need to be so bright?"

He followed the direction of her gaze. "That plane?"

"This hat."

She could feel his eyes return to her, then shift upward to inspect the logo above her forehead. He grimaced. "My wife's design."

"The plane is not very bright. I surmise that it's painted matte Air Force-gray similar to the aircraft that delivered my team. An Army-tan plane would have a somewhat higher albedo."

"Coast Guard would be the brightest."

"Yes," Miranda agreed, though it seemed a redundant observation. "The USCG's planes are high-gloss white and orange as they're meant to be seen, not to be hidden."

"You're with the FAA?"

"The NTSB. And the hat *is* very bright."

"You got a name, lady?"

"Yes." Like the question of *Where are you?* the asked question never garnered the desired information. Or perhaps it was some curious regionalism. She decided to short-circuit the cycle that invariably evoked and supplied her name even though he hadn't asked for it.

"Miranda Chase? You do the investigation on Eames' Cessna 208?"

Two years ago. Fourteen passengers (only licensed for thirteen though not relevant to the incident's cause). Final ground contact eleven thousand feet on Pikes Peak in Colorado. No survivors. Airport of origin...ah, Aspen.

She nodded carefully, unsure of the pilot's pending reaction.

The approaching plane had finally resolved from a point of light to a bullet shape as it approached. It *was* Air Force-gray as she'd anticipated.

"Read that report. Eames was always a sloppy idiot. You nailed it in one, Ms. Chase. That man was a pilot error waiting to happen since the day he left the womb. Probably botched that departure as well."

She'd had no doubts about the accuracy of her report, but she liked that the pilot seemed pleased. That would increase the care he was likely to take when transporting her and her team. She had no idea if she was supposed to say anything about his opinion regarding Eames' birth.

Instead, she turned back to the helicopter. "What else would you include on a preflight checklist for this particular model that isn't there?"

He eyed her, then the helicopter. "That's an easy one, but it would be hard on you for a while."

"What's your suggestion?"

"Make every dumbass pilot out there be a hundred percent responsible for their own bird. Make them not lease it but own it, get the airframe and engine maintenance certification like I did, and have them put their own family's welfare on the line if they do something wrong and the bird goes down on their watch."

"That seems reasonable."

He then smiled for the first time. "Reasonable but unlikely?"

"Sadly," Miranda admitted. "Why would that be hard on me?"

"Because of all the idiots falling out of the air until it thinned the herd. Darwinian selection of every dumbass not smart enough to take care of his own equipment."

"Or her own equipment," Holly joined them from where she'd been chatting with the others. "I like it."

Miranda didn't. "Though I find little fault with your hypothesis, I'm not in favor of anything that *increases* the number of aircraft crashes."

He chuckled. "I expect not. I'm Brett Vance," he held out a hand, which he used to shake hers with too much strength and energy.

She responded with her own name, again, because she couldn't think of what else to say. It left her right arm vibrating like it had just been through a crash of its own.

"C'mon, Ms. Chase. I'll really walk you through this bird."

And he did. Not just the preflight, but strengths and shortcomings. He fetched a ladder and they peeled back engine cowlings. He showed her how to inspect the rear-rotor drive shaft bearings with a mechanic's eye rather than a pilot's.

When Major Jon Swift showed up, she and Brett were lying together under the belly of the helo between the skids.

They were discussing the paths and percentages of force-transference vectors through the hull's skin material versus the internal structure in the event of a hard landing.

"Hi, Miranda," Jon knelt on the other side of the skid's open frame.

She waved but kept listening to Brett about the structural changes AgustaWestland had made to the 109 before certifying it for skids rather than wheels.

4

"WHAT DO YOU THINK HAPPENED?" BRETT CALLED OVER THE intercom as they climbed toward the site—the audio system from PS Engineering, very high end. She'd also always like the SIG headsets for their comfort and sound insulation.

"I never conjecture prior to a crash investigation," Miranda hadn't wanted the copilot seat—because she didn't want such a clear view of the crash prior to assessing terrain and other external factors—but Brett had insisted. The rest of her team, Jon Swift, and Brett's nine-year-old son Jeffrey were seated in the back. They were clear of the airport and beginning the mile-high climb to the crash site.

Now she could see the anticipated switchover to the dark conifers. Several fourteeners revealed themselves to the south—each popping into view like a giant Jack-in-the-box, which she'd never gotten over her fear of though she'd finally learned how to hide her reactions.

"Well, you aren't going to find the answer up there. I've

been flying fire crews in all morning and there's not much to see. I was first on site around four a.m. this morning."

Miranda didn't want to hear this. It was in the wrong order. She hadn't even begun the site investigation and suddenly she was receiving information from a witness, typically the very last step in her information-gathering process.

She always approached a crash in spheres of influence. Weather and terrain at the outermost; the pilot's intellectual process (or lack thereof) at the very innermost. Eyewitness accounts were only the slightest shade removed from those of the pilots themselves—assuming they survived. She'd never found either source to be wholly reliable, emotionally neutral, or even, on occasion, coherent.

But she couldn't think how to stop Brett Vance.

"I was in the oval office when—"

"The Oval Office? Why were you meeting with Roy?" And furthermore, President Roy Cole was sixteen hundred miles from here. "And how did you get here so quickly from DC?"

He glanced over at her for a long moment with a slight frown. She wanted to ask Mike what it meant, but he was in the back and wouldn't be able to see his expression.

"The toilet. The room with the oval piece of porcelain. My *oval* office."

"Oh." Other than Mike, she had very little experience with Coloradan colloquialisms.

"Anyway, that's where I was when the world lit up like daylight. Actinic white, like welding flame, not a gas fire."

Following his detailed analysis of the A109's strengths and weaknesses, she knew to trust Brett's word on the spectral temperature of the light. A fuel fire, even an explosive one, trended deeply into the yellows and oranges. Even at its hottest, it would never be described as actinic white.

"I live just down there," he nodded toward sprawling homes scattered among the trees at the base of the mountain's ski area. "Old home, nothing fancy, but we like it and I didn't want to sell off to the developers. We're just two miles from the top of Snowmass, plus a mile down."

A direct line of two-point-two-three miles—eleven seconds at the speed of sound.

"Counted thirteen seconds before a big boom rolled in— real sharp."

Thirteen seconds would imply that his distances were inaccurate or his accelerated excitement level at the explosion had caused him to count inaccurately. Assuming he knew the elevation difference between his home and the top of Snowmass mountain, thirteen seconds would place his home two-point-four-five miles horizontally from Snowmass, not two miles.

Though such an inaccuracy seemed unlikely in Brett Vance's case.

Oh! She'd neglected altitude. The speed of sound slowed in thinner air: nine percent slower at Aspen's elevation and almost fourteen percent at Snowmass' peak. If she integrated the speed of sound over the distance, thirteen seconds was surprisingly accurate for a human observer without a stopwatch or other aid.

"By that time I was out on the back deck. Not much to see until the two lower fires, sparked by the wings, started working. Early in the season for fire. Normally, the undergrowth is still damp from the snowmelt, though it was a dry winter. Whatever the conditions, the fire grabbed hold and burned up the slope hard and fast. Swept right over the crash site. Nothing much left to burn anyway after that explosion."

Miranda decided that she was willing to accept Brett's observations, pending further observation, despite the early stage of the investigation.

"ARTCC Denver said," Mike had been on the phone even as he'd boarded the helo, "that the flight reported a depressurization event at Flight Level Three-niner-zero and basically augered in at over four hundred knots. Thirteen crew."

Brett nodded, "Mountain Rescue has twelve of them off the mountain. Bits and pieces of them anyway. Can't find the last one anywhere."

Over four hundred knots, almost five hundred miles an hour, he didn't need to mention that there hadn't been any survivors.

"Wow! Look at those wings. They're totally trashed!" Brett's son Jeffrey's high voice sounded over the intercom.

"You'll have to pardon my boy, he's quite the aviation enthusiast—"

"I'm gonna be a pilot, just like my dad!" Jeffrey declared loudly.

Brett's tone shifted deeper, "—who rarely knows when to keep quiet about it."

"Yet his assessment is wholly accurate." Miranda inspected the wings herself, though that too was the wrong sphere of a proper investigation. Everything was all out of order but that seemed to be out of her control. The wings were relatively intact, which indicated that they'd separated from the diving aircraft to fall at a much slower pace. "Those wings *are* totally trashed."

"See, Dad. I told ya."

Miranda remembered her early days of flying, begging rides and free lessons from anyone who flew out to visit their family.

Jeffrey's enthusiasm reminded her a lot of herself. "What else do you see, Jeffrey?"

Brett slowed to a hover at the same altitude as the wings' final resting place.

"Jeff," the boy announced. "Just Jeff."

He was silent long enough that she was wondering if he was awaiting a response from her. But then he continued.

"I see four engines. One still has a couple of its propellers. By the angle, I'm guessing four blades?"

She glanced down and saw that he was correct. Which meant that it might by a Hercules, but it wasn't an AC-130J Ghostrider. She turned around far enough to look at Jon, who just shrugged in confusion.

"Good guess," Miranda shifted her attention back to Jeffrey. "Does that tell you what plane it is?"

There was another long silence before he answered tentatively, "C-1300 Hercules? Like the Disney movie?"

"C-*130* Hercules. *Just* like the Disney movie." It had come out the year after her parents died and she had watched it innumerable times. Not for the conquering of evil, but for Zeus challenging young Hercules to become a "true hero." Her own father had always pushed her to excel, no matter what her learning and behavioral challenges. But it was Father Zeus who had given her the words for the goal she'd striven to satisfy ever since. Father Zeus' words combined with Father Sam Chase's demise in a plane crash had driven her to be the best NTSB crash investigator she could be. *A true hero.*

"What happened to it?"

"That's what we're here to find out. Do you want to help?"

"Really?" His squeal hurt her ears over the intercom; there was no questioning his excitement.

Brett looked over at her sharply. He mouthed, *Are you sure?*

Miranda replied aloud, "Of course I'm sure. Or I wouldn't have offered."

"Please, Daddy? Please? Please? Please?"

Brett sighed for reasons that eluded her.

"Jeff. You are *not* to bother Ms. Chase with too many questions."

"Questions are helpful. That is our job: to ask questions until we find answers."

Suddenly Brett truly smiled for the first time. "Don't say I didn't warn you."

"Warn me of what?"

But a chuckle was his only answer.

She recognized Jeff's passion for aircraft and wanted to nurture that. It was all that had sustained her after her own parents had died in a crash. His father was a pilot in a very dangerous environment.

Miranda wanted Jeff to have that passion as well—in case it was ever the only thing left for him to hold on to.

5

At her suggestion, they dropped Jeremy and Jon near the wings to inspect them.

Brett landed the rest of the team—including Jeff, with more admonishments to behave—at the top of the mountain before gathering up a load of firefighters to deliver back to the bottom of the mountain now that the fire was beaten.

The char was thick on the air. Every step puffed up a small cloud of ash from the burned vegetation. For a moment, the morning breeze would swirl it aside in a brush of fresh mountain air—and then it would drive a cloud of ash up the hill.

Jeremy handed around paper masks.

Brett had been accurate when he'd told Miranda that there wasn't much to see. Actually, the problem was that there was so much to see and most of it was very small—and scattered widely. Any attempt to map the debris perimeter would involve tracking far and wide. Very little of the area was truly vertical but, beyond the broad crown of the peak and the few ski trails, much of it was quite steep.

The tail section had landed below a particularly steep headwall. Climbing gear would certainly be advisable for safety.

"Looks like my game," Holly swung loose her pack and propped it on a steel pipe sticking out of the ground.

As Holly began pulling out climbing gear, Miranda circled the pipe twice but was unable to identify it. Five inches across, eight feet showing above the soil. The upper end appeared to be shattered, as if the metal hadn't even had time to deform due to the suddenness of the blow. She looked down to inspect what Holly was doing.

"Do you always bring climbing equipment?"

"Jon said the crash was on a mountaintop in Colorado. So I tossed in a bit of gear just in case. I brought a second set. Want to join in?"

"I never learned to climb."

"I'll go with you," Mike stepped up.

"You?" Holly sneered. "Don't tell me. Stephanie Garr was also into rock climbing?"

"Mandy Becot. She's a romance author. She uses actual written words, so you probably wouldn't know about her."

Even Miranda knew about Mandy Becot. "She's amazing."

"In more ways than *one,*" Mike turned away from Holly before winking at Miranda.

She hoped that Holly's eye roll was the intended response, even if he wasn't in position to witness it, as that's what she delivered him.

Once Holly and Mike had on climbing belts and hard

hats, Holly threw her body weight at the embedded pipe. It didn't budge. Within moments, she'd lashed her rope around it, and the two of them disappeared off the edge of a steep embankment strewn with parts of what appeared to be the rear ramp and tail section. Hopefully, somewhere in the scattered debris below would be the black boxes.

The top of the mountain was suddenly very still.

She and Jeff stood alone together at the very top of the ski area. A hundred feet below and well to the east, a small team of firefighters were using shovels to toss dirt on one of the last hotspots. Other than that, the fire was gone. It had burned fast and hot, leaving behind blackened soil, the scent of char, and little else other than tiny bits of a very large airplane. The timberline lay perhaps eight hundred feet below, near the level of the wings' final landing places.

"It's awful quiet," Jeff whispered.

"It is." A light breeze brushed cold air over them. She reached for her pocket anemometer...but wasn't wearing her vest. Very unusual for her. She'd been distracted by so many things. She pulled it out of her pack.

Slipping out her personal notebook, she made an entry to remember to speak with Jon about how it was possible that he liked seeing her clothed—yet that didn't somehow preclude him wanting to have sex again. Then she put it away and slipped out the anemometer.

"Can I have one of those?"

"My anemometer?"

"No. What's a amonometer? I want a vest with all the cool pockets for stuff."

"I only have this one. I'm sorry. But if you decide you need a tool, you just ask. Until then, I'll carry them."

"Okay. What's a amanonometer?"

So, she showed him how to measure windspeed, direction, and relative humidity, and how she noted down each item.

"Cool, what's next?"

Miranda surveyed the hillside covered with twists of metal. "Let's see if we can find the cockpit of the plane."

6

"I don't see anything particularly wrong," Jeremy was looking at the twisted remains of the port-side wing.

"Other than the thirteen dead?" Jon knew the bodies were cleared off the mountains, wouldn't even have been here by the wings. Still, thirteen fellow fliers? That hurt bad, a feeling he'd never grown used to.

"I mean the wing. Nothing looks particularly wrong with the wing."

Jon had to agree with Jeremy's assessment. But he couldn't help glancing away from the wings and up the hillside.

However, there was a lot wrong with Miranda. He just didn't know what it was.

After three months apart, she'd barely acknowledged him at the airport. She didn't strike him as fickle, though she'd been very cozy with the pilot, both on the ground and riding up front with him. Then taking his son with her up to the main crash site and dumping Jon downslope with Jeremy when the main crash was up above.

He'd thought their last round of e-mails had gone well. Or well enough. She was even more challenging to communicate with remotely than in person.

"Something strange is going on." And he didn't like it at all.

"You mean other than the wings being ripped off the sides of the Hercules, crashing into a mountain, and bursting into flame?" Jeremy was photographing the root of the starboard wing where the distortion of the metal was consistent with being torn off in flight. "I'd have to agree. I'm seeing no intrinsic damage to any of the wing's structure that isn't caused by impact with the rocks or trees it landed on. Flaps and ailerons are relatively intact and I'm seeing no stress shearing in the hinge points or control rods."

Jon sighed and looked back down at the big wing. Fifty-seven feet long, it had been twisted and bent like a foam toy. The breached tanks had spilled fuel, but it hadn't been an explosion. The metal around the tanks was crumpled inward by the impacts, not blown outward from inside. The fuel had leaked, caught fire, and that had ignited the forest fire that had burned the mountaintop. Actually, they were above the tree line, so it had been a brush fire, but still destructive.

Jeremy stowed his camera. "I think we should check one of the engines next. See if we can find any sign of thrust reversal on the propellers or over-revving. Maybe a flameout." His tone went very wry at the end—a sense of humor about something mechanical was a surprise.

"Yeah. Sure," Jon answered in kind. Then looked at Jeremy in surprise. They knew it was a depressurization event by the pilot's report. So, was Jeremy teasing him out of a bad mood? Or just making a joke?

Either way it worked and they began a methodical investigation of the wing.

But talk about a flameout. Had he said something wrong while trying to flirt with Miranda over the phone this morning? He should know better, but it was how he'd connected with other women in the past. Except Miranda wasn't *other* women. He was attracted to her precisely because she *wasn't* like other women.

Most women saw "handsome Air Force major" and thought: stability, status, and meal ticket for life. Miranda seemed to see Jon Swift: crash investigator and pilot. That alone was a rare gift.

He wanted to go up the hill and confront Miranda, but he knew that the first thing she'd ask about would be the wings. And the second would be the engines. But these...

"Hey, Jeremy?" he crossed over to the base of the broken-off wing, while Jeremy use a thermite cutting torch to snip off a piece of the distorted wing strut. Leave it to Jeremy to have the coolest tools always at hand.

"Yeah?" Jeremy pulled out a sample bag for the cut-off piece, tapping the part against the soil to cool the cut first.

"Everything okay with Miranda?" *Real subtle, Jon.* Though with Jeremy, direct was probably the best approach.

"As far as I know. Did you know that she cleared our entire crash queue? We're completely caught up. Or we were for one night before this accident came in. That seemed to worry her a bit. But other than that, she seemed okay." Then he narrowed his eyes and looked at Jon. "Why?"

Why? Probably because he was an idiot who worried too much.

"No reason." Lame. He glanced up the hill again.

"Miranda won't like it if we aren't thorough."

"Duh!" He did know that. Jon glanced up the mountain again.

Miranda and the kid…Jeff?

What was that about?

He'd tried to point out that taking a kid onto a crash site was—he'd chosen the word "unusual" rather than "totally inappropriate."

In response she'd simply proceeded as if he'd never said a word. Damn, but once she made up her mind, that was one seriously determined woman.

He and Jeremy were halfway through the engine analysis, with him recording fracture patterns as Jeremy called them out, before he felt something was wrong. He'd learned to trust that instinct.

"Hold it, Jeremy."

Jeremy froze with his arm extended all the way into the forward air intake of the engine to hold a flashlight while he inspected the primary intake fins.

"What's wrong here?"

"Other than the crashed plane?"

"Other than the crashed plane."

Jeremy extracted his arm and they both looked around. After thirty seconds of inspecting everything, their gazes met and they shrugged in unison.

"Okay. Describe everything you see."

"That's how Miranda does it." Jeremy made it sound as if Jon was cheating.

"That's where I got the idea."

Jeremy grinned. "Isn't she amazing?"

"She is."

Apparently Jon's agreement was a little too emphatic. Jeremy shifted back to being watchful before he began. He did Miranda's thing of starting with the weather and terrain, then working his way inward.

The wings.

Leading edge.

Flaps.

Ailerons.

Propellers.

"We're standing in front of the Number Three engine. It's an Allison T56 turboshaft with two blades remaining."

Jon waited for the feeling to return, but it was none of those things.

Jeremy just watched him.

"Ever get the feeling that it's too..."

"Neat?"

"Yeah," Jon tried it tentatively, but...yeah. "That's it. Somehow, this big messy crash spread across the entire top of a national ski area is too neat."

"You're right. I think. At least maybe it feels that way. Like the Hawkins C-130A crash back in '02 made sense."

Jon nodded. The forty-five-year-old, first-generation C-130A had been converted into an air tanker for fighting wildfires. After the Air Force was done with it, it had spent fourteen more years dumping nine tons of flame retardant thousands of times. The repeated stress of so many massive unloadings was finally too much, and one day the wings had just given up and broken off the plane in midflight, killing the two pilots.

A depressurization event could cause a very wild ride, and perhaps even a crash. But these were military pilots. And he knew from being one, just how good that meant they had to be.

"It *doesn't* make sense."

"Whatever it is, Miranda will find out why," Jeremy declared with absolute faith.

"Makes the crash kind of like her, doesn't it?"

"How?" Jeremy froze, halfway back to shining his light inside the engine again.

"She's all neat and perfect, except for the parts that really, really aren't."

"Don't say that!" Jeremy launched to his feet. "There's nothing wrong with Miranda! Ever! She's amazing. Don't you ever say anything against her. She knows more about plane crashes than anyone else alive. Anywhere. If I know about them to the top of a molehill, she knows them to the top of Everest! To the moon! And back!" Then, at a complete loss for how to make his point stronger, he stabbed Jon in the chest with his finger-long flashlight hard enough that Jon was lucky it wasn't a sword or he'd have been run clean through.

"Okay, Jeremy. Okay." He held up his hands until Jeremy calmed and finally returned to his engine.

Jeremy was wrong on one point and so very right on another.

Miranda had many things wrong with her, but they were also part of her charm. He'd never met such a literal-minded person. Or one who threw herself into *everything* with a hundred percent of her focus and passion—whether a plane crash or sex. ...and could so completely ignore anything else during those moments.

Duh! Like his arrival while she was inspecting a helicopter's structural design. So maybe that hadn't been about him even if it felt like it had.

But Jeremy was right about something else.

Miranda was the *very* best at plane investigations. He'd been a crash investigator for the Air Force for the last ten years. He knew enough to tell the difference between expertise and mastery. Yet she was like Yoda of the Jedi—operating at a whole other level beyond even that.

Yes, there was something really wrong here; he could feel it.

But while he couldn't see it, Miranda would.

"I've got to talk to her."

Jeremy began banging on something inside the engine with a wrench.

"I need a radio," he spoke louder.

"*What?*" Jeremy shouted as he continued banging loudly inside the engine with a force that seemed completely unnecessary.

"Hope your eardrums hurt!"

Jeremy's banging was now too loud for him to have heard Jon.

He spotted the radio clipped to the side of Jeremy's pack. He made sure the volume was up, then placed a call up the mountain.

7

Miranda led Jeff along the debris trail that spread across the top of the ski area.

"This is bad," Jeff kicked at the tangle of wires and foot-diameter pipes in front of them. It was no part of any airplane. The long pipes had one end bolted to concrete footings but had been bent and twisted despite their size. A heavy one-inch cable of woven steel snaked among the wreckage. Other curious parts—like a giant, steel wagon wheel four meters across—were caught up in the tangle. All of it was blackened to some degree.

"It is?" It was certainly broken, but she had no frame of reference to make any sense of its goodness or badness.

"This is the top of the Cirque Poma lift. They gotta fix it or I won't be able to ski the double black diamond trails here next winter."

"Double black diamond?" It was only one of the things she didn't understand about the boy's statement.

"The experts-only trails. Dad wouldn't let me ski those until last winter. They're the best. Don't you ski?"

"I live on an island. My home is fifty-seven feet above sea level in a temperate maritime environment. I remember six times in my whole life when snow deeper than my ankles stuck on the island for more than a day."

"Really? No snow?" He looked at her as if she was an alien come down from another planet.

"Not very much, especially in the rain shadow of the Olympic Mountains."

"Are they big?"

"Not as big as these mountains, but yes."

"And you don't ski on those mountains?"

"No, I don't."

"Weird." The boy pointed down the slope along the tangled wires. She could see a line of tall poles descending the mountain. "This is a Poma lift. It's…I dunno…like a Frisbee lying flat at the end of a long stick. Maybe a giant ski pole dangling from the wire. You put it between your legs and you kinda sit back, but not too much. The Poma, like a palm on your butt," Jeff giggled, "drags you up the hill on your skis."

She couldn't picture that. "I thought they just had chairlifts."

"Chair lifts, Poma lifts, T-bars—those are really hard to ride alone as a little kid…" His tone said that *he* could do it just fine. "…rope tows—they're the worst but they're only on kiddie slopes and I haven't skied those since I turned five—and gondolas. Some places have J-bars. All kindsa things."

Miranda slipped out her notebook and made an annotation to investigate types of ski lifts. It was uncomfortable that she knew nothing about the technical operations of a ski area yet had to investigate a crash at one. That lack of knowledge made it much harder to determine any possible relevance of the damaged lift to the crash.

"How come you don't know this stuff?"

"Because I've never been at a ski area before. You'll have to be my expert in that. I have experts in computers, structures, and people. You can be my ski area expert."

"What *do* you know?"

She led him over to what must have been the lift's final anchor pole. It was significantly bigger than any of the ones she could see on the slope below. "See the burn marks on the pole? What do they tell you?"

"I dunno. That it got burnt?"

"See how on this side, there's no paint left at all. It's completely gone, then there is soot on the bare metal. Around the back, the paint is scorched and sooty, even a little blistered, but it's still there." She pulled out pliers and a sample bag. Then she freed a thick piece of the paint and bagged it, before holding it up. "This corroborates what your fath—"

"It what it-ates?"

"Corroborates…matches what your father said. The burn pattern tells me that the main explosion was from that direction—it literally blew all the paint off this side of the pole. Then the whole pole was exposed to fire because it's soot-marked on both sides. But the paint survived on the back side. By taking this sample back to the lab, we'll be able to create an experiment to test how big an explosion was needed to peel off all of the paint on the other side, well before the fire even arrived here to put soot on the front and blister the paint on the back."

Jeff squinted at the bag. "You can do all that from that little paint chip?"

"A little paint chip and a large Poma pole." She pulled out her tablet and photographed it from several angles.

"Cool! Show me more stuff."

Using the pole as a guide, they headed toward the center of the explosion.

8

"SHE'S NOT ANSWERING. YOU SURE YOUR RADIO WORKS?"

Jeremy didn't answer him. Whether it was because he'd actually crawled partway into the Number Four engine or because he was intentionally ignoring Jon for some reason, it was hard to tell.

He tried the radio again, "Miranda, pick up, damn it!"

Holly's voice came back over the radio. "No swearing on the airwaves, Major Swift. The FCC doesn't like it."

"I don't need sass. I need to talk to Miranda."

"If she's not answering you, mate, there's a reason."

"Can't you just hand your radio to her?"

"Be glad to, except we're chasing some tail, airplane tail," he could hear her grin. "She and Jeff are chasing the cockpit. Keep an eye out. We found the last body—this poor sap makes thirteen. I called Mountain Rescue and they're coming back up for it. Also, tell Jeremy that it looks like someone took a hammer to the black boxes. We'll need him to see if there's anything to recover."

"Jeremy's—"

"A hammer?" Jeremy asked from right next to his elbow, making him jump.

"Heard *that,* did you?" Jon snarled at him.

Jeremy winced but didn't answer him.

"Figure of speech, my young Padawan," Holly teased. "It's awfully beat up."

"Be careful disconnecting the main power buss."

"Think *that* was done by the crash. We're taking pictures and video, but you'd barely recognize it as an airplane's *derrière.* This empennage is never flying again."

"It doesn't matter," Jon broke in. "It's the wrong plane."

"It's what?"

"It's as if there's something wrong with the crash site. Or maybe with the plane."

"Yeah, it's in more pieces than it was built with."

"No, it's something more than that. I just don't know what."

"Ooo-oo!" She made a noise like a haunting ghost. "There's something *spooky* about the plane. Don't be telling Miranda that it's the wrong plane, mate. She'll snap off your head faster than a saltie chowing down on a chihuahua."

"A what on a—"

"Big nasty crocodile in Australia," Jeremy explained.

Jon unkeyed the mike.

"Of course," Holly came back with her accent even thicker, "none of the three of us is so shit-for-brains that we'd tell her something like that in the middle of an investigation."

"Now who needs to watch their on-air language?"

"I'm Australian. I'm allowed. Anyway, we're leaving that one for *you* to explain to her."

"Well, she's not answering," Jon was going to throttle the whole team if they kept this up.

A silence stretched out long enough for Jon to become aware of a bird call that...sounded as if it was very upset about finding its home burned up.

Jeremy reached for his radio. Resigned, Jon gave it to him.

"I've got at least another hour here," he reported to Holly. "I have to go through two more engines and I want to look inside the port wing."

Holly took a moment to answer. "Mike's almost done cutting free the black boxes. Nothing much to learn here without collecting every single scrap and rebuilding it. We'll climb up and make sure nothing happened to Miranda. Meanwhile, this is a plane crash and our job is to investigate it. Finish what you're doing."

"Roger that," Jeremy made a show of returning the radio to the pouch on the side of his pack rather than returning it to Jon.

It was enough to bring his sense of humor back as he turned to help Jeremy once more with the engine investigation.

9

"WHAT KINDA GUN HAS SUCH A BIG RIFLE BARREL?" JEFF DID indeed ask numerous questions as his father had implied, but as he listened to the answers and appeared to be absorbing them, Miranda found no dissatisfaction in the process.

She glanced at the barrel and other remains of the gun still attached to it. "It's from a 40 millimeter L/60 Bofors autocannon." That finally told her what variation of C-130 Hercules plane it was. An AC-130 gunship.

"Autocannon? That's like an automatic cannon?"

"Yes."

"It automatically shoots cannonballs? Like a pirate ship?" His streams of questions were curiously logical from a certain point of view—a person filled with infinite curiosity and only limited experience. Once she'd realized that, she'd discovered an ongoing interest in what he'd ask next.

"Forty-millimeter shells. That's about an inch and a half across. But yes." Miranda had never been fascinated by weapons. She could use them, her father had insisted, but only to put down a suffering animal on her island.

"Cool!" Then Jeff knelt in the char to stare into the open end of the barrel.

"Don't do that!"

Jeff froze and looked at her. "Oh, right! Just like my .22, I gotta make sure there's no round in the chamber. I never thought of that on a cannon. I thought they were different. Do you think pirates ever looked into their cannons?"

"Not while they were loaded. Not unless they wished to become dead pirates."

"Right. *Whups, I looked in a cannon just as it fired. Ker-Pow!*" He splatted his palms against his face, covering his eyes as he staggered in a small circle. "Where's my head? Where's my head?" Then he shifted to inspect the Bofors' feed armature. "So how do I check that?"

"You have to wait for a professional."

"But you know how, don'tcha?"

She did. All of the rounds that had been in the feed had exploded in place, shredding the mechanism designed to handle and load a hundred and twenty, foot-long, two-pound shells every minute.

The mechanism to release the feeder from the firing mechanism in case of a jam was still sufficiently intact to operate. Between them, they were able to open the breech. A round still sat in the firing chamber.

She slipped it out and showed it to Jeff.

"Oh man. Please don't tell Dad. He'd be all angry if he knew I'd almost looked down a loaded barrel."

"I'll try not to."

He looked up at her cautiously. "You'll *try?* That doesn't sound like much of a promise."

"I sometimes say things I shouldn't. I try to stop myself, but I'll be too late and it just comes out."

Jeff nodded. "I do that. Like you want to gobble up the words after they're gone."

Miranda liked that image, but couldn't think how to do it. Jeff reached out a hand for the shell and she handed it to him.

"Wow! That weighs more than my rifle."

"If you have a standard .22 rifle, it probably weighs six pounds. This is only two pounds. But its density—small size for the amount of weight—makes it feel heavier than it is."

"You *do* know science stuff," he handed the shell back.

"I do." She set it beside the shattered loader and placed a yellow warning marker on it before taking a picture of it and the shattered mechanism.

"What else?"

Miranda looked around at the shattered remnants of an AC-130 Hercules gunship. Even the rocks showed the two-event markings: explosion, then burn. Here it had peeled all of the moss and grass off one side of the rock and only scorched what was on the back side.

They had walked less than a hundred meters from the pole.

The paint had been blasted off this side of the pole, but scorched the *opposite* side of the rock.

"Where was the center of the explosion?" They must have walked right through it.

Jeff looked at the pole, then he looked down at the rocks

she'd just been studying. "We passed it. Or maybe circled 'round it."

"Good observing. Now let's go find it." They carefully retraced their steps. Twenty meters back, she knew they'd arrived.

Debris lay in radial patterns outward, yet nothing remained on the exact spot. For at least ten meters around, the surface rock had been shattered by the impact of the plane—but not a single piece of it remained in that circle. Beyond that, a field of twisted metal, structural scraps, even the occasional airplane seat were spread far and wide. Nothing stood higher than two meters in the entire visible debris field.

She pulled out her tablet and shot a panorama from this point.

10

Additional study verified that they were indeed at the epicenter of the explosion. The shape of the impact crater on the rock, though shallow, was distinct. It was several times longer than it was wide. In its final tumble, the plane had landed lengthwise before it was blown apart.

Jeff held the tape as Miranda took measurements and noted them down on the form. She let him be in charge of winding up the tape and carrying it.

Brett's report of actinic-white light suggested that it was the explosive shells that would have been aboard. Based on the scattering field and the location of sections of the heavier lower parts of the hull, it appeared to have landed on its side, the one away from the guns. The shells storage would have struck first, blown the fuselage upward and outward.

Then she looked at the slender pole buried into the ground that Holly had tied her rope to. It had bothered Miranda that she couldn't define the piece as any element of the C-130 Hercules.

Now that she knew what type of plane it was, she knew what the slender pole was. It was the barrel of the M102 howitzer, driven deep into the ground. The guns must have been blown aloft, tossing the Bofors and GAU cannons aside and launching the howitzer's barrel high enough for it to javelin back to earth. Not a part of the cargo as she'd thought.

"No assumptions," she remonstrated herself.

"Dad always says that."

"What?"

"No assumptions. He tells me to always kinda look at things and figure them out."

"Mine, too."

"Would he like my dad?"

"He's dead."

"Oh." Jeff went back to inspecting the ground.

She'd said it. It wasn't something she said very often; it hurt too much. But now, it was mostly just fact and it didn't feel as if her world had ended all over again merely because she'd voiced the words. Just as if the day was less bright.

"How'd he die?"

"In a plane crash."

"This one?" Jeff's voice was so soft she could barely hear it.

"No. A long time ago."

"Could *my* dad die in a plane crash?" She could barely hear the whisper over the morning breeze.

"Yes."

Jeff grabbed her hand, squeezing it hard enough to hurt. "No! You gotta fix that! You gotta make it so that he doesn't. Can't you fix that, Ms. Chase? You know stuff. You gotta save my dad. Yeah? Pleasepleaseplease?" His face was screwed up in such distress. The sheer force of his will had her looking in his eyes, perhaps because it was so reminiscent of her own unforgotten pain. Just as hers had, while she'd begged Tante Daniels to take back the news of her parents' deaths, his tears began to flow.

She squatted down in front of him and he threw his arms around her neck. Miranda could only kneel there and clutch her tablet as he clung to her.

How was she supposed to explain the devastating hole in her life and that it actually *could* happen to him?

"Pleasepleaseplease..." Jeff continued to almost pray through his sobs.

"Jeff," she tried to pry him loose.

"Jeff," she pushed harder, but he clung about her so hard that he was actually choking her.

"Jeff!" Miranda shoved him back hard enough that they flew apart and both landed on their butts on either side of the explosion's epicenter.

The air was briefly filled with a puff of scorched carbon. She raised a hand and saw that it was well-blackened from arresting her fall.

At least the shock seemed to cut off his pleading as he looked at her with big round eyes.

Miranda had learned to fly from her father. She'd often wondered about his final thoughts as he plummeted from the sky with no way to control the plane and save himself, and especially Mom.

"Is your father a good pilot, Jeff?" Even at thirteen she'd known it was ridiculous, but that hadn't stopped the nightmares of her father scrambling for the 747's stairs to the cockpit and diving to the controls to save everyone—and failing. TWA 800 had been blown in two at over thirteen thousand feet. The greatest pilot in history couldn't have saved that plane. Or her parents.

"He's the best ever!" Jeff shouted. At her? At the world?

So was mine. But some instinct told Miranda to keep that thought to herself. "As long as he can reach the controls, then he'll probably always be safe."

"Really?" Now he was begging her.

How could she know? How to explain to the child she herself had once been, what she now knew to be the hard truth of death?

"*Really?*" An escalation of pleading. She didn't want another choking embrace.

She wouldn't lie, not even to an upset child.

How to explain what she knew in a way he'd understand? Then she remembered what she'd done when she'd finally stopped crying over her parents' deaths.

"Do you know why I study plane crashes?"

Jeff bit his lower lip and shook his head.

"I don't do it to learn why a plane crashed."

"You don't?" That earned her a frown that she hoped meant he was really listening.

"No. I do it to make sure it never happens to anyone else again. At least not for the same reason."

Jeff stared at her hard, but she didn't feel the need to look away from him.

She waited him out. That fierce concentration was something she knew very well from herself.

Finally, he nodded. "Teach me how to do that."

From somewhere deep inside her, a laugh came up. A

sad laugh that also had tears, though she blinked those back even as she swallowed the laugh—barely managing not to choke on it. It was a drive she knew that, once embraced, would never let him go. One that blocked out all other possibilities.

She'd spent a lifetime crawling through the remains of dead planes and past dead people. It wasn't a task she'd wish for anybody.

"Maybe you'll fly planes someday. Or help build safer ones."

"I wanna learn why they break."

She sighed—to herself—for his sake. "Well, that can be useful to understand if you want to fly them or make them safer, too."

"Show me."

"Well, next we need to get to the cockpit to do that."

He jumped to his feet. "Let's go!"

Then he looked around in every direction.

"Uh! Which way is it?"

She pointed in the direction opposite from where they'd found the tail and the scorched pole.

Jeff grabbed her hand and led the way.

11

JUST AS THEY WERE TURNING AWAY, HOLLY AND MIKE CAME UP over the ridge by the howitzer barrel.

Jeff kept tugging at her hand, but Miranda stopped and waited for them to pack up their climbing equipment and join them.

Mike set the battered orange case of the CVDR, cockpit voice and data recorder, at her feet.

"What happened to it?" It was incredibly battered.

"You should have seen the tail it came out of." Holly tapped the radio in Miranda's vest. "Isn't it on?"

It wasn't. Yet another thing she'd missed. This was a very...confusing wreck. She took a deep breath and centered herself. Then she began her usual process of tapping all of the pockets on her vest. When she reached the radio, she sighed and turned it on. Lastly, she tapped her chest, then had to look down in surprise. Not even her NTSB badge was in place.

"Someone been distracting you?" Holly gave Jeff a punch

on the shoulder. Thankfully without the usual force she unleashed on others. "You been asking a lot of good questions?"

"Maybe," Jeff grinned up at Holly.

Miranda fished out her badge and placed it so that it faced outward.

"I'm Miranda Chase. Investigator-in-charge for the NTSB."

"Well, I'm glad we got that cleared up," Holly joked.

Mike was laughing as well for some reason.

Miranda ignored them both and pointed at the steel pipe Holly had tied her rope to. "That's the barrel of an M102 howitzer. And we also found a Bofors L/60 autocannon, or the remains of one."

"That confirms it," Holly nodded to Mike.

"What?"

"From down at the wing, Jon was whining that something was wrong. Must have picked up on it being an AC-130 gunship rather than a standard Hercules."

"All that's missing is the GAU-12 Equalizer rotary cannon."

Holly shrugged. "We crossed paths with the remains of a 20 mm Vulcan cannon."

Miranda looked at her in surprise. "That's—"

"What's all that stuff mean?" Jeff asked.

"It means that the plane that crashed here wasn't one that should be flying anymore. That it still has the Vulcan cannon means that it was an *old* gunship and they were all retired by 2001."

"You mean another plane crashed, too?" Jeff's panicked tone was back.

"You're thinking is upside down. Maybe this will help." Holly grabbed him by the ankles and hung him upside down. "Do you always ask so many questions?"

Jeff's panic turned to a half giggle.

"It means," Holly explained still holding Jeff aloft, "that this plane isn't one that should have been flying. That's all. It's still the plane what planted its nose here so hard. Got it?"

Jeff nodded from his inverted position. "Got it."

Mike stepped in and grabbed Jeff around the waist to set him back on his feet.

"Remember to keep thinking upside down." Holly's order earned her another giggle.

Miranda let her mind consider the surrounding area.

Right side up or upside down, there was only the one reported crash.

But it was a plane that shouldn't have been seen outside of a storage boneyard.

So where had this gunship come from?

12

When Miranda had raised her question about the gunship's origin, Holly had shrugged.

"Like I told that guy panting on your trail, a crash is a crash."

The guy...? Miranda shoved the thought aside as irrelevant.

Holly was right.

But the more Miranda investigated this crash, the less sense it made.

They found the very nose of the cockpit by following the trajectory of debris.

It had survived more or less intact. Its second landing—after the initial crash and then the brief flight due to the explosion—had plowed through a perimeter fence of orange plastic mesh. Jeff said it was there to stop people from skiing down the wrong side of the peak and into a dangerous wilderness area *with avalanches and cliffs and things*.

Past the fence, the cockpit section had tumbled down a

rocky slope that had severely battered the exterior but left the interior surprisingly intact. It had landed nearly right side up. Out its missing windows towered the true peaks of Snowmass and the Maroon Bells mountains reaching another two thousand feet higher than the top of the Cirque where the plane had crashed.

They'd checked that it was firmly wedged and wouldn't be falling off any cliffs before Miranda led the way aboard. This section was surprisingly intact. The ladder itself was badly warped, but still usable.

The view when she stepped into the cockpit was somewhat surreal.

Without the windshield glass, it was a disconcertingly clear sight from inside the plane. Both mountains were still snowcapped and close enough to imply imminent impact— if the Hercules could still have flown.

The QAR, quick access recorder, in the dashboard had survived. She extracted it for Jeremy to analyze when he joined them. Everything was...

"What's missing?" It had been one of her father's favorite questions. He trained her how to see what wasn't there as much as what was.

Holly came up and looked over her shoulder. "Other than the bodies?"

"Other than the bodies." There were yellow tags marking where Mountain Rescue removed the two bodies of the pilots.

The two of them looked over everything, but Miranda could see that Holly didn't know what it was either.

She pictured the cockpits she'd investigated at other crashes. There were few signs of fire that swept through the interiors of so many crashes, but that was not definitive.

The only burns were the scorch marks of the initial explosion that had launched the cockpit through the fence and down the slope. None of the brush fire had reached here over the back side of the Cirque's crown.

"When Dad shoots a deer, it can be really messy." Jeff had been playing with the circuit breakers. She'd recorded the position of each before allowing him to pull and reset them, making small explosive noises with his mouth each time he pushed one in with a sharp click.

"Really messy how?"

He didn't look up from the breaker panel. "Well, there's always blood. And if you don't get a heart or brain shot—Dad says you got to kill them right away like that to be kind —it can go everywhere." Click. *Pow!* Click. *Boom!* Click. *Ker-Pow!*

Miranda looked down at her feet.

"No blood," Holly whispered.

"These bodies were dead before the crash. Maybe they died at altitude."

"Not just dead," Holly corrected her. She reached out to muss Jeff's hair, who batted his hands at her to make her stop. "Kid got it all aces. But not dead like recently. Otherwise there would still have been blood."

"Their seatbelts were unbuckled," Mike poked his head in through the pilot's window making the mountain view seem more like a painting than a pending crash. "The FAA wouldn't approve."

"The FAA has very limited jurisdiction regarding military flights," Miranda replied, but it was a knee-jerk reaction. The reality was that Mike was correct. In fact, one of the bodies had been removed from *behind* the copilot's seat if the marker was accurate. She couldn't think of any professional pilot she'd ever met who would unbuckle and try to hide behind their seat, not even with the plane past any possibility of recovery.

"That's majorly pear-shaped." Holly tapped the two emergency air masks. The pilot's was looped around the control yoke. The copilot's mask was still stowed as if it had never been used.

"You like *that,* Holly? You'll love this," Mike pointed off to the side.

Miranda had had trouble keeping Jeff from playing with the main panel, so she scooted him out ahead of her.

Mike led them about twenty meters away around a rough outcropping.

There stood the front, port-side passenger door for the Hercules all by itself. The base was jammed against the ground and the two sides of the frame had been caught by two boulders. Unlike most commercial airliners where the door opened outward, the C-130 passenger door pulled inward, then slid upward on tracks. The entire door frame had survived intact and landed upright wedged in the rocks.

Looking through the open door was even more surreal than the cockpit windows. One step beyond the threshold was a hundred-meter drop. Yet the big door was perfectly intact, though she expected it would topple and fall at the lightest touch.

Holly had a firm grip on Jeff's shoulder to make sure he stayed back with the rest of them.

Mike pointed east where the sun was high enough to

shine through the door and out toward the true top of Snowmass peak beyond.

"I spoke to the folks at Denver ARTCC again. The Air Route Traffic Control Center was very helpful. The actual flight controller was very upset, but made it through the post-incident interviews before the shift supervisor took her home. I managed to chat with the assistant supervisor who did the debrief."

"Get her home number while you were about it, mate?"

Mike merely sniffed at Holly's comment. "*He* said that the flight declared a depressurization emergency at thirty-nine thousand."

"Opening this thing," Holly eased up to the door, "would be one spectacular depressurization event. But if they were masked up, it shouldn't have been that big an issue."

"The assistant super says that Shadow Six-four's flight path nosed down and never came back up. In fact, there was no significant maneuvering before the pilot called total loss of control and stopped responding—other than a final curse. Wings ripped off about ten seconds later, up around twenty thousand feet."

Miranda looked back toward the cockpit.

Something else was missing from the cockpit. More upside-down thinking. She liked that phrase enough that she knew there was no need to write it down.

There was no blood. There should have been brown stains of dried blood after the force of the impact. That was missing.

The seat belts should have been buckled. Both masks should have been used...

And...

"Come along, Jeff. I want you to help me find something. If it's here, it should be between the cockpit and the center of the explosion."

Jeff ran to her side as she explained what she was looking for.

13

Jon stared at the message on his phone. It was a long one and he had to scroll several times to read it all. When he got to the end, he couldn't believe it and scrolled back to the top. But he'd read the header correctly. This hadn't been some ordinary flight.

"Jeremy, we've got to go." He began packing his gear.

Jeremy stuck his head out from under the port wing where he'd been inspecting the exhaust port of the Number Three engine. "I'm not done yet."

"Doesn't matter. We've got bigger problems. I need to get up the mountain." Then he began stuffing Jeremy's tools into his pack.

"Hey!" Jeremy scrambled free. "You've got to organize it or it doesn't all fit."

"Fine, then you do it. You have thirty seconds." Jon threw up his hands, then shouldered his own pack.

"Where's the fire?" Somehow, though his pack had been half emptied and laid out across the top of the wing, Jeremy had everything stowed and had slung it into place while Jon was still adjusting his straps.

"In Washington, DC," Jon said grimly, then turned to climb up the steep slope. It was steep enough that in many places it was only a matter of reaching out to touch the rising ground. "People really ski down this?"

"I'm a computer and airplane nerd from Seattle. What makes you think I'd know?"

"I'm a SEAL's kid from San Diego who decided to be a black sheep and join the Air Force. You've got to know more than me."

"Not about skiing. I can't even waterski. Besides, isn't the Air Force Academy in Colorado Springs? That's where the Olympic ski team trains, right?"

Jon could waterski, but had never liked the cold so kept his mouth shut.

He knew they were about six or seven hundred feet from the top. That shouldn't take long. He might not have skied at the Academy, but he'd certainly run more than enough in the foothills of the Rockies.

He made the first hundred feet before he had to stop, his pulse thundering in his ears.

"What the hell?" he managed to gasp out.

"Altitude," Jeremy gasped as well. He was glad to see that Jeremy was in no better shape.

"Then how do they climb something like Everest?"

"Again, what makes you think I'd know? Supplemental oxygen above the eight-thousand-meter Death Zone. Most teams do a four- to six-week acclimatization for altitude at Base Camp."

Typical. Jeremy seemed to know a lot about everything,

even if he couldn't ski. Jon made it another fifty feet up. Reminding himself it was just five stories didn't help.

Jeremy dropped to sit beside him. Jon didn't even remember sitting down.

"Why are you..." Jon had to drag in another deep breath, "...giving me such a...hard time?"

"Am I?"

Jon decided that an eye roll would use less oxygen than speech.

Jeremy seemed to be studying the peaks lying to the north for a while. "I didn't know I was." It didn't sound as if he was lying.

"Well, you've been grinding on something since the moment I got here. The hammer. Banging the engine. Insisting that every camera angle I used wasn't optimal. Stuff," he finished lamely.

"Huh!" Jeremy's grunt was thoughtful. Or was it another brush-off like Miranda had given him?

They rose to their feet and made it up another seventy-five or so. They should be halfway up the slope and it looked good. He pushed an extra twenty-five and came over a rise. After a short meadow that looked almost level, though he'd bet it wasn't, the mountain rose up high above them.

"It got taller," Jeremy gasped out. He pulled out an altimeter, studied it, then turned it to Jon. According to it, they were still over four hundred feet below the main crash.

Jon turned to look back down at the wings. They were smaller, he was sure of it. Just not much. Upslope, the top still looked very, very far away.

They had to work together to get around an outcropping and not be tipped over backward by their heavy packs.

When they were sitting atop it, with their legs dangling out into space, Jeremy pulled out his water bottle, offering it to Jon first.

He drank deeply before returning it and felt better for doing so.

"You're upsetting Miranda." Jeremy said as if it was simple fact, again studying the horizon.

"I'll be damned if I know how."

"You like her?"

"Yes."

"A lot?"

"Uh-huh." Jon slowed down on his answer.

"And you're sleeping with her."

"Not sure that's your business, but yes. When our schedules allow."

Jeremy hadn't looked away from the distant peaks. And again he stopped talking. But if Jon was judging correctly, he wasn't angry. His profile looked puzzled.

"Do you wish it was you sleeping with her?"

"*What?*" That finally had Jeremy facing him. "No! Why?"

Jon finally figured out what was going on. He should have seen it right away. Jeremy worshipped Miranda. *Anyone* touching her would be just plain wrong in his world. Like watching your parents kiss. Not that his parents ever had.

But he couldn't just let Jeremy off the hook, even if he hadn't realized that he'd been chapping Jon's ass for the last few hours. He pushed to his feet, ready to tackle the next section.

"She's pretty hot, you know. Wouldn't blame you if you wanted to."

"No-o! I— Not with—"

"How about Holly? You like blondes?"

"*Holly?*" His voice squeaked and Jon didn't think it was due to the altitude. "She's...scary."

Jon had to agree with him there.

"So who are you seeing?" The conversation stretched out in stages. They were no longer stopping after each section, but rather step-step-rest, step-step-rest.

"No one."

"C'mon, Jeremy. You're a good-looking kid." Step-step-rest. "How old are you?"

"Twenty-four." Over a decade younger than him or Miranda.

"You're not a virgin, are you?"

"No!" His voice had the defensiveness of someone who'd not had much experience. But then was softer as he continued. "Nancy. Chess club. Graduation night. I was sixteen. I finished MIT at nineteen. Dual masters from Princeton. At twenty-two. I mostly studied." Even those short sentences were more than Jon could have managed while moving.

Then Jon stopped short and looked at him. He'd known Jeremy was smart, but it hadn't sunk in that, much like Miranda, he was a genius at what he did. Jon's main success in high school had been swim team—his SEAL father's realm as if he could ever compete. For his first eighteen years, he'd never been good enough. Without Uncle Drake, then a colonel in the 75th Army Rangers, calling in a couple favors for him, he'd probably never have made it into the Air Force Academy at all. Once there and away from his father, he'd thrived. But it had been a close thing.

Had Jeremy had a chance to thrive yet? Professionally and intellectually, yes. But the rest of him?

"We need to get you a girl, Jeremy. One as nice as you are."

Jeremy blushed in response—his coloring lit far more brightly than could be accounted for by the high-altitude workout. Jon's kid sister was still in her twenties—and hunting for Husband Number Two with all the sensitivity of a battering ram. She would run right over Jeremy and never notice that she'd flattened him. He'd have to give it some more thought. Maybe ask if Holly knew anyone.

He turned back up the slope, too short of breath to speak anymore. They'd moved past step-step-rest. Now they were just in the slow grind of continuous motion that would eventually get them to the top.

But he didn't dare look up to find out how much longer it would be.

14

Jon felt like Sir Edmund Hillary and Sherpa Tenzing Norgay atop Mount Everest—without the supplemental oxygen.

Jeremy had ground out the details in broken sentences and scattered phrases. "Fifty feet to the highest peak in the world, they stopped crawling and stood. Past speech, Tenzing waved for Hillary to be the first ever to stand atop the mountain. He figured it was the white climber's privilege. In reply, Hillary wrapped an arm around Tenzing's shoulders, then, staggering forward, they took the top together."

His and Jeremy's arrival at the top of the Snowmass ski area was far less auspicious, but perhaps equally welcome. Jon had thought he was in pretty good shape. Apparently not.

"Sixty-four percent," Jeremy grunted from where he knelt on all fours with his head hanging down.

"Huh?" Was all Jon could manage. If not for the char, Jon

would have spread-eagled on the ground. Finally reaching the true top past three false peaks had taken his knees right out from under him.

"We only have sixty-four percent of the air up here compared to sea level."

"How much did they have on Everest?"

"Thirty-three."

"Shit." It was all he could say. So much for comparing himself to Hillary. He and Jeremy had barely walked up to an altitude that locals skied at all winter. Of course, skiers didn't live at Pope Field at two hundred feet year-round and carry full site-investigation packs weighing at least thirty pounds.

Then he glanced at Jeremy's big pack and felt even worse about the current state of his conditioning.

He looked up to see the rest of the team and the helo pilot's kid walking the hilltop in a well-spaced line.

Grid pattern search of the debris field. But...

"Hey, Jeremy?"

"Wha..." he trailed off as he spotted the others. "They're not mapping the area; they're looking for something specific already. Isn't Miranda amazing?"

Jon checked his watch, but couldn't remember what time they'd gotten on the mountain. Enough time for the sun to be much higher in the sky and make him thankful for the eyesore hat the helo pilot had given him. It couldn't be more than a few hours and already Miranda was hot on the trail.

Not that it mattered now.

Or maybe it mattered all the more.

The line was coming their way. Jon felt recovered enough

to rock back on his heels, but he wasn't so sure about his knees yet.

"Hey, Miranda," he greeted her as she swung close.

"Hey." But she didn't look up from her search. If he didn't already know that Miranda never missed a thing, he'd have guessed that she hadn't even registered his presence.

Shedding his pack, he pushed to his feet and fell in beside her. "What are we looking for?"

She held up a pilot's emergency breathing system air bottle with regulator. The fat bottle was about the length and size of his upper arm. Separate from the airplane's main system, it could supply approximately fifteen minutes of safe breathing independent of the onboard air system. On a fighter jet, it would be part of the ejection seat system, allowing the pilot to breathe during the descent from a high-altitude bail out.

"Why?"

Miranda stopped what she was doing and looked at him for the first time since his arrival in Aspen. Well, she looked at his left ear, but that was normal for her.

She waved for the others to continue the search.

"There are several anomalies with this crash."

"Including that it killed a three-star general?" That's what had been in the text message that had sent him climbing up the hill.

"No," Miranda shook her head, then her focus seemed to encompass his right ear.

"No? Three-star generals are practically as rare as flying penguins. When we lose one, it's a big deal."

"There are no species of penguins that can fly—assuming we're discussing flight in the medium of air and not the medium of water, where they are far closer to flying than swimming. That actually makes three-star generals *infinitely* more common than flying penguins. One hundred and forty-seven divided by zero is an infinite ratio."

"How in the world do you know how many three-star generals there are?" As soon as he asked the question, he knew it was a mistake. He was sidetracking Miranda, which meant he'd have to let her complete the sidetrack logic before he could get back to the point that, rare as penguins or not, a three-star had died on this mountaintop.

"September 30th, 2018, Department of Defense Personnel workforce reports. The number is also limited by law." Then she simply stopped and waited, catching Jon off guard.

"So what are the anomalies?"

"They're numerous. Based on armament and the cockpit avionics, the plane is an older AC-130H Spectre that was not upgraded."

"I didn't know that any of those were still in service."

"Not since 2001. This plane almost certainly came from the Davis-Monthan boneyard."

"That's weird as hell. It was en route from... Huh! I'm not even sure where. I'm operating from the Denver ARTCC supervisor who called us about the loss of a military aircraft."

Miranda pointed toward the far side of the peak. "The forward personnel door was found partially intact, and fully open. In the cockpit, the bodies were *behind* the pilot and copilot positions. There was no blood, their seatbelts were unbuckled, and—" she held up the EBS air cylinder "—we're unable to locate the copilot's breathing system, but the pilot's was intact and in the seat-side sleeve exactly as it should be."

"What are you thinking?" Jon's head whirled with the stream of information she'd just delivered.

She started to answer, but he held up his hand to stop her.

"Wait. Okay. I've got that. It means that...the bodies weren't actually the crew. They were placed on a plane that was...deliberately crashed."

Miranda was nodding, so he kept going down the logical chain.

"The pilot put on his breathing mask. The copilot took his breathing bottle, opened the door, and depressurized the airplane. He then jumped out in a parachute."

"At thirty-nine thousand feet, which would probably point to a highly skilled individual."

Jon nodded his agreement, then looked up at the bright blue sky. "Three a.m. at thirty-nine thousand, it's not a jump I'd like to make. Then the pilot declares an emergency, dives the plane—perhaps even setting the autopilot to continue the dive."

"I didn't think to check—" Miranda turned to go back to the cockpit.

"No," Jon caught her arm to stop her. "Because the autopilot is designed to recover from dangerous situations automatically. So they wouldn't engage it. He rode the plane down until it was unrecoverable. By that time there would be enough air to breathe. He rushed to the door and bailed out himself. Leaving the plane to die."

Miranda didn't even hesitate. "That is the precise

scenario I had also formulated as the most likely sequence of events."

Jon felt a bit as if he was a little boy who'd just been patted on the head. Also, in matching Miranda, he felt like he was one step closer to understanding her. Maybe...

"Was that what was going on?"

"What?" Miranda blinked in confusion

Is this what Miranda felt like all the time—like she was being constantly hosed down by the sheer flow of information? No filter? He'd asked around and been told to read Temple Grandin's book, *Thinking in Pictures: and Other Reports from My Life with Autism.* If they were going to be lovers... Boy and girlfriend? Accident investigators with benefits? If they were going to be any of those things, then he figured it was worth trying to understand her a bit better.

"Have you been avoiding me all morning or have you just been focusing on the helicopter, then the boy, then the crash?"

"I haven't been avoiding you. We've been working on the same project all morning."

"Then why did you assign me to study the wings with Jeremy?"

Miranda turned to face the team still walking the grid search over the hilltop and he was half afraid she'd rejoin their efforts without answering. Jeremy had taken over her position in the line.

"Because you're good with Jeremy," she responded without turning. "Holly doesn't give Jeremy time to slow down and think, and Mike tries but he isn't very technical and having to explain things to him slows Jeremy down too much."

"Oh, okay." And also, now that he'd kicked his ego to the curb, it made good sense. More than he expected Miranda to make about people. "It was just that we haven't seen each other for three months, and you didn't seem to be very happy to see me."

She turned back and for just an instant studied his eyes. He now knew how atypical that was. "Was I supposed to stop the investigation and make a gesture to indicate that I'm glad to see you again?"

"Well...yeah."

Then she pulled out her notebook and wrote a neat note that he could just make out.

Show people (e.g. Jon) that I'm glad to see them after time apart.

He could also see the note above that: *Discuss (Jon): attractiveness versus varying states of undress.* He was absolutely looking forward to that one.

"Is it too late to make an appropriate gesture? Like..." she flipped to an earlier page, "...a laugh too long after the joke?"

"Never too late to show you care about someone."

Miranda simply stepped into his arms and placed her face against the center of his chest. He wrapped his arms around her and held her close even though she didn't hug him back. Jon made sure the embrace was firm for her sake...and his. He liked the feel of her in his arms. There was something very right about it.

He breathed in the scent of her. Northwest wilderness, and—he tried not to sneeze in her hair—the carbon of the mountaintop fire.

The crash.

Crap!

15

"YOU SAID THERE WERE A BUNCH OF ANOMALIES." JON released her from the hug and she missed it. That wasn't something that had happened to her before. If she'd missed his hugs, did that indicate that she'd missed Jon as well? She supposed that it really did.

"I said there were *several* anomalies."

Previously, Miranda had learned to tolerate hugs, partly because Holly insisted on delivering them so fiercely at such unexpected moments. But she liked leaning her face into Jon's chest and not thinking about anything else for a brief time. It was one of the only places, other than sitting alone on her island, where Miranda had ever found that that she could just be...quiet.

Now it was time to deal with the crash.

"Acknowledging that it is far too early in the process to discuss conclusions..."

Jon nodded his agreement without interrupting her flow.

"In the past you've asked me to create a 'most likely

model' against which to compare findings rather than waiting until all of the findings were complete."

Holly and the others, including the boy Jeff, came up beside Jon. With a slight shake of her head, Holly indicated that they hadn't found the copilot's emergency breathing system cannister.

"So, hit us with your conclusions. Then we'll see if they pan out."

"Not conclusions; incomplete hypotheses." Miranda toyed with the regulator of the EBS cannister that she still held as she sought a way to explain what looked so clear in her head. "I need to clarify beforehand, the best-fit scenario has a distinct problem in that it is inherently illogical."

Holly shot her a thumbs-up as if that was a good thing. Jeremy and Jon both nodded for her to continue. Mike knelt by Jeff and whispered to him, "She means that her ideas don't make any sense, but she thinks she knows what happened anyway."

Jeff nodded hard in sudden understanding and waited.

"The airplane, despite a probable origin at the Davis-Monthan boneyard—"

"Actually, it's still officially there," Jeremy chimed in. "I checked the logs against the aircraft number on the tail and the cockpit. It's still recorded as being in storage on site."

"Which means we need to have a little chat with Colonel Arturo Campos," Holly snarled out. She'd never liked him. Miranda had...briefly.

"—despite the plane's *origin* at the Davis-Monthan boneyard, it reported a depressurization event last night—"

"At precisely three a.m. according to Denver Center," Mike added.

It had taken her over six months working together for her to accept their interruptions without losing track of her own thoughts, but rather allow her team to add to them on the fly. It was disconcertingly like having part of her brain be external to her head.

She reached for her notebook to log the curious image for future consideration, then spotted Jon's smile that seemed like it knew more than it should. She decided that making the note wasn't important enough to interfere with her consideration of the crash scenario. Besides, she was unlikely to forget the externalization of her thoughts with the constant reminders the team provided.

"If that depressurization event was caused by the opening of the passenger door at—"

"—thirty-nine thousand feet—" Mike inserted again. "Oh, then it would be deliberate."

"Who would deliberately tank a nice old gunship?" Holly appeared disgusted. "Know more than a few ex-mates I wouldn't have minded targeting with a Spectre if someone had just given me the use of one. That's as dumb as doing a dance on a dingo's tail."

Miranda forged ahead. "The cockpit has bodies, but not in their chairs. And there's no *messy* blood," she nodded to Jeff to acknowledge his contribution.

He tried to stand up even taller than his four-foot-five.

"So we can theorize that the corpses were dead before the crash. But the perpetrators of the crash assumed too little evidence would remain for that to be ascertainable. This crash was deliberately created to make us all assume that the named passengers aboard are dead so that the Air Force would not pursue their whereabouts while they carried out a very different mission. I would surmise that it is one not authorized by the military establishment."

"Whoa!" Jon gasped out. "I didn't think about the last part of that."

So she stopped.

He narrowed his eyes at her. "Not whoa, just...*whoa!*"

Holly delivered one of her trademark punches to Jon's arm, causing him to stagger aside. "Not *whoa* like stop, Miranda. *Whoa* is also an exclamation of surprise."

Jon punched Holly back. Her attempts to avoid flattening Jeff sent her careening into Mike, and he barely kept them both from going to the charred ground.

Then Jon smiled. "What she said. Keep going, Miranda. I think you've got it right so far."

"You hit a *girl?*" Holly practically roared as she regained her balance.

"Nah!" Jon winked at Miranda.

What was it with people winking at her and giving eye rolls as if she understood some hidden message?

"Unless Ms. Holly Harper is admitting to actually *being* a girl...rather than a royal pain in the ass."

"Pain in the *arm,*" Holly grinned at him. "I ain't kicked your behind yet to be a PIA, jet jockey."

"Don't tempt me...*girl.* You were saying, Miranda?" Then he turned his back on Holly with what Miranda estimated to be a certain degree of rather foolish lack of caution.

She waited a moment, but Holly didn't take advantage of the situation.

"If the people were already dead, then who was flying the plane?" Jeff looked puzzled.

"Exactly the correct question," Miranda acknowledged. "I would conjecture—"

Holly kicked Jon in the behind, but not too hard. Jon didn't turn, instead muttering, "Total PIA!" and grinned.

Miranda did her best to ignore them both.

"—that the copilot removed his EBS cannister from its holder by his seat and was using it to breathe when he opened the personnel door on the Hercules."

"Did he fall out and die?" Jeff's voice quavered.

"No. If he planned all the rest of it, he must have had a parachute. He kept his air cannister and simply stepped off the plane and opened his chute. That's why we looked for the EBS. It should still have been in its holder, just like the pilot's was. It wasn't. So, taking it with him or her is the most likely explanation as to why we didn't find it in our first search."

Jeff formed a big O with his mouth but appeared safely calmer.

She held up the cannister. "The pilot didn't take his. He used the system built into the plane until he was at a low enough altitude to not need it. Once the plane was doomed, he probably followed the copilot out the open door. Mike, call Denver again."

"For possible signs of parachutes on their radar. Got it!" He pulled out his phone.

"So nobody died in the crash?" Jeff sounded hopeful.

"We don't know that, but it looks that way."

"But where did they go?" Jon pulled out his phone and handed it to her.

Miranda read the list of names. It didn't mean anything to her except... "These are some very high-ranking officers to be all on an old AC-130H Spectre gunship at the same time. The gun crew would have to be majors and colonels rather than airmen and staff sergeants."

Holly moved to look over her shoulder, then pointed at a name. "That one. That's the body we found. Little bit of a thing not much bigger than Jeff. Colonel Vicki 'Taz' Cortez. We read her dog tags, not much left identifiable after the crash and fire. Sorry, kid," she nodded to Jeff as if charred corpses were just a normal part of the job. They rarely were for her team, but sometimes she arrived fast enough to see them before the remains were removed.

"S'okay." Jeff returned the nod with a hard swallow.

Mike finished his call. "They looked at the radar imaging again and there were two very small additional radar signatures after the declared emergency. They thought it was just screen noise it was so faint. The first one—appearing at thirty-four thousand feet, which must be our copilot—landed somewhere along the highway north of Aspen. The other might have been debris, as it appeared after the wings ripped off, but it had some lateral flight before it disappeared into the back country. If that was the pilot, his rate of descent was far too fast and I'd guess he didn't make it. Maybe he had a parachute failure." He waved to the south.

"Major Danny Gonzalez and pilot-in-command Lieutenant Colonel Luis Hernandez according to this list." Jon looked around the empty mountaintop, marked by little more than the barrel of the 105 mm howitzer still sticking up out of the ground. "Ejecting pilots. Fake bodies with real dog tags so that no one would bother to check the remains more carefully. Jesus, what a mess."

"Not fake bodies, but ones that were a close enough

match to not arouse suspicion over false dog tags. After all, a fake body would be easily identifiable because it would be probably be built of metal and plastics that were..." She tapered off at Mike's amused smile.

Too literal. *Again.*

Jon took his phone back and stared at the list of names before growling out, "Then where the hell is my missing three-star, General Jorge Jesus Martinez?"

16

GENERAL JORGE JESUS MARTINEZ, JJ TO MOST PEOPLE—
though few were actually close to him—sat in *the* most
sought-after spot on Santa Catalina Island just off the coast
of Los Angeles, California. The bench seat at the very end of
the stout wooden Green Pleasure Pier offered the premier
view of the harbor.

It was also the closest place available to monitor what
was occurring in the offshore flight test range immediately
north of their position, while masquerading as a civilian.

In late June, the water was rife with pleasure boats of the
wealthy and oblivious—the ones who thought nothing of
what kept them so safe in their little pleasure ground. The
great round casino commanded the harbor from the far
point. The harbor town of Avalon, filled with shops and
restaurants priced to scalp even the most wary tourist,
wrapped along the waterfront just waiting for the next cruise
ship to moor outside the breakwater.

"Why did we fight so hard to protect this shit?" Either his

foul mood or Taz made sure that this corner of the pier was all theirs. He suspected it was Taz. Despite being only four-foot-eleven, when she wanted to, she cast a danger signal that seemed to drive people well away without their even realizing it.

She didn't answer, instead doing a slow sweep of her mirrored Ray Bans. They weren't Aviators, like most of the Air Force favored—they were sharply octagonal. He sometimes wondered what she saw through them. It made her look even colder and more calculating than he knew she was—which was saying a lot.

He'd picked newly minted Airman Vicki "Taser/Taz" Cortez as his adjutant when he saw how she performed during 9/11. Five-foot-nothing of slender Mexican with skin darker than his, had been a pillar of calm fury in the aftermath. She hadn't let her anger at what bin Laden had done to their country control her as it did so many others, but she'd looked poised—like a silent Doberman Pinscher ready to be unleashed at the least provocation.

Not once in the nearly twenty years since had now-Colonel Taz Cortez made him second guess his choice. Something about her made everyone else shy away. He liked that in an assistant.

Bouncing her to OTS had paid off as well. Taz had taken to Officer Training School like an AIM-9 missile to a Russian MiG. No officer listened to an enlisted, but even when they outranked her by three or four grades, they now listened to her.

Death walking, more than one obstinate officer had called her after surviving a meeting with her. They were rarely obstinate after the meeting. In addition to being highly organized, she was one of the most effective weapons in his arsenal for navigating DoD politics—because if nothing else, the Department of Defense was *intensely* political.

"We fought so hard to protect this shit because it used to be our sworn duty," she finally answered him.

"Still is our duty." Yes, he'd sworn to protect these clueless Americans against all comers.

" '*I will support the Constitution*,'" she quoted from the officer's oath.

" '*Against all enemies, foreign and domestic*,'" it was an old argument. They had walked away from their sworn duty to the US Air Force, but it was in their commitment to defend the Constitution—just not the way those political wranglers in DC ever thought about it.

Another crowd swirled to the head of the pier to prepare for one of the sightseeing, diving, whatever-just-give-us-your-money tours embarking down the ramp to the low dock before them.

He took the final bite of his crab empanada from Maggie's Blue Rose at the head of the pier. He'd have been fine with a corndog or a burger, but Taz didn't eat that way. Whenever they were out of the office together, he knew the food would be superb. Even in places she'd never been, she could always zero in on the very best. She'd nailed it this time for certain.

While they waited, she'd been methodically working her way through a spread of tacos: grilled shrimp, skirt steak, lobster, and carnitas. Even after twenty years working together, he'd never understood how she could eat more than a six-three airman after a thirty-k run.

His empanada brought back memories, as such things

always did, of his mother's cooking. Even after they'd found a steady place—as permanent farm hands, not just seasonal pickers—east of Stockton on the baking flats of the north San Joaquin Valley, she'd let him crank the *molino.* Grinding corn into masa for tortillas—another thing lost. Nothing had ever matched her carne asada tamales or... Yet another memory he didn't have time for.

"Are they in position?"

Taz looked just like any other tourist fooling with her phone while she ate. Except her phone included full encryption capability, and had a special app to pick up broadcasts on US Air Force frequencies. Her headphones appeared to be wired, but that was actually the receiving antenna.

"Yes, they've just entered the Point Mugu Sea Range."

He'd been watching to the north. The area between Santa Catalina Island and Santa Rosa Island to the north was a no man's land that belonged to the US Navy. Despite the nearby Los Angeles population, marine and flight charts forbade all civilian entry. The US Coast Guard caught a surprising number of narco-submarines transporting cocaine out of Colombia because they wandered into the forbidden zone and became easy to detect with no other shipping about.

Edwards Air Force Base and Naval Base Ventura County were only two of the airfields that did testing there. The Navy out of San Diego were common participants as well. Even Maverick had gone down there in *Top Gun.* Though the movie had failed to explain how he'd gotten in trouble in the dry Sierra Nevadas, but crashed in the Pacific.

Today they were doing acceptance testing on the Block

30 upgrade to the AC-130J Ghostrider. It was the newest gunship in the fleet. He'd made sure to be on the development team. He'd also made sure that, today, it flew with *his* pilots aboard.

Taz handed him a Bluetooth earpiece. He pulled out his own phone so that they would look like some bored father-daughter duo doing side-by-side play on their separate phones.

"This is Shadow Three-five commencing the first run of Test Suite Alpha-Bravo-Two-Seven-Five." Major Mark "Tango" Torres reported to the observer team that would be flying in a nearby plane to monitor the Ghostrider's performance. His voice sounded clearly over the earpiece.

"Roger."

There was no other cross chatter.

How many missions—hundreds, thousands—had he sat and listened while others risked their lives? Too many.

After today he was done with that as well.

He'd selected his entire team for one very specific mission. It wasn't a mission of mere duty. It was one that included a deep personal stake for every individual.

For now, all he could do was listen to his men do their jobs.

17

Tango Torres kept an eye out as his copilot, "Gutz" Gutierrez, set up on the first run.

The Block 30 upgrade to the Ghostrider had included some nice tactical and weapons control enhancements. It also included an advanced active denial system that could suppress all of a hostile's communications for a range of over five kilometers—including both cell phone and radio.

But the centerpiece of Block 30 was the HEL-A.

The High-Energy Laser-Airborne could deliver a hundred-and-fifty-kilowatt beam against a tracked target. Ground testing had shown it effective against anti-aircraft missiles and other aircraft. It was also powerful enough to destroy cars and disable boats and other ground targets.

Tango wanted to see it burn.

The twin-prop C-12 observer plane that hung just off their rear quarter was crowding close to see as well.

Perfect.

The first two passes occurred without incident. They

fried the electronics of a small drone, which proceeded to splash down into the ocean near a recovery boat. Then they cooked a target on a small floating dinghy.

Rosa Cruz was on laser control and clearly enjoyed her new toy.

Tango's camera feed in the cockpit showed that the six-foot dinghy didn't just get a hole, its plastic hull melted and shriveled like an ant under a magnifying glass aimed at the sun. Or maybe the jump from the hundred kilowatt to the one-fifty was just that big a change.

Nah, it had to be Rosa.

He liked that about her. She was always a bright fire in any darkness. Her laugh could light up a room, and her body was a gift from Sweet Mother Mary.

They often raced their Kawasakis out into the deserts that surrounded so many US military bases, then fucked each other until even the rabbits were envious. He had to readjust his flightsuit at his body's reaction to even thinking about her bent forward over his Ninja 1000 sport bike. She'd peek at him over her shoulder through that lush fall of brown-black hair, and wiggle that fine ass like a marshaller waving two bright batons and guiding him straight to the gate.

Gutz lined the Ghostrider up on the third run and Tango reported the start to the observers. He knew that the general would be monitoring their status. Everything was scheduled to fly off-plan in just moments.

Rosa flashed "Ready" from her midship control station.

If their maneuver didn't work, it would be her job to finish it.

The AC-130J had just the pilot and copilot on the flight

deck. Down the left side behind them were the weapons. First, the five tons of HEL-A laser where the 30 mm GAU-23 autocannon usually sat. Back under the wing lurked the monster 105 mm howitzer.

Integrated into the rear cargo ramp were ten drop tubes. Most were filled with guided sixteen-kilo glide bombs in ten-round magazines, but several also had small surveillance drones that could be launched in flight, provide over-the-horizon data, and then be discarded.

On the right side, across from the laser, were the weapons control stations. The loaders in the bay kept the guns fed, but the weapons control team aimed and fired them using all of the visible light, infrared, and radar information fed to them by the sensor technician.

Tango had always been a flier and there were few machines more complex than a big military plane. From the first time he climbed into one, it had just been a part of him; every upgrade made perfect sense. Weather and threat radars, status on the four big engines, and every other one of the hundred thousand pieces that made an AC-130J Ghostrider fly.

Too bad there was no way to go down on Rosa while she was firing the big guns or for her to do him extra hard while they were flying. Rosa was wild and had a laugh that burst out at the most amazing times. Out in the desert, she'd let loose a wolf-howl as she slammed into her peaks.

Or maybe there was a way to tap that in flight.

After all, they were permanently exiting the United States Air Force at the end of this run. Who knew what could happen after they joined General JJ's Air Force. No one called it that to the old man's face, of course.

Or to Taz's.

Damn but she was one hard-bodied bitch. The general had to be tapping that himself, even if the rumor mill said not.

He imagined Taz would be hard, fast, and deathly silent. *Yeah, idiot. Then she'd snap off your head and drink your blood like a praying mantis bitch.*

He counted down the seconds, did the last five aloud for Gutz because it was always a shock when they blasted the first round out of the big 105.

On cue for their last-ever training run, the big gun spoke from the Ghostrider's belly with a bang that shook the length of the aircraft. Even though he wasn't flying, he rested his finger on the control yoke. He felt Gutz make that automatic correction for the recoil. The gun's mount was so well buffered that beginning pilots couldn't even feel it. But he and Gutz had been flying the ACs together for almost a decade, and the recoil was there even if the "experts" said it was impossible.

Rosa began calling her laser shots as Pierre Jones kept the big howitzer barking at targets. Not like the guy was all tall, lean, and elegant. He looked like he'd walked into several too many squid bars just to have a brawl with way too many Navy boys. But he could shoot almost as well as Rosa, which was all Tango cared about. Turned out he wasn't a bad sort to grab a beer with either.

"First round, dead center of Target B," Pierre announced —B for boat. It took the big gun's crew six seconds to clear and reload the howitzer.

In the meantime—

"In-bound Hellfire."

Rosa's laser responded. Silent and invisible.

But Tango saw a spark of light four miles away at the ten o'clock position out the windshield. It would be the explosion of the destroyed missile—heated to ignition by a one-second burst.

"Target M," M for missile, "neutralized," she reported.

"Now!" Tango called out.

Gutz slipped out of the planned flight path slowly, easing toward the observer plane that was following close on at the seven o'clock position and just a little high to stay clear of the big Ghostrider's turbulent wake.

"Hey, go easy there, Shadow," the observer's pilot called across.

"Oh, roger that," Tango answered as Gutz slid clear— then eased back even a little closer.

"Everything okay over there?"

"Just fine," Tango did his best to sound even more at ease than his usual slick self. He nodded to Gutz that they were close enough now. "Just a few little air pockets. We're gonna—"

Gutz twisted sharply left and traded speed for a little more altitude. The tip of the Ghostrider's massive wing slammed into the empennage of the observer plane. The rudder and elevator of the little twin-engine crumpled on contact.

"Oh, sorry. You guys okay over there?" Tango watched as the remaining bits of metal flapped uselessly in the wind. He couldn't even see a ding in their own big wing. Probably broke the lens on the green navigation light that they'd never be using again.

"Mayday! Mayday! Mayday! This is Oversight Nine-five-

two. We have a complete loss of control. We're going in at—"
The pilot proceeded to read out the coordinates.

Tango stopped paying attention.

Gutz raised his left hand and Tango high-fived it. The maneuver had been perfect.

Sometimes sacrifices were necessary, the general had been very clear on that. It was both horrible and beautiful to watch the little plane die. He'd lost enough fellow fliers in battle that he could avoid thinking about the men dying aboard her—almost.

Rosa had been ready to unleash the HEL-A laser if they'd missed, but that would be a little obvious. Unlike the Spectre gunship "Coffin Flight" staged over Colorado—where most of them had "died"—no one was supposed to know what happened to their Ghostrider.

Gutz fully feathered the props on engines One and Two. With the left engines now just spinning in neutral and the right engines still at full claw, they entered a counterclockwise spin.

It drove Tango to the right; would have dumped him in the aisle if not for his harness.

It was time to shed their Ghostrider's own excess crew. That was going to be even easier...and far less messy.

Tango got on the radio. "Mayday! Mayday! Mayday! This is Shadow Three-five declaring an emergency. We have lost engines One and Two." Then Tango had an evil thought, "Correction: One, Two, *and* Three."

Gutz feathered the prop on Three and scowled at him. Keeping tight control on a C-130 Hercules with only a single outboard engine was going to be a major challenge.

Tango only grinned back.

It made up for the time Gutz had informed him there was a hot missile on his tail when it was only a F-35 Lightning II jet passing through the testing range. Explaining away that particular evasive maneuver to the flight leader had taken some serious song and dance. It was bad form to blame the other guy.

Tango continued his report as he watched the little C-12 Huron finally auger into the Pacific Ocean below. "Engine Four controls are nonresponsive. Entering hard spin." With just the outermost engine running at full power on the right wing, that was becoming dangerously accurate.

"We've got about thirty seconds," Gutz said calmly. But he didn't bring any of the other engines back online—that would have been cheating. Ronny Gutierrez hadn't come by his nickname only because of his surname. He was a stone-cold flier in any situation. Stone guts. Tango had always liked that about his best friend.

Tango keyed the onboard intercom.

"All hands! All hands! Abandon the aircraft. I repeat. Abandon aircraft immediately."

18

Even knowing what was coming hadn't fully prepared Rosa Cruz for the sudden pitch change when Gutz took out the observer plane. It slammed her against her safety harness so hard that it knocked the breath out of her.

For half a second she froze in fear.

No.

Her newly discovered fetus wasn't at risk. Still too small to be harmed, even by such a hit. Her PSR, Pink Stick Revelation, was less than forty-eight hours old. *No one* knew.

Then the Ghostrider pitched nose down and entered a hard spiral.

At the controls for the M102 Howitzer, Pierre yelped.

"We're going down?" He cried out sharply enough that her eardrum hurt.

"Big, brave master sergeants with over a dozen years in the service are not supposed to squeal like little schoolgirls." She knew it was a faked emergency and couldn't resist the opportunity to tease her fellow gunner.

"Well, excuse me, Tech Sergeant Rosa. It's my first-ever crash."

"Oh, then squeal away."

"No, you've broken the mood now." He sniffed in a deeply offended way as he safetied his weapon.

She matched him move for move. She half suspected that he'd squealed completely for her benefit. He looked like a tough guy—the kind that came from a longshoreman's bar, not UC Berkley. His nose was even crooked. Every time she asked about it, he had a new story.

A grandma I was helping cross the street took umbrage at me feeling her up and smacked me with her purse. But she was a seriously hot octogenarian.

Doc took one look at my face when I was born and decided this would be an improvement. It did add to his dangerously capable look.

I did this dive off the high board in school. You should have been there to see. It was just beautiful. But I was paying too much attention to Mary Beth McAllister's bikini cleavage and dove before I got to the end of the board. Landed nose-first right on the end. She was even less interested in my nose going where any man's would want to after that. Blood! Snot! He'd made gushing motions as if it had been a geyser's worth.

The spiral was getting harsher than she'd expected.

"I think we're in real trouble."

"No shit, Tech Sergeant Rosa." Pierre could always make her laugh.

Tango totally tapped her wild animal fantasies.

Gutz, however, was like a long pull on a bottle of good tequila—the burn slow, deep, and powerful.

She'd hinted once or twice about a threesome, but

neither alpha bull liked the idea at all. Now she didn't know which one the birth control had failed on, or how to explain it to either of them.

Now the baby was going to choose for her.

She and Pierre had fun flirting, but there was one critical thing he didn't know about her that the other two men did.

Rosa was one of the three people on the plane who had sworn their allegiance to three-star Lieutenant General Jorge Jesus Martinez.

19

Tango's call of "Abandon aircraft!" galvanized Pierre into action.

Before Rosa knew what was happening, he'd unsnapped her harness—without even copping a feel he'd declared as his heart's truest desire in such a jovial tone that even her normal high-alert guy-dar didn't mind. Dragged to her feet, they were slammed against the starboard hull by the plane's spin. At the last second he twisted to take the brunt of the blow. She landed chest-to-chest hard against him, driven together by the pressure.

"Tech Sergeant Rosa," he always said her name that way, this time with a heavy dose of surprise. "I'm forced to question your timing if this is going to be the moment that you finally throw yourself at me."

In a moment that should be full-blown panic on his part, and carefully displayed panic on hers, he still flirted.

But he didn't leave her time to respond.

He pushed off the hull against the pressure of the spin's

centrifugal force. Keeping a hold on her arm, he dragged her up-pitch across the plane's cargo bay to the forward personnel door.

They arrived as the four gun operators and the sensor tech were donning their parachutes.

Pierre released the emergency door handle and opened the door. The roar was deafening. The hot California sea air slammed in and buffeted them against each other.

Pierre grabbed his parachute from the emergency rack.

No—he held it to her like an evening coat to slip her arms into. Only then did he pull another for himself. Hard to imagine Gutz or Tango doing that for her.

The plane's death spiral was getting worse.

The gunners began dragging themselves against the force of the spin, and then over the threshold to get clear of the plane. The long looping flight scattered the gunners widely into the air.

What would Pierre be like as a lover?

She actually regretted that she wouldn't have a chance to find out.

In moments, it was just the two of them rapidly buddy-checking each other's harnesses. She'd gone along with the farce of her escape. But there were only moments left. The ocean was getting very close.

What would her next choice be if she hadn't sworn to follow the general?

But she had. For reasons that, she reminded herself, were good and valid ones.

Pierre snugged the harness across her chest—above her breasts. Most asshole jokers tried to snug it below them, which always hurt like hell when the chute opened.

Yet, a stupid plastic stick with a small pink cross had changed her world entirely. She wasn't used to all the thoughts her Pink Stick Revelation had stirred up in the last forty-eight hours.

She wouldn't change her career-ending choice. But she'd like to know...

"Just this once," she shouted over the wind's roar screaming in through the open door.

"Excuse me?" They were each holding onto the door frame with one hand and the other's harness with the other. Checks were complete.

She grabbed his hand, shifted it onto her breast and used the wind's leverage to drive them together so that she could kiss him.

Pierre convinced her that she'd been missing out for the six months they'd been flying together. Missing out bad!

Even this simple contact aroused everything in her—the animal, the lover, and the something deeper. The mother? *Yikes! Scary-ass thought. But there anyway.*

"Sweet Jesus, Tech Sergeant Rosa. I'll definitely see you later. But I have to go help the pilots."

"No, wait. I—"

Pierre used the leverage of his hand still filled with her breast, and the leg driven between hers—she hadn't even noticed when he'd done so, but could feel herself pushing against his thigh—to leverage her out into the slipstream.

A flail, and she managed to grab the doorframe at the last second. The wind slammed her hard against the hull. She couldn't hear the release, but could *certainly* feel when her left shoulder dislocated.

She tumbled backward away from the plane. It

continued to soar away, in a long southbound loop as she fell.

Mierda! Not the plan.

Out of options, she yanked the ripcord with her good right hand and was slammed hard in the crotch by the harness. Between that and the screaming pain in her shoulder, it knocked every bit of need Pierre had aroused in her right out of her system.

Every bit of *physical* need.

A glance aloft. Parachute was full and flying clean. The ocean was still a few hundred feet below.

But her brain was still in high gear.

Which one of the three men would make the best father? That was a question she'd never asked herself before. Now that she had, the answer was pretty damn obvious.

There was only one problem.

She was supposed to be the third person left on the plane, not Master Sergeant Pierre Jones.

20

THE SPIN WAS STILL PULLING HARD AS PIERRE STUMBLED UP the ladder to the cockpit level. It was raised eight feet above the main deck, tucked inside the upper curve of the nose.

The two pilots were sitting in their seats as calmly as if nothing was happening.

"All clear. Let's go!" He held onto the handrail several feet behind the pilots' seats and shouted above the roar that echoed through the plane. Between the big engines and the open door just at the base of the cockpit ladder, he could barely hear himself.

Tango might have said something like, "About time." But Pierre couldn't have heard that right.

Rather than yanking off his harness, Gutz reached forward to the control cluster.

Pierre wasn't a pilot, but he'd been aboard planes for his entire Air Force career. Gutz unfeathered the props on three of the engines. Suddenly the doomed Ghostrider was flying perfectly. It eased out of the spin less than fifty feet above the shining waves.

To the airmen who'd parachuted into the water, it would appear that the plane had gone down out of sight.

"Good. Let's get the fuck out of here," Tango eased back in his seat.

The plane was fine.

They were...*stealing* the goddamn plane?

It was the only thing that fit.

While he'd been briefly enjoying the best feel-up ever—despite the flightsuits and parachute harnesses—the pair of pilots had been hijacking two hundred million dollars of airplane.

Pierre slapped for his sidearm, but he'd lost it somewhere in the rough and tumble of getting Rosa to safety. A quick scan around revealed that the only handy weapons were the pilots' sidearms.

Bad gamble, Pierre.

Tango shouted over his shoulder. "Close the goddamn door, Rosa. We've got a long flight, my favorite piece of poontang. And Tango is so gonna nail you with his monster harpoon. I'm gonna fuck you right up against your console the whole way to base."

Gutz twisted hard to stare at Tango.

Blind shock. Easy to see in profile from his position behind them.

Pierre had known that Rosa slept with Tango Torres. Apparently she'd also slept with Gutz Gutierrez without letting on to either one. And now she'd kissed him like she meant it? *What the hell?*

"First in front, then behind, then I'll give you primetime

Tango right up your perfect ass." Torres kept checking over the flight instruments, wholly unaware of his copilot's attention.

Gutz's shock slid over to fury.

Frozen in the aisle two steps behind the seats, Pierre saw the motion.

His shout was instinctive—and incredibly stupid.

Gutz had pulled out his sidearm. But he was right-handed and sitting in the right-hand seat belonging to the copilot. He had to bring his weapon clear of the control yoke and fully around his body.

Pierre's shout was enough warning for Tango.

In a single action, Tango looked at Gutz, registered the fury so deep only death could wear it, yanked his sidearm, and shot Gutz in the head.

Blood splatter painted the side window lurid red.

Gutz's dying shot went wild, shattering the windscreen directly in front of Tango.

In turning to shoot his copilot, Tango had twisted far enough to spot Pierre.

He tried to keep turning, but was trapped by his seat harness from bringing his weapon to bear.

Pierre stumbled backward, tripped, and landed flat on his back. Padded by the parachute, it was only *remarkably* painful.

Tango switched hands to aim around the side of the pilot's seat.

His shot passed through where Pierre's heart had been half a second earlier.

Pierre rolled left and tumbled down the stairs to land facedown on the cargo deck.

Everything hurt, but he was safe—Tango had to fly the plane.

But it would take Tango mere seconds to engage the autopilot, then he'd come hunt Pierre down.

The wide-open door beckoned. Though the ocean was so close that survival would be a fool's gamble.

He looked at the open door. Remembered the feel of Rosa Cruz in his arms for even a moment.

Dying was going to suck.

But if he jumped, Tango might still get away with stealing the Ghostrider. Better to destroy it than let such a powerful weapon fall into the wrong hands.

A quick scan of the deck and he couldn't spot his stray sidearm.

The solution wasn't hard once he refocused inside the plane.

He leapt to his feet, then remembered Tango's gun and ducked.

Still clear.

It took three hard kicks to break free the final mirror assembly on the laser, the mirror that turned the final beam ninety degrees to send it shooting out through the hull. The broken piece now dangled out of the way and the laser was a wide-open weapon aimed at the inside of the cargo bay itself.

He ducked behind the weapons officer consoles.

Perching in Rosa's chair, he could feel his fingers echoing hers. She'd drilled the keystrokes into him until they were reflex.

Targeting? Didn't matter. Lock in whatever was set.

Burn power? Max.

Burn time? Continuous.

Fire?

"Damn straight!"

He punched the button just as a shot rang out.

The supersonic shockwave of the bullet snapped close by his ear.

Near miss.

Around the back of the console, he did a racing dive over the broken laser assembly and out the open door.

He hit the air at three hundred knots.

The monster thirteen-foot-diameter, six-bladed propeller spinning at a thousand RPM passed within an arm's length.

The plane's broad tail within two.

He yanked the ripcord and the parachute harness tried to gut him.

One wrenching heave, three seconds of float time, and fifty-seven feet later, he slammed into the chilly California ocean water like it was made of steel.

21

"Why hasn't Tango reported?"

Taz's stillness said that she had the same question.

JJ studied the northern skyline.

The planned escape route for the Ghostrider had been straight down the channel. There were so many military flights in this area that one more, even one below the radar, was unremarkable. Sometimes hiding in plain sight was the best practice.

And in thirty-six hours, none of it would matter. That was all the time he had left. It was all he needed.

Then, on the far horizon, he spotted a black dot, moving low and fast just as it should be.

"Radio trouble?" But he knew it was wrong even as he said it.

Taz shook her head. He'd always liked that her instincts checked with his. When it mattered, they rarely disagreed. Moments later he could see her scanning motion stop as she too locked onto the dark blemish low against the horizon.

There was their bird.

The Ghostrider was supposed to be headed south between the island and the mainland.

But it wasn't "making any trees."

He remembered his father using that phrase on their small sailboat on Camanche Reservoir in the hills above Stockton. If two boats were approaching each other, the trick was to watch how the other boat moved compared with the background. If it seemed to be moving faster than the trees behind it, then it would pass in front of you. Slower, it would be behind. When it seemed to sit dead still against the background but kept getting closer it meant that your angle of approach and speed worked out for a collision course.

He hadn't learned the math until he'd joined the Air Force and he'd forgotten the details by now.

But one thing was certain: the Ghostrider was coming quickly in their direction—*exactly* in their direction.

22

Tango Torres stood at the open passenger door, the frame edge in one hand and his M9 pistol in the other.

"How did it all go to shit so quickly?"

No one answered him, of course. The gunners were gone, even the one who'd snuck up behind them in the cockpit. No chance to identify who.

Rosa too. That wasn't supposed to happen. She'd been tasked with making sure they dumped everyone else except herself.

She'd been two-timing him with Gutz?

That was the total shits.

He hoped Gutz was miserable in the sack.

Had been...

Shit!

Sharing the same holes, even with his best friend, was just a gross thought.

And now his best friend was dead too. Gutz had tried to *shoot* him. *Over a piece of tail!* Even one as fine as Rosa's shouldn't have made that happen.

Well, he still had to save the plane or the general would be some kind of pissed. The whole plan hinged on delivering this Ghostrider.

He stepped back from the door and closed it.

Double-check. No one by the big guns.

He crossed between the laser and the M102 howitzer to make sure that Rosa hadn't magically reappeared at weapons control.

Tango made it two steps before a searing pain sliced into his leg.

He screamed as he collapsed backward.

The whole outside of his left leg was charred flesh —burned!

Right through his fire retardant flightsuit. Some blood dribbled onto the deck, but most of the flesh had been cauterized.

It looked like someone had put his thigh on the fucking broiler and forgotten about it for an hour or two.

Goddamn fucking hell it hurt so shitting much!

Then he saw it.

Part of the laser assembly looked smashed. No. Broken off and dangling aside.

No wonder he'd been cooked, he'd just walked into an invisible laser beam.

A master alarm began beeping up in the cockpit.

That was never good.

For half a second he figured Gutz could handle it...except he was dead and couldn't even handle his own dick.

He'd deal with the laser later.

First, get to the cockpit and—

God, standing up hurt worse than anything ever in his life!

He was drenched in sweat by the time he made it to the cockpit, hopping one-footed up the ladder, and collapsed in his seat.

Gutz's blood was everywhere.

Shit!

He should have shot the guy in the balls.

Tango tried to look out the window, but all he could see was star-cracks. Gutz's shot hadn't gone through; instead the bullet had lodged exactly where he needed to be looking as if Gutz was giving him the finger from the afterlife.

He almost smiled at that, but then went to put his feet on the rudder pedals and screamed instead.

Smashing a finger against the Master Alarm stopped the damned beeping.

Red lights all in a clump. A wide variety of systems, but all in the tail.

He twisted around to look behind him.

The back wall of the cargo bay was glowing red.

He should have dealt with the laser. Without whatever was broken off, it was firing at the back of his plane. The beam wasn't narrow, maybe because of the missing part, but it was still heating the shit out of everything. A hundred and fifty thousand watts was a hella big lightbulb.

In addition to the back of the plane, which he needed, it would also be toasting the racks of gliding Viper Strike bombs still perched in their drop tubes.

The laser took too much power for there to be a breaker in the cockpit, it had to be shut down at the weapon itself.

Tango was gritting his teeth in preparation for getting up

and going back down that goddamn ladder, when the yoke went lax in his hand.

He gave it a wiggle.

He still had side-to-side control, but up and down? Gone. The laser had burned through something critical in the empennage control system. *Several* somethings for there to be a total loss of control despite all the backups.

The big-bellied plane eased down, skipped on the waves like a red-hot puck on an ice rink.

Ahead was...invisible through the shattered windshield.

To the right, Gutz's blood was drying across the windows. To the left...

A cruise ship towered above him—a ten-story wall of white.

The plane skipped on the water again, slamming his leg hard against the side of the chair.

He was past screaming.

There was only one thing left to do.

He pulled out his sidearm and shot Gutz Gutierrez in the balls.

"No fucking Rosa in the afterlife, you bastard. That's Tango's poontang."

He holstered his sidearm and then did his best to keep the wings level.

23

AFTER TWO DECADES AT HIS SIDE, TAZ REMAINED AS STILL AS the general, no matter how loudly her instincts said to run.

The AC-130J Super Hercules Ghostrider grew bigger alarmingly quickly. It must still be at full cruise speed of four hundred miles an hour—a mile every nine seconds.

Moving at over half the speed of sound, the roar of the propellers still hadn't reached the waterfront. All around her, she could hear the merry laughter of people on holiday. The whining child who wanted another ice cream. The two girls with the massive boob jobs and too tight bikinis being so perfectly casual as they strolled along.

The Ghostrider passed between two parked cruise ships that were moored out beyond the breakwater. The massive ships towered several times its height.

It skipped. Planes were supposed to hit the water and die. Out there. Beyond the breakwater.

It skipped again.

For a moment it wavered and dipped the starboard wing toward the water.

Maybe it would hit the north breakwater...

But no. It lifted a wing just enough to clear that outer barrier.

From behind her sunglasses, she kept an eye on the general.

The man was made of stone. She'd served him for nineteen years. Had been the first to swear allegiance when he asked, because from eighteen she'd known no other life.

The general didn't dismiss her due to her small size like so many others in the Air Force. Instead he'd listened when she spoke and trusted her at every turn. He was a real show-don't-tell male. If he'd ever thanked her for her years of unflagging service, she couldn't recall it. But he kept her by his side. That was enough.

He'd also never asked a single question about her past. Scrubbed clean.

So, if he wanted to die sitting at the end of Green Pleasure Pier, killed by an errant AC-130J Ghostrider gunship, she would sit beside him and die as well.

The plane skimmed over a line of small sailboats before coming down for the last time.

The left wing slammed into a hundred-and-fifty-foot luxury motor yacht. The plane twisted away from it—leaving one engine and forty feet of wing embedded in the yacht as it burst into flames. Only a few people made it off the deck by diving overboard. They surfaced into a burning hell as the fuel from the wing tanks spilled over the water's surface and ignited.

Then the right wing snapped both masts off a hundred-foot schooner, remaining attached long enough to shear off the cabin down the entire length. The spinning propeller passed along the boat like a giant shredder. No one emerged from that boat.

The Ghostrider slammed head-on into the massive rock pile that formed the southern breakwater of Avalon Harbor. Five degrees more to the right and it would have come straight at them.

The cockpit was rammed back into the fuselage with all the ease of an Army boot stomping on an empty Budweiser can. The stubs of the wings, along with the remaining inboard engines, broke off, swung forward, and wrapped either side of the pier in a flaming embrace.

The explosion hit moments later. The munitions, which were supposed to be safe in even the worst crashes, lit off with a resounding boom that hurt her ears and would have blinded her if it hadn't been inside the plane's hull.

The tail launched backward into the deeper water.

The remains of the fuselage launched upward from the rear, flipping end-over-end onto the top of the pier. Several score of tourists who'd been disembarking from the latest ferry from LA were crushed instantly. They were the lucky ones.

Those still climbing off the ferry were inundated in gouts of flame and burned alive.

The force of the shock wave knocked her into the general's lap.

Once it had passed, he placed his hands on her shoulders and helped her sit back upright. It was the only time he had ever touched her other than pinning on her next rank insignia at each promotion.

The fireball climbed upward.

"Something must have triggered the entire load of glide bombs."

She could barely hear the general over the ringing in her ears. The entire length of the southern stone breakwater was now on fire. Flames began sheeting out over the water as more fuel spilled from all the ruptured tanks. At the current rate of spread, the wooden Green Pleasure Pier would be aflame within the minute.

General Jorge Jesus Martinez rose to his feet. When she rose as well, he placed her Bluetooth earpiece in her palm, then began walking toward the land.

"Colonel Cortez?"

"Yes sir?" From long practice, Taz strode at time-and-a-half to keep up with his long legs.

"I'm going to need another Ghostrider and I suspect another laser operator."

"And pilots." The screams of the injured were finally starting to rise. Or her hearing was coming back.

"I have plenty of pilots. But that laser is very new and very rare. Technical Sergeant Cruz was one of the few qualified to operate it."

"Plane and a laser operator. I'm on it, sir."

She gave it a moment's thought, pulled out her phone, and began placing calls.

This was going to be very tricky, since she was supposedly dead in a Spectre gunship high in the Colorado Rockies.

24

"How am *I* supposed to know where your general is?" Miranda squinted at Jon.

The sun over Aspen had risen high in the sky, but Jon stood just two steps away and almost due south, aligning his head and the sun closely. Even the wide brim of her HeliSee hat was marginal at best for distinguishing him from the blinding background.

"The question was rhetorical, Miranda." Jon sighed.

"Then why did you ask it if you didn't want to know the answer?"

"I very much want to know—" He growled deep in his throat. "Never mind."

"That's not something I'm very good at." But Miranda's reply was lost under the beating of rotors from the arriving AgustaWestland Trekker helo.

As soon as it was shut down, Brett climbed out. He flipped open the side-hanging equipment cage and opened the big cooler he'd tucked inside.

"You know the annual Aspen Food & Wine Classic is going on in town."

Mike gasped. Jon shrugged his indifference. Miranda glanced at Holly and Jeremy, but they had no more idea than she did.

"You got a burger in that lot?" Holly headed to the cooler.

Brett snorted. "I've got Gail Simmons' favorite. Grace Parisi's Grilled Gruyère and Sweet Onion sandwiches. Does that count?"

"Not even close, mate." Holly may have scoffed, but she snatched the one in Brett's hand. Biting in deeply, she sighed happily, grabbed another, and spoke as she chewed. "Still warm. Now that's fair trade."

Miranda had a half of one of those and some of Caroline Glover's summertime chopped salad with flatbread. And the treats just kept coming.

"And," Brett announced as he pulled out a brown paper bag, "one of Mom's bologna sandwiches on whole wheat with yellow mustard, American cheese, and a box of raisins on the side. You've been behaving, Jeff?" His son nodded eagerly as he took the bag and dug out his sandwich.

"Yes, he identified a key insight into our investigation," Mike explained, sparing Miranda the need to interact.

Brett rubbed his son's head affectionately. It reminded her of her own father and the hours he'd spent challenging her mind with cryptographic puzzles and elaborate thought games. He'd rarely touched her, and never so easily. But that had been her own hypersensitivity to touch.

Hadn't it?

She was fairly sure it had been her who was broken and not him.

Was she still?

The disconcerting power of Jeff's embrace. He'd wanted to be held when he was afraid. What had she wanted when she was afraid of something? She couldn't remember.

Brett spread out red wool blankets, with a thankfully small Helisee/Heliski logo in just one corner.

For a while, the only sound on the hilltop was the soft breeze humming against the rotor blades and the occasional territorial bird.

Jon's shoulder brushed pleasantly against hers.

He seemed to be doing it on purpose. When he saw that she'd caught on, he simply leaned in to her. It made eating the sandwich much more awkward, but it was very comfortable.

Mike and Jeremy shared another while Holly sprawled on a third. Brett and Jeff were sitting on the helo's cargo deck and both swinging their feet.

The food was good. The sun warm through the cool breeze. Jon's touch made it easy to just drift and not think about much at all.

"The real prize," Brett cut off her non-thoughts. "I managed to score some of Lisa Donovan's peach hand pies." He had Jeff hand them around.

Each was indeed the size of Brett's hand—at least twice the size of hers—thick with a flaky crust. Mike was making ecstatic noises and Holly's eyes were closed in bliss. She tried the corner of one and rather liked it. The peach seemed to swim into her taste buds and embrace them before continuing on their way.

On their way...

Jon's question, rhetorical or not, regarding the general's

whereabouts still remained. But she had so little to go on. Generals, especially high-ranking ones, were not a common occurrence in her world.

Except...

She pulled out her phone and dialed Drake.

"Hi, Miranda. I only have a minute. The Saudis are being stupid again and are really pissing off the Iranians. Allies or not, I wish that I could just flatten their asses once and for all. What are you up to?" She'd rarely heard the Chairman of the Joint Chiefs of Staff being so brusque. But she preferred this to his peculiar jokes any day.

"We are eating gourmet hand peach pies and attempting to trace the location of General Jorge Jesus Martinez. Can you offer us any assistance?"

"With the pies?"

"No, with the general."

"Too bad, I could use a treat right about now. JJ? What do you need him for?"

"There is some doubt regarding his present corporeal state."

"What?"

"We have a report and hard evidence that he's dead, yet reason to believe that—"

"JJ's dead?" Drake gasped. "How can he be dead? He and I were just fighting over a beer and nachos a week or so ago."

"Why were you fighting over a beer and nachos? Couldn't the restaurant serve you two orders?"

"What? No. Yes. Sure they could have. I meant that he and I were arguing, while having a beer and nachos."

"Not two beers and nachos?" That made more sense when she tried to picture it.

"Miran*da!*"

She'd learned that when people hit the last syllable of her name extra hard that they were frustrated. She had the notes of repeated observations in her notebook to support that conclusion.

"Well?"

"There was a plane crash and—"

"That can't be right."

"Drake, I—"

"You've got to be wrong on this one. JJ can't be—"

Miranda had finally learned how to deal with these kinds of situations. She placed her phone on speaker and handed it to Holly, who sat up to take it.

"—dead. I know that he's a pain in the ass sometimes. Seriously old school, even more than me. But he's a top man who—"

"Mr. Chairman," Holly just cut him off as if he wasn't the country's highest ranking general and the Chairman of the Joint Chiefs of Staff.

"What?"

"Sir, with all due respect, you really need to learn to shut your yap and listen when Miranda's speaking. She didn't call for some friendly jaw."

"Ms. Harper, you don't begin to underst—"

"*You* don't want me hanging up on you *again,* do you?" Something Holly seemed to delight in doing.

"She'll do it, Uncle Drake," Jon was chortling. "So, as Holly would say, 'Hush up some'."

"No self-respecting Aussie would say such a thing," she protested, then turned to the phone. "Just cut the yabber, Mr. Chairman."

Drake sputtered, but stopped talking. Miranda had never been able to confront such a wall of words. They always made her feel shaky and small, as if the world was peppering her, like when she forgot the lid on a pot of popping corn—a thousand little hits that didn't particularly hurt, but made it impossible to think of anything else.

"Do it up, boss." Holly tried to hand back her phone but Miranda didn't trust her grip, so she clenched her hands together, which was the only way to keep them still at times like these.

"We have two proofs of his death. His dog tags on a corpse and his name on the crew list for the crash."

"What kind of crash?"

"An AC-130H gunship. But—"

"Are we still flying the Hs? I thought—"

Holly pressed a finger down on one of the number keys, making it emit a long beep.

Drake stopped talking.

Holly answered him. "It was stolen from Davis-Monthan's boneyard, except it wasn't, because according to the official records—that Jeremy hacked—it's still there. But it isn't. It's now spread all over the top of the Colorado Rockies. Now pay attention to the next part."

At Holly's nod, Miranda continued. "But we have reason to believe that this crash was fabricated. No, correct that. The crash is real, but we have reason to believe that it was deliberate, and the thirteen bodies aboard were not the individuals identified by the dog tags and crew roster."

"No way would JJ be a part of something like that. You never met a patriot like him. Somebody's messing with you. Look, I've got to go. The President is waiting. Find JJ. If you can't find him, track down that Colonel Taz Something. Taz Cortez. Scary as shit half-pint Mexican chick. She's always at his side. JJ uses her like a tactical nuke. I've watched her destroy career officers during a single interview. Woman's relentless."

"Get a taste of that yourself, Chairman?" Holly sounded delighted.

"Thank God, no! JJ takes me on himself. We go way back to when we were both still punk majors. Besides, he's hit mandatory retirement age. His party is tomorrow night—all the joint chiefs and half the Pentagon will be there. Even the President said he might drop by. If he does, I'll think even better of him because JJ has always been a real thorn in Roy Cole's side...and every President before him. Find him. Let me know as soon as you do. Maybe this is some elaborate hoax for him to get out of his retirement party, except he wouldn't be a part of anything that isn't strictly by the book. I'm gone." And he disconnected.

The phone gave a small chirp of Call Ended. Now Miranda could finally take it back when Holly handed it to her. She slipped it into the proper vest pocket.

"So, what's next?" Mike asked and they all looked at her.

As if she was supposed to know.

25

"I mean, it's a beautiful day here atop the mountains of Colorado," Mike continued.

Miranda didn't need further proof that weather was not a factor in the crash. The crash was deliberate. It was the first deliberate military crash since Captain Craig Button had committed suicide-by-pilot with an A-10 Thunderbolt II in 1997. Though since no one had actually died during this crash...

"We have a picnic and have had a fire," Mike waved a hand to indicate the scorched mountaintop. "We could tell ghost stories—appropriate, as thirteen bodies were found here even if they didn't die here."

"We do have a shattered plane to investigate," but she didn't sound convincing even to herself.

"But if it was deliberately crashed?" Holly left the question dangling.

"Not much point except as a scientific study."

Brett pointed his peach hand pie down toward Aspen.

"Owners want to know if they can start the cleanup? It may be late June, but summer is very short at this elevation. They want to get crews up here clearing the mountain and fixing the Cirque Poma by winter—which comes early on this mountain."

"Yay!" Jeff cheered around a mouthful of raisins. "Double black diamonds, here I come!"

Mike smirked just a little. "Do I see a lot of airlift bonus for your birds?"

Brett nodded. "Won't mind the extra work. Already have a pair of heavy-lift Chinooks on call if I can get the contract."

"Smart man," Mike nodded.

Yes, Miranda already knew that about Brett.

Jon's phone rang and he stepped away to answer it.

His distance made it the first time since he'd crested the ridge that she felt she could think. The man was very distracting, even when he wasn't doing anything. She pulled out her personal notebook and made an entry for later consideration if that was a bad thing or a good one.

Jeff led Mike away to show off the remains of the Bofors L/60 and M102 howitzer they'd found earlier. Brett tagged along.

Now it was just Holly, Jeremy, and the dry wind riding fast and cool over the mountaintop.

"Think we'll learn anything more here?" Holly asked softly.

Miranda considered, but finally shook her head. A deliberate crash was a criminal investigation, not a problem for the NTSB.

That felt wrong but sounded right. Would it be better the other way around, if it felt right but sounded wrong?

"This is weird." Jeremy had perched on a nearby boulder in a way that reminded her of the caterpillar in *Alice in Wonderland*. He wasn't blue, three inches tall, or smoking a hookah atop a magic mushroom, but the similarity was there. He had his computer out and cables running into the black boxes that Holly and Mike had recovered. She could also see the card reader for the Quick Access Recorder drive that she'd recovered from the cockpit.

"What did you find, Jeremy?"

"Magic."

She doublechecked, but he definitely wasn't sitting on a mushroom.

"This plane magically appeared about five minutes before it crashed. There are no recordings on either device prior to their initial contact with Denver Center air traffic control. No handoff from Salt Lake Center, nothing."

"Did they erase parts of it?" Holly looked over his left shoulder. Miranda moved to look over his right.

"No. There's no background noise even. The media are factory fresh. Turned on just to capture the crash. I don't even have the opening of the door. And I should, right there." He stabbed a finger at a time mark. "At least that's when they reported the depressurization event. The door must have already been open specifically so that the event wouldn't be recorded in the data stream."

Miranda could see the spikes consistent with voice communication, but there was no mechanical record of the door opening.

"They turned everything on to just capture the crash but wanted to keep their point of origin and flight route hidden," Holly was nodding to herself as if that somehow made sense.

"They wanted us to focus on the dead, assuming that no one would read these devices until they were sent back to the NTSB lab."

Which, Miranda knew, would have been the proper procedure. But Jeremy's ability to quickly access the information had proven useful on a number of occasions. It had saved their lives in the New Mexico desert.

"Why would someone do that?"

Jon hung up his phone and joined them. "Because they knew they had to keep the best crash-investigation team in the business distracted."

That didn't sound quite right, but Jon continued before she could think of why.

"Brett," he called out and the man turned from where he'd been repacking the cooler. "On my advice, they've called off the Air Force investigation team for this site. You can tell the owners that they're good to start clearing the mountain. They're to coordinate with Peterson AFB over in Colorado Springs."

Brett shot a thumb's up and got on the helo's radio to pass along the news.

"Miranda, there's another—"

"Hang on, mate," Holly rose to her feet, brushing pastry crumbs off so that they showered over Mike. "What Air Force investigation team?"

"The one coming to investigate the crash."

"But I thought we were investigating the crash?" Jeremy covered his face as Mike brushed Holly's and his own crumbs onto Jeremy.

"You are. You were. You are." Jon looked at her as if she

knew what he was talking about. "I told Miranda earlier that—"

"Not about another team." She didn't like that someone didn't trust her team.

"Yes. No. I started to. We don't lose a three-star general without upsetting a lot of people."

"Penguins."

Now the team was looking at her strangely.

"We were discussing the ratio of flying penguins in a known population versus the number of three-star lieutenant generals and—"

"That's easy. An infinite ratio. You're dividing by zero," Jeremy peeked out from under his hand to see if another shower of pastry crust flakes was inbound.

"That's what I told him. He was—"

"Miranda," Jon didn't hit the last *-da* hard, but it sounded as if he wanted to. "They launched a full team in our direction the moment they found out that JJ Rodriguez was aboard."

"Supposedly aboard," Holly corrected him.

"Right. I never had a chance to mention it because when I got up here, you were already deep in the investigation."

"Been just sitting here through lunch, mate." Holly's sneer was accurate.

"Right, sorry. I should have said. Anyway. They're called off."

"But didn't we just decide that there's nothing further to investigate here as it has a known cause—intentional destruction?" Mike found some more crumbs that Holly had gotten on him. Jeremy ducked aside before they were showered over him.

"It doesn't matter," Jon sighed.

"Why not?"

"Because, Miranda, there's another crash. Far worse than this. An AC-130J Ghostrider Block 30, flying out of Edwards Air Force Base—we're sure of that much this time—just plowed into Avalon Harbor on Santa Catalina Island off LA during a planned testing flight. At least fifty confirmed dead, but probably a lot higher."

"How long ago?"

"Just over an hour. A lot of things are still on fire. Multiple engine failures. At the moment of trouble, they clipped the observer plane and it went down with all hands as well. Then they spilled people in parachutes over twenty miles. While fighting for control, they wandered out of the test zone, ultimately ramming the pier at Avalon. Looks to actually be an accident, as the plane was under only marginal control. The pilots never got out."

Miranda felt a chill, not just from the cool Aspen air.

First a Spectre and now a Ghostrider? Two gunships down within hours of each other—built forty years apart but both AC-130s.

She hated plane crashes, but she'd wager that she'd like this one even less than usual.

26

Once aboard the helo, Jeff had asked if he could go "help" with the California crash. Before Miranda could even consider the request, his father shut that down.

"You can watch it on TV. It'll be the only thing on all the news channels."

For the rest of the short flight down the mountain, Miranda struggled to fit together the pieces.

The AC-130J Ghostrider had several unique features that were unfamiliar. The biggest change was the laser system. She needed to go inspect one so that she'd know how to understand its possible effects. Beyond its five-ton mass, she knew little about it.

She also needed to inspect the new crash.

And if there was still an undead general involved, then...

Miranda felt torn in all three directions. And a part of her wanted to return to the top of Snowmass and study the unusual effects of such a complete and destructive impact.

When she stepped from the HeliSee helicopter back

onto the ground at Aspen airport, Jeff clasped her around the middle in a hard hug. She held his shoulders tightly for a moment—an almost hug—before she tried pushing him back. He went more easily this time so neither of them landed on their butts, though she kept a firm hold on him until she was sure of the success of that strategy.

He looked up at her face. "I'm gonna learn everything and then I'm gonna come work for you, Ms. Chase. We're gonna save planes together."

Brett had come up behind his son.

"Dad, for Christmas I want a vest with a lot of pockets and tools. A notebook to write cool stuff down in, and an anonymommenator."

"It's only June, short stuff," Brett said, keeping a hand on Jeff's shoulder.

"It's what I want," Jeff insisted. "Don't forget the aniometer. It's important."

Again, Brett's eyebrows raised above his aviators as he turned his attention to Miranda. "Seems you made quite the impression."

"I'm sorry." Miranda pictured Jeff's terror over his father's possible death and his commitment to spend his life investigating dead planes and dead people. "I didn't mean to."

Brett tipped his head to the side, started to speak, then cut himself off.

Mouth curved down, unhappy frown. The old childhood lesson came back to her, but she didn't know what else to do. She'd already apologized.

She turned for the waiting US Air Force jets, but halfway there Jon stopped her with a hand on her arm. A light touch that was so hard to ignore. It was there but it wasn't and that jangled against her nerves.

It had taken her a long time to learn how to deal with it —she pulled her arm away.

"Oh, right, sorry. Can we talk for a minute?"

"Jon. I can't think about our relationship at the moment. It's one factor too many for me to—"

"It's not about that."

"—process at this time. Oh. What is it?"

"It's about your team."

Everyone else had continued over to the two waiting Air Force planes and dropped their packs on the pavement.

"What about them?"

Holly glanced back at her. Somehow Miranda knew that she was offering to backtrack if Miranda needed help.

She shook her head.

Holly shrugged, lay down on the pavement in the shadow of the plane, and rested her head on her pack as if ready to take a nap. But something in how Holly tugged down the brim of her HeliSee hat told Miranda that Holly was watching them and was ready to come running if needed. Though she couldn't imagine why that would happen.

Jon tapped his phone in his pocket. "I was speaking with the general in charge of military crash investigations. He wants to bring your team onboard."

"We already are onboard. Over sixty-four percent of my team's investigations have been military- or military personnel-related over the last eight months. That's up from my prior lifetime average of forty-two percent."

"Life, the universe, and everything."

Perhaps ignoring anything she didn't understand would be a useful tactic. At least things that people said. She would continue paying attention to the "voices" of the equipment and systems she investigated. But people, at least those she associated with the most, were becoming less comprehensible rather than more with increased exposure. Plotting the axial curves of familiarity versus comprehension decay over time would be an interesting challenge.

"My commander wants to bring your team on full-time. Military contractors for both disaster recovery and—"

"We work for the NTSB."

"I know that."

"*I* work for the NTSB. Your request doesn't make sense. Thirty-six percent of my work is still in the commercial aviation sector. You'd want me to stop that?"

"Yes. And it makes perfect sense from our point of view. Your consistent ability to accurately assess site crashes in unprecedented time frames would be a real asset to—"

"No. Both myself and my team work for the NTSB." Miranda tucked her suddenly cold hands under her arms. It made no sense—it was far warmer down here at Aspen's elevation than atop Snowmass, yet her hands hadn't been cold up there.

"Look, Miranda. As contractors we can pay you far more than the NTSB can—"

"I'm already wealthy. Jeremy's parents are Microsoft millionaires many times over. No, this conversation is over."

"But Miranda—"

"Hey boss," Holly was standing at her elbow. "We'd better get a move-on right soon, I'm thinking. Crash in California and all."

"Yes." She let Holly guide her toward the planes.

"That was looking a bit intense," Holly whispered.

"No. It was just...wrong." She'd trusted Jon. And now he wanted the military to absorb her team? She'd been reading NTSB reports since she was thirteen and writing them since twenty. She'd never wanted to be anything else.

Why would Jon suggest such a thing? Didn't he know her at all?

27

The two Air Force jets were still waiting—the one that had delivered her team and the one Jon had arrived in. With only five people, they could all easily fit aboard either one.

If only she could be on both planes, then she could be in at least two of the three places she needed to be. Unless, perhaps, two of the places happened to be near each other.

"Jeremy, where is there another AC-130J Ghostrider? A Block 30 with the laser."

He pulled out his tablet and answered within moments. "There are only two other Block 30s built so far. One at Eglin in Florida for testing. The other was just flown from Eglin to Andrews in DC. Apparently a demonstration tour for the House and Senate Armed Services Committees."

Miranda stopped with one foot on the first step, then turned to face Holly. She had an idea...and a reminder that — "You once said that we just investigate crashes. That it's what *we* do."

"Actually, you said it, Miranda. I just agreed. You're still right."

"So, you and I are going to the crash."

"It's what we do," Holly nodded. "What about these three amigos? You," she pointed at Jeremy, "are obviously Martin Short. Mike is definitely in the Steve Martin role. Jon, that leaves you playing Chevy Chase."

Once again, Miranda had no idea what one of her team members was talking about. Except she was fairly sure Steve Martin was a banjo player; she wasn't a fan of bluegrass music.

The three men lined up side by side. They slapped their right hands to their own left shoulders, then left to right. Hands on their hips, they turned their heads and coughed as they did a pelvic thrust. Then they began a quick shuffle step where they tried to dance around each other in figure eights, instead colliding hard enough that they all would have fallen to the ground if their combined momentums hadn't canceled each other out.

Holly was laughing.

Then the three of them lined up and shouted out, "The Three Amigos!"

Miranda decided it was definitely better not to know, and made a note in her notebook about the potential long-term viability of ignoring obscure cultural references.

Jon's phone rang again.

"Holly and I are going to investigate the crash on Catalina Island," Miranda told the others once she'd finished her note and tucked the notebook back in its pocket. "Jeremy and Mike, you're going to Washington, DC. I want you to investigate two things. Mike, talk to Drake to get more information about General JJ Martinez. Jeremy, I want you to study the AC-130J Ghostrider at Andrews. We need to understand the modifications, especially those introduced in the Block 30 upgrade."

"Cool!" Jeremy shot her a double thumbs-up, almost losing his tablet to the pavement.

Mike looked less certain. "Perhaps…" He tipped his head as if cracking his spine, a very Holly-like gesture.

Holly picked up his thought before Miranda could ask, "Perhaps…*not* Drake. He's more stubborn than an Aussie shepherd dog. Sounds like his claws are dug in pretty deep on the subject of General JJ."

"Precisely my thought, Holly. Wow! You do have a brain in that pretty head of yours. I thought it was just for show." Mike dodged behind Jeremy before Holly could take a swing at him.

Miranda would trust to their judgment on that. "How about Lizzy? She's close to Drake and may know something." She was the only other general who Miranda knew in DC.

Holly snorted, "The director of the National Reconnaissance Office? I'd bet that General Elizabeth Gray knows far more than her boyfriend suspects. When are those two gonna do more than have a naughty anyway?"

"A naughty?" Miranda could help herself.

"A bangaroo. A good time in the sack. She needs to be making an honest man out of him some day."

Jon rejoined them, "Where do you want me?"

Hopefully he'd been informing his commander that Miranda only worked for the NTSB: past, present, and future.

Where *did* she want Jon?

Jon was an able crash investigator, but so were she and Holly, and they'd both be in California. Mike's specialty was people, not aircraft, and Jeremy still suffered from her own old failing of too narrow a focus.

"I need you with Jeremy and Mike." He frowned for a moment, but then he glanced at Jeremy and it switched to a broad smile almost immediately.

"Got it! Wherever liberty is threatened, you will find—"

"—The Three Amigos!" They all shouted it in unison and fired pretend guns made of fists and fingers into the air. Their bright HeliSee hats looked nothing like Mexican sombreros despite their oversized brims.

"No, I don't want you to fight. I want you to…"

Holly rested her hand on Miranda's arm just long enough to stop her. "It's a quote from a comedy movie named *The Three Amigos*. They're just big boys. Let them have their moment."

"Let's ride!" They shouted again, grabbing their packs and storming aboard one of the airplanes. They jostled each other like five-year-olds as they struggled to all go up the narrow gangway together.

Jon, last aboard, blew her a kiss from the entry before ducking inside. One of the pilots rolled his eyes as he leaned out to pull up the gangway from inside—yet another misdirected expression. In moments, the plane was taxiing toward the runway.

She and Holly climbed aboard the second plane like normal people.

Once they were seated and their plane was moving as well, she asked Holly if she should watch the movie for cultural reasons.

Holly snorted, "Are you kidding? I'd rather watch a water buffalo sleep in the sun."

Miranda thought about that as they lined up for takeoff.

Why would anyone want to watch a water buffalo sleep in the sun?

28

Pierre Jones checked the hospital hallway in both directions. He felt like a geriatric patient. His entire body was mostly a big bruise. The docs couldn't believe he'd survived his low-altitude jump, never mind without serious injury.

No guards. Good sign.

He peeked into Rosa Cruz's room—the number he'd gotten by total subterfuge from the nurses' station...he'd asked.

She was awake.

Her smile lit brightly when she saw him in the doorway. It was a very powerful weapon on a lovely woman clothed in almost nothing and already lying in a bed. A sling held one arm, completely immobilized with a crossbody strap just below her breasts. That was something of a deterrent. And she wasn't his lover, but rather Tango's...and Gutz's.

"What are you in for, Rosa?" He hadn't heard she was injured.

She flinched briefly and that lovely smile wavered for the length of a single heartbeat before she covered it.

Please don't let that flinch be because of what he expected it was. What he *knew* it was. He wished he'd phrased his question differently so that he could deny noticing anything. But he hadn't...and she'd flinched.

Rosa knew that he knew something. But instead of addressing that, she shied off and answered the hospital question.

"I was the last one they picked up. They said they hadn't even been looking for me until after they found the 'last person out'—which must have been you. I was in the water long enough to become marginally hypothermic. And the shoulder." She raised her arm ever so slightly, winced more understandably this time, then lowered it again. "Dislocated. Fixed, but I'm strapped in for a week. I didn't know it was possible to be so cold. I'm warmer now, but still under observation. They said I should be free in a few hours. You that sent them back for me?"

"Of course." He himself had been picked up by a group of jet skiers, making the seventeen-mile crossing from the mainland to Catalina. They'd spotted his chute and pulled him out of the water. The instant he'd come to, he'd called in his best guess at Rosa's position.

"Are you okay?"

He shrugged yes, then wished he hadn't. Wouldn't surprise him if his whole body turned black-and-blue from how hard he'd hit the water.

As to Rosa, there'd been a long gap between the cluster of gunners and her own departure from the plane. Long enough for them to end up in a brief clench and—

Pierre cast the thought aside and took another step closer, both physically and to the elephant question in the room of her being a conspirator in a hundred-million-dollar hijacking.

"What did you tell them?" He knew that she would have been through the same level of debriefing he'd faced. Two officers and a video camera, cross-questioned on every moment from the first alert until they were hauled from the water.

She looked aside quickly and spoke low and fast. "That I don't know what happened to the plane. That you helped me with my chute and pushed me out the door before going to help the pilots. Which was incredibly brave."

"You heard?" He tipped his head toward the sea. They were in LA's main VA hospital. The Pacific lay just a few miles away across Santa Monica.

She nodded and that's when he saw how red her eyes were.

"Did you love him? Them?" Not that it was any of his goddamn business. But maybe it was. "Is that why you were helping them?"

Rosa nodded. Then shook her head. Then shrugged helplessly. "No. That's *not* why I was helping them. *Love* them? I... They were both very good to me...in different ways."

"But they didn't know about each other."

She shook her head. "Neither one would have liked it. I don't know what I was doing. Mama always said that my older twin brothers and I were like three puppies in a pile."

"So you tried to recreate it with Gutz and Tango?"

"Maybe. Mostly I was just not thinking. Life by default.

Neither of them would ever have accepted another man. I was juggling them but it was close to coming apart. I knew that if they found out it was going to be ugly."

He was on the verge of telling her just how ugly, brains spattered in the cockpit of a crashing hijacked plane, but thought better of it. In fact, he hoped that she never read the official report because he'd told the investigators about it— saying he hadn't heard what woman they were fighting over.

Then he noticed the position of her hand. Her fine fingers, that were never still as they danced across the keyboard of the HEL-A laser firing console, lay on her abdomen just below the sling.

Perfectly still.

29

"Who's is it?"

"Who's is *what?*" Rosa jerked her hand aside but she knew it was too late.

"Neither one knew." Pierre said it as a flat accusation.

She wilted. "I don't either. It was a birth control failure, not a plan. I guess now, without a DNA test that I can't ask for, I never will." She wanted to cry again, but she'd done enough of that. And that hadn't even been for Tango or Gutz, not really. It had been for the overwhelming madness that her life had become.

Her hand returned to her belly of its own volition. She'd heard about that, but never really believed. It was ridiculous.

Except both of her child's potential fathers just died. And wasn't it obvious that Pierre had something he wasn't telling her about them. But she trusted him; she probably didn't *want* to know whatever he was hiding.

He slumped down in the visitor's chair with his hands jammed deep in his pockets, scowling in the vicinity of his boots. Papa did that sometimes, when things had been hard at his work. She knew from watching Mama that there were times to let a man sulk, but there were times to just break it apart.

"You're doing a crappy job of flirting with me right now, Pierre."

He barely smiled. "Half of that was because I thought you were 'safe.' Saw you with Tango and knew you weren't available. Easy to have some fun when you don't think it means anything."

He was right, it had been fun. From the first moment they'd met, both seasoned AC-130 gunners, arriving together on the factory floor in Marietta, Georgia, to watch the first Ghostrider slide off the line. A lot of classroom hours because firing a HEL-A laser wasn't at all like firing an M102 howitzer.

A month in the classroom, then five more of shakedown. Their Ghostrider was to be the first to be declared mission ready—available for combat after today's tests. Not counting General JJ's plans to do just that with it, simply not by following any orders but his own.

"What was the other half?"

"Why did you kiss me?" Pierre grunted out.

She could feel the heat flash to her face as she looked away.

"You don't mind telling me that you're okay with lovers in pairs without a single blush, and you can't tell me why you kissed me like that?"

Rosa still wasn't sure, though she'd given it a lot of thought. "How did you *really* break your nose?"

"Weird-ass question."

No argument from her. Why was that suddenly important? But it seemed like it was.

"Local swimming pool. Seventh grade," he grumbled out. "*Carmen* McAllister's seventh-grade bikini curves could boil your hormones. Well, mine anyway. Watching them go by, I walked square into the high-dive board's support pole. Broke my nose, tripped, and fell on the pool's concrete edge hard enough to break my arm, *before* I fell in and had to be rescued by the lifeguard."

"Was she impressed?"

"My aunt sure was. Almost laughed herself out of her one-piece—which would have been gross as hell because she makes heifers look svelte. She still roars with great brays of laughter when she retells it at every family gathering over the last fifteen years. Carmen never even noticed me: before, during, or after." His grimace spoke volumes.

She couldn't help but laugh despite everything else that was going on.

And there it was.

Not the humor, something both Gutz and Tango lacked —though Tango thought he was funny as hell.

There was a kindness there. And an honesty.

"Why didn't you tell the Air Force investigators about..." She couldn't quite bring herself to say it.

"Your part in the conspiracy?"

She could only nod.

"Needed to hear your side of the story first. Were you coerced? What?"

And there was another piece of it. Tango wouldn't have hesitated to throw her under the wheels if it meant saving his own ass.

"*Why*, Rosa?" And she realized that he liked her far more than he was willing to admit even to himself.

Again she looked away, because there was no way to speak to the pain on his features. She made a show of patting her stomach. "I wasn't coerced. But then *this* changed the world. I've known for," she glanced at the wall clock, "fifty-three hours and nine minutes. It changes your world in ways you can't imagine. The...two of them were good fun but..."

"They'd have sucked as husbands," he finished her sentence more harshly than she would have.

She bit her lower lip and nodded yes to the opposite wall. *That* was absolutely without question.

"Then you kissed me like... Oh, give me a fucking break, lady. Are you suddenly reeling me in for someone else's kid in the middle of all this shit?"

"No!" She twisted to face him, and the pain came crashing right through the drugs as if they weren't even there. She'd forgotten about the dislocated shoulder.

As she lay there trying to catch her breath, she *did* realize it was far easier to picture Pierre with a child than Tango or Gutz.

And he respected her for more than her ass and breasts.

Despite outranking her, at the end of training Pierre hadn't even hesitated. He'd simply pointed at her and told their commander, *She's the best damn gunner I've ever seen. If you don't put her on the laser, you're an idiot.*

"No. I'm not asking you to be my child's father. I'm just trying to get a grip on a world that is suddenly overwhelming the crap out of me. I did absolutely nothing wrong before you threw me off the plane."

"Other than take part in a conspiracy to steal a Ghostrider, and then failing to report that to your commanding officer."

"Right," she sagged back against the bed. "Other than that."

"Spill it, Rosa."

There was no path out that made this right. Sick of all the games and lies, she might as well go down for the truth.

"It was our commanding officer who came to *me...*"

30

THEIR FLIGHT WAS FAST APPROACHING CATALINA ISLAND. THE airport, perched on the crest of the island, had never been one of Miranda's favorites. Its primary asset was that there was no regular commercial air service to the island, so accidents here were rarely called in to her department.

The general aviation group, however, received a disproportionate numbers of calls here.

Instead of a long, flat safety area at either end of the runway to accommodate early landings and overshoots, there were steep cliffs. A sudden downdraft, quite common across the rounded island top, could make someone land in the cliff face propeller-first, rather than on the runway. Required approaches were steep and precise.

Also, the runway itself actually draped over the crest of the island's highest point. Once down, landing planes couldn't see the other half of the runway because of the central highpoint. There were numerous skid marks from excessive braking at midfield as it appeared that the runway suddenly ended far too soon.

It was even possible for two departing planes to choose opposite ends of the runway and not see each other until they were well into their takeoff rolls.

No, she'd never been a fan of Catalina Airport.

And yet she was here for a plane crash that had nothing to do with the airport. Any C-130 Hercules could have easily landed on the short runway, would have sufficient power to fight the toughest downdrafts, and was tall enough to see the whole runway for almost the entire distance.

Instead, an AC-130J Super Hercules Ghostrider had tried to act like America's largest seaplane since the Spruce Goose —until it rammed into a massive stone pier.

As they flew over the harbor, she noted eerie similarities to the Aspen crash—aside from them both being AC-130 airframes.

There was far less of the plane visible than there should be for an aircraft of its size.

"Look," Holly was pointing out her window. "Part of a wing and engine are jammed into that big yacht. Looks like there's another piece over there in that sailboat."

Indeed, there was a Hercules propeller snagged in the sailboat's rigging. Both masts lay overboard, but a section of the wing remained there. That accounted for some of the missing plane.

"That fire is creeping me out, mate," Holly shook her head.

Miranda would trust to Holly for naming the emotion. Again, the evidence of fire was widespread. None of the buildings ashore had been burned, but the two piers were badly blackened—the stone outer pier with char and burnt buildings, and the wooden inner pier was now little more than blackened stumps sticking out of the water. Several fire engines ranged along the waterfront.

Then the view was cut off as their plane turned onto final approach to land at the airport.

Ever since her first-ever military investigation—a downed C-5 Galaxy at Joint Base Lewis-McChord—fire had never bothered her particularly. Except she *hated* the destruction of evidence crucial to an investigation.

The view when they deplaned was refreshingly like her island in Washington State. This was far more familiar than the jagged peaks of Aspen. Rather than the towering Douglas firs of home, Catalina had brown scrubby slopes on the few hilltops that reached higher than the lofty airport. But in every direction that had a view, the sea shone brightly. It wasn't the midnight blue of Puget Sound, but rather the true blue that was still the Pacific without the brighter tropical tones.

It smelled different. Dry brush rather than sharp conifer, but—

"Hope you're not in a hurry," one of the Air Force pilots remarked as he tied down the airplane.

"Why is that?"

"We're ten miles from town here. A taxi can take half an hour each way on these roads. If there's one available at all with that mess down in the harbor."

Holly stepped in. "We're with the NTSB. Of course we're in a hurry to get down there, mate. Sooner's not within a dingo's whisker of fast enough."

The pilot shrugged and went to walk away.

But Miranda saw something coming their way from the mainland.

A speck, bright in the sky and easy to spot. A rotorcraft.

"Captain. Could you please call that US Coast Guard helicopter and reroute them here? I presume that they're on their way to the waterfront and we won't be much out of their way."

By the time it had come close enough to the island to resolve into more than a bright dot, it began turning in their direction.

Holly held up a hand palm out.

Miranda tried to slap it high-five, but it didn't work very well. Maybe the ability to do high-fives was genetic like so many other things that she couldn't do right.

"Hold up your hand, Miranda."

She did, reluctantly.

Holly slapped it just hard enough to tingle, but not enough to hurt.

It appeared normal.

"Do that again."

Holly shrugged and repeated the gesture. Miranda studied the angle of attack and pivot moments at shoulder, elbow, and wrist.

"Now hold up your hand."

Holly did as she'd instructed.

Miranda moved her joints through the observed motions at one-quarter speed.

Shoulder and elbow initiating the motion, hand lagging behind. As the shoulder stopped, the elbow continued with the hand shifting for correct angle of impact.

She repeated it at full speed. While her aim was off, there

was still sufficient contact to create a similar tingle and zing on her skin's surfaces.

Miranda lined up to try again, then saw the look on the face of the pilot, who had rejoined them. She wasn't sure what it meant. So instead, she slipped out her phone and snapped a photo of him to study.

As the pilot blinked in surprise, she turned the phone to Holly. "What is that expression?"

Holly offered the pilot one of her grins. "Half disbelief and half thinking that you're off your rocker."

"Only half?"

At Holly's laugh and nod, Miranda felt relieved. She'd always estimated that she was seventy to eighty percent off.

The big HH-60 Jayhawk variant of the Black Hawk settled close beside them, its white-and-orange paint job shining brightly next to the far duller Air Force jet.

It settled just long enough for her and Holly to scramble aboard. There were the pilots, two crew chiefs, a medic, and a man who reminded her a little of a gloomy troll hunched in the dark.

31

Master Sergeant Pierre Jones had been sitting on the hospital's roof trying to figure out how his life had gotten so much more complicated than it had been this morning.

He'd started the day off looking forward to a series of tests on their new aircraft. Any airtime was good time as far as he was concerned. And that had been before he'd remembered he'd be flying those hours sitting beside Tech Sergeant Rosa Cruz. Beautiful, funny, and all-Christ competent.

Finding out that their unit commander was in on it just made the whole thing the shits. Then all the rest...

Right about the time he'd decided he'd just sit there on the hospital roof helipad until he turned into mulch, a medical crew had raced out from the elevator and shooed him aside.

A landing Coast Guard Jayhawk had disgorged multiple victims.

Burn victims.

"Avalon?" he'd asked one of the crew chiefs.

"More to come." He'd helped the woman heft her end of a stretcher as they shifted the first of three from the cargo bay onto a rolling gurney.

"Need a lift." Maybe the answer he was looking for was at the crash.

"Not a taxicab."

He'd pulled his ID. "Master Sergeant Jones. I was on that plane until I had to bail out. Need to get back out there."

"Still not a taxi." But then she'd focused on his face.

He didn't know what he looked like. He'd bet it was about right for having just reached Hell's intake and registration desk. Apparently the crew chief thought the same.

"Shit!" She'd waved him aboard, then yelled forward to the pilots. "We got a hitchhiker. Crash investigation."

Which wasn't quite accurate, but he'd take it.

He sat in the corner of the Jayhawk's cargo bay and did his best to stay out of the way as the crew re-stowed their medical gear during the short flight and prepared for the next load of victims.

They stopped at the top of the island and picked up a small brunette and a shining blonde.

"*Still* not a fucking taxi service," the crew chief muttered to him as the bird lifted again.

He nodded his agreement. Not that it mattered.

The thing that Pierre couldn't imagine was how to explain what he now knew. And by his silence, he too was complicit as sin. He still wasn't clear why he'd kept his mouth shut when he shouldn't have.

The investigators had asked the key question, *Do you*

have anything else to add that might be relevant to this crash investigation?

He'd evaded with, *Not at this time.* But no way was that going to save his ass if there was a court-martial.

And there was a three-star general in the middle of the mess? That was *way* above his pay grade. He was just a master sergeant and had never actually met a three-star.

His aunt always said that he was damned because he hadn't been to church since his own baptism—usually accompanied with another of her braying laughs. But this time?

"I really am going to hell."

The blonde passenger was close enough to overhear and grinned at him. "Not as fast as the poor bastards who were on that plane." Her accent was smoothly Australian—which was almost as sexy as Rosa's soft Spanish.

"Perfect. Just perfect. Means I get an express nonstop flight. I was last one off the damned bird." Maybe that was the problem. Had he actually gone down with the plane and this really *was* hell?

The blonde studied him for a long moment, then turned to her small companion. "We got a live one, Miranda."

Turning back, the blonde stuck out a hand. He shook it because he didn't know what else to do.

"Holly Harper. National Transportation Safety Board. Pleased as two peas in a pod to meet'cha."

32

"HI, LIZZY."

General Elizabeth Gray was Lizzy to very few people other than herself. Miranda Chase was one of them. She had been from the very first moment they'd stumbled into each other the same night she'd met Drake.

It hadn't hurt, much, when Miranda had proven her ability to analyze crash images even better than she could herself.

And Miranda's abilities as a pilot—no textbook written said she should have survived that emergency landing on the National Mall when her plane was sabotaged. Lizzy had studied the flight. Ten degrees more bank, five degrees less flare, even a half second of hesitation and she'd have been dead. But Miranda had done it perfectly. The former combat pilot in her couldn't help but respect the woman.

But what she'd liked most was Miranda's unflappable focus. She'd faced down Drake, the President, and even the CIA director in the time Lizzy had known her. Her friend's self-confidence had helped Lizzy bolster her own in her new role as the NRO's director. And she *loved* managing the National Reconnaissance Office; from satellite launches to global image analysis, every part of it was a joy and a challenge.

But the members of Miranda's team calling her Lizzy? Barely maybe. And definitely not in her outer office in front of her chief aide, Captain Thorsen.

"Hello, *Michael*. Jeremy. Jonathon." All three men had intensely bright hats dangling behind their shoulders from loose chin straps around their necks.

"Wow, that's a hell of a sparkler, Lizzy," Mike persisted in being cheery. "Matches your eyes." He laughed at his own joke.

She didn't. Her eyes were Eurasian dark and her engagement ring shone brilliant blue.

Thorsen twisted around to look at her hand, then looked up at her with surprise. Of course he hadn't noticed; he was a male. But Mike had, and now announced it to the world. It would rip through the three thousand employees of the NRO in hours—their job was generating and handling vast amounts of information, after all. Gossip moved even faster than news of a new Russian jet.

She'd been trying to keep the Air Force-blue diamond turned toward the inside of her hand. Mostly because every time she looked at it, it freaked her out.

Last night, Drake had taken her back to the Metro 29 Diner where they'd had their first date. He'd done the whole bent-knee proposal thing in front of the crowd, waitresses, and everybody (thankfully no other military personnel). There'd been no press, of course. And it had been over the same "patriotic" banana split they'd shared the first time—strawberry, vanilla, and blueberry ice creams. It was all alarmingly romantic, especially coming from the Chairman of the Joint Chiefs dressed in jeans and a black t-shirt.

At fifty she was too old to have squealed with delight. Thankfully she had an excuse as her big five-o birthday was still four months away—she'd met him on her forty-ninth.

Married on her fiftieth? Wow! There was a startling thought.

But she didn't need her private life rubbed in her staff's face.

She herded the three men into her office and shut the door. Circling around her desk, she sat, then waved them to settle across from her.

"So, Old Drake finally popped the question." Mike looked very pleased.

"The Chairman of the Joint Chiefs of Staff General Drake Nason's private business is none of yours, Mr. Munroe."

Mike seemed to finally catch on—mostly. His smile barely abated as he bowed his acknowledgement before sitting in a chair.

"And that's General Elizabeth Gray to you until I say otherwise. Are we clear?" She hadn't really used that tone of voice since she'd been a combat flight leader.

He blanched white, "Yes ma'am."

Maybe it had been overharsh, but she was past caring.

Just this morning, she'd managed to excise a real prick—brother of the CEO for a major defense contractor—that the former director had put in charge of space launch acquisition. The idiot shouldn't be allowed to launch a rowboat off a car trailer. It was only the third time in her life she'd had to recommend an officer for a court-martial offense for failure to obey a direct order to stand down, *and* sexually abusive language. She'd stripped his security clearance and had him escorted out of the building under heavy guard less than an hour ago.

Her tolerance for more bullshit was at a low ebb at the moment. Let Mike spin for a bit.

"May I offer my congratulations, General?" Jon asked carefully.

"On my becoming your evil step-aunt?" She hadn't yet had time to think about the fact of Drake's extended family. His two sons and daughter—with a granddaughter, she was going to be a step-grandmother!—were enough for her to contemplate. "Yes, you may."

"My congratulations, Aunt Gray." Jon kept it that succinct, but offered a nice smile with it.

"Thank you, step-nephew-to-be."

Jeremy squinted at her. "Is 'step' the correct term? Once you marry General Nason, then you will technically become Jon Swift's aunt. There is no genetic lineage consideration as the connection is through Drake's brother, not your genes. And that would imply—"

"Jeremy," Jon stopped him before she had to. Though even in her present mood it was impossible to be angry at someone like Jeremy.

"Oh, right. Why we're here—that's what I need to focus on. Gotta remember that," he mumbled to himself. Then he spoke succinctly, which wasn't like him at all. "We need to find out everything we can about Lieutenant General Jorge Jesus Martinez."

"Why aren't you asking Drake...General Nason?" She'd

never get used to this. *Screw it!* They were engaged and *she* could call him any damn thing she wanted. "Jorge is one of Drake's oldest friends. Ahh, *because* Drake is one of his oldest friends. But what do you need to know about him?"

The three men all eyed each other, then Jon spoke up. "We need to know why we found his dog tags on an incinerated body-double at a crash of a decommissioned and stolen AC-130H Spectre gunship on a mountaintop in Aspen."

Lizzy carefully showed nothing as she waited, but Jon didn't continue. Somehow, impossibly, that was a complete thought. She hadn't become the head of the NRO, or one of the rare female generals, by revealing her thoughts. But it didn't stop her thinking them.

JJ dead. But not dead. He'd faked his death?

"Where is Taz? Colonel Vicki 'Taser' Cortez?" She'd had a run-in with Taz just a few weeks ago. The woman hadn't been on the attack, exactly, more of an exploratory probe—a hard one. She'd been after a feed for a certain type of intel, without carrying orders from the general granting her access to that type of intel.

"She also had a dead body-double. We're guessing that she's still with the general?" Jon asked the last with a shrug. "We were hoping that you might know something."

"Also without an official request," Lizzy sighed.

A special assignment for General Martinez, had been all Taz would say. Lizzy hadn't doubted that it was the general's request, but it had sounded as if the general didn't want a paper trail. Lizzy had refused to play along. She'd been busy, tried to push Taz aside—finally throwing her out of the office—almost bodily. In retrospect, there was little doubt that Taz had gone elsewhere and managed to get what she needed. She certainly hadn't tried again.

And now she too was undead?

On the up-and-up or not, Lizzy didn't like the way this was feeling.

"Actually," Jon drew out the word, then smiled before she could think about ejecting him just as she had Taz. "As the Air Force major in charge of this investigation, I would be glad to make it an official request for assistance, as long as we can do it expeditiously. That's why we came to you. Though any personal insights wouldn't be amiss."

"JJ's a complete hard-ass. No matter what Drake says." Lizzy knew it was judgmental but that didn't make it any less true.

"So you should have gotten along just fine," Jon's smile made it a joke without it quite being one.

She turned away and stared at the walls for a moment. She'd left them bare, with no stamp of her own. The previous director had made such a thing about past glories that he could barely lay claim to. She didn't want to mimic that but she'd had more of herself in her workspace when she was an image analyst. Maybe that's what had made Mike, Taz, and many of the directors treat her so casually.

Fine. They needed a reminder of who she was, she'd give it to them.

Lizzy picked up her phone and punched Thorsen's extension.

"I want two framed posters for my office. That F-16 poster with General LeMay's quote about the love of freedom, except have them make it up with my old Viper as the image. Make the other one from the NRO's latest sat launch for the

KH-11 spy bird. That one on the Delta IV Heavy out of Vandenberg last January." One that she'd overseen personally.

"May I also suggest a USAF flag beside the national one —it is your lineage—and a display case for your medals and patches. The 79th Fighter Squadron Tigers is a great patch. You need to put those in people's faces—hard. Ma'am."

"Remind me that you need a promotion soon, Thorsen. Thanks." She hung up and turned back to face the others.

"So, if they aren't dead, you need to know what they're up to." She pulled over a keyboard.

"Uh-huh," Jeremy nodded eagerly. "And we also want a tour and orientation on the AC-130J Ghostrider that's sitting over at Andrews."

That stopped her and made her turn to face him. "Why is that?"

"I'm not sure, but Miranda seemed to think it was important. See, the plane that went down in Aspen was an AC-130H Spectre gunship. It's a version of the C-130 Hercules that—"

"I know what a Spectre is, Jeremy."

"Right, okay. Well, the one that's currently burning in Avalon Harbor on Santa Catalina Island, unless they've put it out by now in which case it *isn't* still burning, was an AC-130J Ghostrider based on the Super Hercules that—" He slowed just enough to take a breath and add a grimace. "— that you probably know all about, too. To properly investigate the crash, Miranda wants to know about the laser and any other upgrades. And I saw that there was a Block 30 here in DC at Andrews—oh, I already said that—so we thought we'd kill two birds with one stone and come see you and it. And that was a really horrible analogy, wasn't it? Since two Hercules *birds* have gone down in the last fourteen hours. Curiously, both crashed on stone: the top of the Snowmass ski area is mostly rock, and the stone pier in Avalon harbor, and...shutting up now."

"The second crash was a Block 30 that went down?" She hadn't heard about either one, but her usual concerns were space and what she could see of foreign military actions from there.

Mike's smile was back, but he was smart enough to keep his mouth shut.

"How the hell did that happen?"

"That's why we're here...General Lizzy." Or not. Mike was incredibly convinced of his own cuteness. His charm and beautiful smile might work on others, but it wasn't cutting him any slack in her office. She just ignored him. And she ignored his puzzled frown at the failure of his so-civilian tactics.

33

Lizzy led the way to the UH-1N Twin Huey helicopter that the USAF 1st Helicopter Squadron at Andrews had sent over. One of the nice benefits of being an agency director; her time was rated as too valuable to be wasted stuck in traffic.

It landed inside the loop of the NRO's running track, close by the grass volleyball court.

Drake had a good eye. Her diamond exactly matched the Air Force-blue paint job and her gold band matched the helo's gold side-stripe. There was no clear diamond to match the white tops of the Huey, but she preferred the simplicity of the ring with just the single stone and the smoothly twisted setting suggestive of the contrail of a jet barrel-rolling through the sky.

Now she finally knew how to explain to her mother why she'd waited so long to get married. Not like her three sisters hadn't already provided multiple grandchildren, along with four divorces and six marriages. Lizzy had waited...for Drake.

They all clambered aboard and the helo lifted for the fifteen-minute ride to Andrews.

A text chirped on her phone.

"According to the NSA," she read out, "Taz placed a called approximately five hours ago from—oh shit—Avalon Harbor."

She'd already checked her satellite logs while they were still in her office. There'd been no surveillance over Aspen or Santa Catalina at the time of either crash. *We aren't in the habit of surveilling non-military civilian territory.* Mike hadn't been pleased, but Jon was military and had nodded in understanding.

"They found three call starts, none over twenty seconds. It was locked down with the full SCIP encryption, so we can't trace them. All they know was that two of the calls were to the Pentagon."

"Before or after the crash time?" Mike asked while the rest of them were still processing the information.

"Within five minutes after. Three minutes, fifteen seconds actually."

"Three-fifteen." Mike sat back and spoke as if to himself, "Did she bail out at the last second? Was she ashore, witnessed the crash, and needed to report it? Or was it because the crash was unplanned and she then had to act quickly? I'm guessing the last."

"What about JJ?" Jon asked. They'd all taken to calling General Martinez by his nickname. It would have felt very disrespectful, but she was doing it herself despite barely knowing the man.

"Let's see," Mike looked out the window as they crossed over the Potomac, but she guessed he wasn't sightseeing the National Mall. "She wasn't on the crash. It was too destructive. If she bailed out at the last moment, she'd have been in the ocean and wouldn't have had time to be placing a secure call that quickly."

Lizzy found herself nodding. She'd never had to eject, but she'd practiced water landings by parachute. The first five minutes were all about dealing with the parachute and trying not to drown.

"If we theorize that she was there to witness the results, she could have been reporting to the general. But that three-minute delay... No. She must have conferred with the general before the first call. They saw the crash together. It was unplanned. And he issued new orders for her to carry out. That's the best fit."

Lizzy was still trying to get over Taz being undead from the initial crash, *and* on the site of a second major air crash.

How had Mike already...

Lizzy almost laughed. Once again, she'd underestimated Miranda's team. They were the very best at what they did, even if she didn't always understand how they achieved their results. It wasn't all Miranda. Jeremy was a technical wizard. And Mike probably saw motivational interactions the same way she understood the tactical implications of orbital dynamics—as a single gestalt.

Mike looked at her. "Are JJ and Taz the sorts to just hang out at a place like Catalina Island?"

Lizzy had met Taz just the once that had led Lizzy to throwing the colonel out of her office. She'd never met JJ, but Drake had talked about him enough for her to feel that she knew him.

"They're more likely to take a vacation at an active bombing range. A rock has a greater sense of fun."

"So..." Mike was now studying the cargo bay ceiling. "Why were they there? They were there to observe something about that plane. Maybe the crash made it so that they never got the chance?"

"Then why did she make the phone calls immediately afterward?" Lizzy could almost see it... "Oh."

"Right," Mike acknowledged.

"What?" Jeremy asked but Mike ignored him.

"There's some reason they really want that plane. There are only the two others. One here at Andrews. Where's the third Ghostrider?"

"Eglin Air Force Base," Jeremy somehow knew.

Mike slapped him on the shoulder and refocused on her. "If I was Taz and the general just sitting on the Avalon harbor, and they somehow were involved with the crashed Ghostrider... Taz is looking for another one for her general. They *need* a Ghostrider for some reason. General Gray, you better call Eglin and get them to put a guard on that one they have down there."

Lizzy did.

As she finished, Mike's phone rang and he punched for speaker.

The 1st Helicopter Squadron's birds weren't like the President's birds from HMX-1 or even the gold-tops of the Army's 12th Aviation Battalion. They were stuck with aged Hueys and boasted little more luxury than padded seats.

Leather armchairs and mood lighting were for others. The Air Force's 1st HS was for getting work done, but they did have decent sound insulation. It let her hear the conversation without too much straining.

"Hey Mikey," Holly's voice sounded from the speaker. "We've got a chap here, took a parachute-assisted swim in the Pacific. Last off the AC-130J Ghostrider. Says that two pilots went down with it, everyone else got out."

"You still have him there?"

"Bolted to my hip. He's not as pretty as you, so I figure he'll be less trouble."

"Ask him if there was a Colonel Vicki Cortez or a General Martinez on the flight." Oddly, Mike ignored her side comment. Maybe under certain conditions he really was all business.

Holly finally answered. "Neither name means anything to him. He's been with the crew for six months."

"Shit!" Mike glared at the phone as if trying to see Holly and the man through it.

"He doesn't swear much," Jeremy commented. "I think Mike's cursed like three times since I met him. Something must be really weird on this one for him to—"

"Sitting right here, Jeremy, and I could do without the running commentary, buddy. I'm missing something, but I don't know what it is."

"You'll get it, Mike!" Jeremy announced with absolute confidence.

"Too many missing pieces," Mike scowled out the window as they settled onto the parking area close beside the AC-130J Ghostrider at Andrews Air Force Base. "Keep working him, Holly. We're missing something here. It's important."

"Roger that." And she was gone.

34

WHILE HOLLY WAS STILL ON THE PHONE, MIRANDA HAD LED Master Sergeant Pierre Jones out onto the stone quay, nose-to-tail with the Hercules. The big plane had flipped end-for-end, landing on its back with the rear closest to land. That placed the tail closest to Pierre's and Miranda's noses.

The remains of the plane's nose were at the ocean end of the quay. The remains of the rear end of the cargo bay were the closest piece to land. The broken off tail section still remained in the water nearly two hundred feet off the end of the stone, only a lone fin sticking above the water like a dead, giant shark.

"Did you observe any problems with the weather?"

Pierre squinted down at her, then waved a hand at the sky. "Clear and calm. So calm, there isn't even any real wave action."

Miranda knew that oil and fuel spills could calm rough waters, making assessments deceptive for a wide area around a water crash. However, the spilled fuel had burned off and there were indeed no underlying waves that she could see on either the ocean or the harbor side of the pier. It was a surprisingly tranquil day on the Pacific Ocean.

"The terrain wasn't an issue," she continued working her way down her mental checklist.

"Not until they rammed the end of the pier."

She nodded. That was an accurate assessment and she noted it down.

Diving equipment would be necessary to investigate the debris perimeter. In fact...

The next Coast Guard helo dropped a dive team on the cleared area at the head of the pier. All she had to do was wave to Holly and point at the divers.

Holly made a hand sign as if holding something the size of an aircraft's black boxes and rushed over to convince the Coast Guard to go after those first.

It was so awkward splitting the team across the country. She only owned the one black box reader, and it was in Jeremy's pack in Washington, DC. But still, the Cockpit Voice and Data Recorder's recovery was the next essential step. Rather than her usual preference of working on her own, she was actually adapting to their extended abilities.

This she did take time to note down. Pierre Jones didn't appear to mind waiting; he just stared glumly at the inverted fuselage.

Now Miranda allowed herself to look at the crash site itself.

Other than scorch marks, the stone pier itself actually looked little the worse for wear from the Hercules collision. There had been two buildings on the top that were now little more than scorched foundations, but the stone remained.

The nose of the Hercules, however, had been flattened and driven back into the fuselage. The plane's hundred-foot length—roughly eighty without the tail section—was now closer to fifty feet long. The entire front end all the way back to the wings had been pancaked.

There was unlikely to be anything recoverable from the cockpit, even the QAR. Unlike a black box—designed to withstand a minimum of thirty-four hundred g's and a thousand degrees centigrade of fire—a quick access recorder was meant as a simple backup device.

"Poor bastards," Pierre was shaking his head.

"Who?"

"The pilots. They're in there somewhere. Be a miracle if they ever even find enough to bury."

That also meant that the HEL-A laser she wanted to inspect would be unrecoverable as well, it was normally mounted close behind the cockpit opposite the weapon control stations.

This was the moment, shortly after the death of both her parents, when people had tried to say comforting things to her. She'd never enjoyed it much, but Mike had been teaching her that such things were reasonable offerings to a grieving person.

"I'm sure...it was quick."

"I sure as hell hope not. They were both *absolute* bastards."

35

WHICH PIERRE KNEW WAS AN UNFAIR ASSESSMENT.

Tango and Gutz weren't bastards. They were jet jockeys. Classic, macho, half-a-century-after-their-time, pig-headed jet jockeys. *No way* either of them would have stepped up when they found out Rosa was carrying their kid.

"Cheap. Two-bit. Arrogant..." He could feel his teeth grinding.

"Why were they bastards?" The NTSB investigator asked without quite looking at him.

He certainly wasn't going to try explaining how they'd both leave Rosa in the lurch. But the rest of it?

Screw it, his ass was toast now anyway.

"They were hijacking the goddamn plane."

"It appears that they weren't successful," the woman said it absolutely deadpan.

Pierre could only look at her in surprise. In his experience, most smaller women did something to compensate for their size: feisty, funny, hiding behind meekness. This Miranda woman didn't sound like any of those.

"No, lady. No, they weren't."

"I wonder why not? If they had successfully convinced the crew to depart the aircraft and the plane was actually fully functional, it should have been an easy task." She stepped forward until she was almost pithed by the jagged metal that now framed the open rear of the inverted cargo bay and peered in.

He moved close enough to track her attention. She was intensely methodical, not just peering into the wreck. Instead, every foot of the rear break came under her scrutiny —top-left to bottom-right. Then she seemed to repeat the process one meter into the hull at exactly the same pace. Then another.

"Um," Pierre couldn't decide what was safe to say and what wasn't. What could he tell this investigator without implicating Rosa? Or *should* he turn her in? Rosa hadn't actually done anything—other than agreeing to go along with everything and then not reporting the general's plan.

Shit!

Could she get away with "under the orders of a superior officer" as an excuse? No, she said she'd volunteered.

Double shit!

And he'd never asked her *why*.

He turned to look toward the mainland. The moment she'd told him that she was part of the plot to take the plane, his brain had shut down—or tried to.

Then it had gotten worse.

Three-star generals leading hijackings?

Pierre was pure USAF. His lineage traced all the way

back to pre-World War II Army Air Corps. And now one of the service's top generals had decided to form his own Air Force.

What was up with that?

Unable to stand it anymore, he'd stormed out of Rosa's room and somehow ended up sitting on top of the VA hospital's roof by the helipad.

"There is a very curious pattern of damage here that I haven't seen before."

"Well," Holly returned to Miranda's side. "It did have the shit blown out of it when it crashed."

Miranda shook her head. "First, such a simple impact, even at high speed, should not have ignited the entire bomb load. Second, look at the effects."

Pierre felt like an automaton as both he and Holly turned to look at the plane, turned back to look at each other, then shrugged in unison.

Miranda continued without appearing to notice. "Look past the obvious blast damage from the bomb's detonations. Note the liquefaction of the underlying materials. Even the metal shows fluid rather than brittle deformation—which is not typical in a blast explosion."

That, at least, he could explain. "That was me." At least he'd told that part to the investigators.

Both women turned to look at him, though Miranda kept staring at his chin until he had to rub it to make sure there was nothing there.

"I had an…altercation with the pilot. Basically, he tried to shoot me when I realized he was stealing the plane. I broke the final mirror off the—" No. That was classified.

"The HEL-A laser," Miranda stated.

"But you aren't supposed to know about that."

Holly just smirked at him.

Miranda turned back to studying the aircraft. "Without the final mirror, a partially unfocused beam would have been directed at the rear of the aircraft. Is it still the hundred-kilowatt version, or did they manage to get the one-fifty configured in time for the Block 30 upgrade?"

"One-fifty," slipped out before he could stop himself.

Holly looked impressed; Miranda just looked at the plane.

"Based on the varying degrees of damage, assuming you used the laser's full output—"

"I did."

"—and a minimum of atmospheric blooming effect due to short range down the length of the plane, I'd estimate that the laser was engaged for thirty to forty seconds."

According to the jet skier, they'd retrieved him approximately two-point-seven miles from Avalon. At three hundred miles per hour, the Ghostrider had flown another thirty-two seconds.

"Who the hell are you, lady?"

Holly shushed him. "Don't bother her when she's thinking. Besides, I can tell you the only answer you'll ever get to that question. 'My name is Miranda Chase. I'm the investigator-in-charge for the NTSB.' "

"Well, that doesn't tell me shit."

"Right. And it doesn't tell you shit that she knows more about your top-secret laser than you do?"

Pierre grunted. Another question he didn't have a good answer to. He thought that he knew everyone on the inside of this project, because the circle was very small—they'd all been in his class at Lockheed Martin in Marietta, Georgia, as either students or engineering instructors.

And now this NTSB investigator, who should be looking after bunged up 737s, was pointing out effects of the HEL-A laser after he'd intentionally broken it? That implied a level of knowledge that even he didn't have.

"Therefore," Miranda turned to face Holly, but didn't quite look at her either, "we have a plane crash that was due to sabotage of a hijacked flight. And we have an earlier crash that was completely intentional. Why am I here? Neither of these are pilot error or aeronautical failures."

"Wait. What?" Pierre hadn't heard anything about a second one.

"I said hush!" Holly turned back to Miranda. "Even Mike can't get what's happening."

"Who's Mike?"

Holly punched his arm hard enough to hurt.

36

LIZZY HAD BEEN A FIGHTER PILOT FOR YEARS. THEN SHE'D shifted over to tactical training. First training other flight leaders, then ultimately their commanders.

But her first love had always been space. Her dreams of leaving orbit had died before she'd been born, with the demise of the Apollo program. She hadn't even tried for the shuttle program—a female fighter pilot had enough hurdles to climb without having to live it down if she failed to make the grade. That a class of only a dozen astronauts was chosen from nearly twenty thousand applicants wouldn't offset that worst of labels among pilots—"failure."

Or so she'd thought at the time.

But when the chance came to jump over to the NRO satellite program, she'd leapt without a hesitation. Everything about it, tactically and technologically, just...fit.

The same way technology seemed to fit Jeremy.

Once aboard the Ghostrider at Andrews, he'd spent less than three minutes inspecting the laser—barely glancing at the big guns. Instead, the moment he'd sat down at the weapons console, it was as if the rest of the Ghostrider disappeared for him.

The depths of his concentration was revealed in his running commentary to Mike.

"Pretty cute, huh, Auntie Gray?" Jon whispered over her shoulder as they watched.

She could only nod. Mike might understand barely a tenth of what Jeremy was saying, but that didn't stop him from being encouraging.

More than that. He asked questions.

"So, how does it fire through clouds?"

"Well, there are several compensators here," Jeremy tapped four separate controls. "It's just a beam of light, so technically a line-of-sight instrument. However, by adjusting the emission frequency and pulse rate, you can—huh, yeah, like that—you can adjust for interference and retain a high percentage of the beam's power for several seconds dependent upon the estimated cloud's water density. Oh, look how they show that. Very cool."

Lizzy saw that Mike wasn't trying to increase his own understanding, but rather was asking questions that would increase Jeremy's.

"He may irritate the hell out of you, Auntie, but Mike's the best I've ever seen at what he does. I still don't get why Miranda doesn't want to directly contract her team to the military. She—"

"You *asked* her that? Jon, nephew-to-be, since when are you an idiot?"

Jon just gaped at her.

Lizzy rubbed at her face. A crew began coming aboard

through the forward door. Despite the size of a C-130, there was little extra space in a Ghostrider.

Five big men entered and headed to the guns. Two more for the cockpit. A small woman in combat fatigues stepped into the shadows by the sensor control station.

Every post had its position and it was soon clear that they were in the way. Even Mike was getting squeezed for his space beside Jeremy.

She led Jon back out onto the tarmac. Night had slipped up on them and the perimeter of security lights around the massive hangar for the Air Force One and Two jets began standing out against the darkness at the far end of the airfield. The cool air was a relief—even in June, DC was heating up. They came to a stop out past the port wingtip.

"Why did you suggest that to Miranda?" Lizzy wondered where the tact had suddenly come from. Because Jon actually was her nephew-to-be? *No.* She was not into nepotism. It was because he was a good young officer and she liked him.

"My commanding general felt that bringing her team on board as full-time contractors would be a good move. Her insights have proven to be essential to multiple investigations. Also, working on existing safety practices would—"

"Don't you know anything about Miranda Chase?"

"More than you might think, General Gray," he responded stiffly. "I've been studying information about—"

"You're as bad as she is."

"But I—"

"No," she wasn't going to let him speak. "Throw out

whatever books you're reading. If you really care about her..."

"I do!"

"Then study *her*. This is me speaking, not General Gray. Damn it, Jon. Yes, she's the best crash investigator I've ever seen, present company included."

"No argument," Jon held up his hands.

"Miranda Chase is a high-functioning autistic, air-crash savant. But don't think that's all she is any more than I'm just some glorified image analyst turned bureaucrat. She's also a woman terrified of change. No. That's wrong. Miranda is a woman mortally confused by change. You weren't around when she first acquired this team. It's been eight months and she's only just now figuring out how to work with them— and I'd wager that's stretching her to the limits every single day."

Jon grimaced. "Yeah, I saw her make some notes to that effect in that little book she always carries."

Lizzy had seen her do that as well. "You have to pay attention to the *woman,* not to wherever the hell your imagination thinks she fits. She *belongs* in the NTSB, and she knows it. If you try to take away the one thing she truly knows, you'll lose. Trust me!"

Jon was hunched with his hands in his pockets. Finally, after inspecting the pavement for an inordinately long time, he looked up at her but didn't lose the hunch.

"Shit! When did you get so smart?"

She could only laugh at that. "Hell if I know! Maybe it comes with the star." She tapped the one on the shoulder of her uniform.

"Huh, got a ways to go then." He rubbed at his own collar point oak leaf. "Guess I know one thing though."

"What's that?"

"My uncle is one lucky bastard."

"He is!" Lizzy counted herself pretty lucky too.

37

TAZ WAS AMAZED THAT IT HAD WORKED.

Her first call after the Ghostrider crash in Avalon harbor had been to locate the other two AC-130Js.

Her second had ascertained that there was no training flight planned tonight for the one at Andrews Air Force Base.

The third had been to file a new training order—to be manned by a very different crew.

Base security had worried her. But apparently their IDs weren't registered as dead yet, so it had been a simple matter to get to the plane. Then she'd almost blown it by nearly stepping in front of General Gray, ducking into the Ghostrider's interior shadows at the last second. That had been too close.

Now she stood in those shadows and watched the two men at the weapons control console.

"But what happens when you're in nonstandard flight configurations?" The slender man asked the seated Vietnamese.

"Okay, watch this, Mike. It's so cool. I'll just set up a SIM space here."

There was a fast rattle of keys that Taz couldn't quite see. She shifted through the shadows as their sensor operator came aboard until she had a better view.

"I've simulated us in inverted flight."

"Put on your seat harness," this Mike person teased the man at the laser console.

The operator took him literally, and snapped in with an ease that showed a deep familiarity with the complexities of a five-point harness. "Okay, here we are in a sixty-degree, inverted bank. Watch what happens."

And Taz watched as the man's fingers flew over the console.

"I don't actually need to key any corrections. Now the M102 howitzer requires compensation for angle of attack, airspeed, and so on. Especially the trajectory from our theoretical inverted position. The howitzer shell will appear to fall upward due to the Earth's gravity pulling the shell down to earth. The targeting information must be inverted with the over-ninety-degree bank angle. But watch the laser."

And Taz studied the simulation as he targeted and fired, nailing the simulated drone.

"See? It's all line-of-sight operations. No gravitational effects. We need to worry about air density, humidity levels, and particulate content like dust, which will scatter the beam," he tapped various pieces of information on the screens that meant nothing to her. "But the angle doesn't matter at all."

General JJ Martinez walked up the aisle from the gunnery positions.

She eased away to join him.

"Did you find us a laser operator?"

Taz considered as she continued watching the two of them. "Civilian contractors by their dress and speech patterns. But definitely the skill set we need."

"Close enough. We're out of time. I'll be up in the cockpit. Get them to come along nicely, if you can." Then he turned on his heel and headed for the cockpit ladder. *Nicely if you can* meant *under duress if necessary.*

She decided on a combination approach.

"Excuse me," she stepped from the shadows.

"Well, hello there," Mike's tone did one of those, *I'm now speaking to a woman things* that made her so sick of the old-guard military. At least it didn't sound demeaning per SOP. No, this Mike's standard operating procedure was "flirt mode" not "misogynistic-asshole mode."

She definitely didn't have time for that and ignored him.

"Are we at your station?" the operator asked. "I hope that's okay. I just can't get over the wonderful control suite for the HEL-A. That's one bad-boy laser but it is configured to be run with…"

He kept going on about the tech at a level she couldn't follow. Taz never had been a technical gal.

The Number Three engine fired to life and began winding up to speed with a throaty buzz. Number Four fired close behind it; General JJ wasn't wasting any time.

Her art was cutting through the bureaucracy of red tape; something she did by leveraging people's weaknesses. His overeager manner gave her the key she needed to turn.

"We're about to run a test flight over the offshore VACAPES Test Range. We'll be night-firing at numerous targets. Would you like to come along for the flight?"

"Like to? *Like to!* That would be fantastic. I mean usually it's Jon or Holly who get to go along on a flight, because I'm not a pilot. But I'd love a chance to study the actual performance profiles of—"

"Good. You just need to tell your ground team." She couldn't do it herself or General Gray might recognize her.

"Ground team? Oh, Jon and General Gray." He shot to his feet...or tried to. The harness slammed him back into the seat. He looked down at it in surprise, which was pretty amusing. She couldn't remember the last time she'd felt that.

"I've got it, Jeremy," Mike patted his shoulder, which also gave Taz the operator's name. How curious for a young Vietnamese man to be named Jeremy.

She could overhear Mike as he shouted out the door that they were going on the "training" flight—at least as far as he knew. She considered coaxing Mike off the plane, but he might prove to be useful leverage later and decided to let him remain aboard.

"Look at this!" Jeremy called for her attention, apparently unable to restrain himself. "See how they're compensating for atmospheric blooming—that's air turbulence caused by the laser superheating the air—by oscillating the beam over the millisecond time frame. That's just so cool!"

He continued displaying different aspects of the weapon. She could feel the energy and excitement coursing through him.

Mike returned. "If she and Jon head back to her office, they'll toss our packs in the hangar office."

"Oh, I need to secure your phones for the flight. Please set them to Airplane Mode and hand them to me. It's a required security precaution."

They both handed them over as engines One and Two came up to full revolutions. The plane eased into forward motion smoothly enough that none of them stumbled.

"I'll just stow these." Taz circled around the other side of the weapon control stations. As the plane taxied to the head of Runway 01, they passed a grass strip.

She heaved both phones into the grass.

Then she pulled out her own phone and stared down at it.

For nineteen years her life had been about communicating the general's wishes to whoever opposed him.

For better or worse, that was over now. This mission was their final play.

She heaved it after the other two, and closed the forward passenger door.

Taz leaned her forehead against the sealed door. For the thousandth time she wished her life was different. Too bad she had no idea what she wanted it to be.

Moments later they were aloft and headed south-southwest—the opposite direction from their filed flight plan to the VACAPES Test Range. She checked in with the man at sensors; he'd already shut down all tracking devices. Now they would look no different electronically than any other general aviation plane out for a night flight.

Time to go break the news to their new laser operator.

38

"I DON'T UNDERSTAND WHAT'S HAPPENING." MIRANDA GLARED at his left ear hard enough to make Pierre scratch at it.

"It is a very rare accident that I must report as 'Cause Unknown.' Those are almost exclusively when the plane was completely lost in the ocean or deepest wilderness. There's only an average of one every year or so, including both commercial and general aviation."

Pierre didn't care about any of that. But when he went to speak, Holly gave him an urgent shake of her head.

"In a crash with multiple causes yet with a clear final result, there typically remain some indicators signifying safety recommendations to be made. *However,* two consecutive crashes of very elite and rare AC-130 gunships, both with *known* causes unrelated to the aircraft? That just isn't right."

Pierre followed her gaze as she looked around the remains. They'd managed to climb about fifteen feet into the remaining fuselage before being completely blocked by the wreckage.

Miranda had explained what they were seeing as they went. Which was pretty amazing as he could barely recognize anything in an aircraft type he'd spent thousands of hours in.

"The bomb racks in the rear ramp were definitely the point of ignition for the final explosion as evidenced by the deformation angles observable in the aft portion of the remaining hull." Yada. Yada. Yada.

Forward of that, their way was blocked by the mass of the M102 howitzer. There was a subtle scent on the air that was almost lost behind the smell of the scorching. But here, deep inside the cargo hold where the fire hadn't reached, it was prevalent.

Bright.

Lacquer?

Yes, he spotted several broken-open rounds of the 105 mm ammunition for the howitzer. M64 propellant. Another damn good reason to get out of here until an EOD team could get it cleaned up.

Immediately past the main gun, they could see the remains of the laser, even if they couldn't reach it.

"Here," Pierre pointed at the elbow he'd busted on the laser. "I only had a few seconds to stop the hijacking. So I busted this and fired the laser on full. I'm guessing that it cooked the back of the plane. The heat probably destabilized the munitions, and the plane's impact with the pier was enough to trigger the explosion that lifted and flipped the fuselage."

He looked up at the crumbled deck plating above their

heads just in front of where the remains of the laser hung. There was a staining he didn't recognize.

"Blood," Holly followed the direction of his gaze. "Dried brown, but definitely blood."

He'd exited the plane uninjured, as had everyone else. Unless...

He pictured the layout of the plane, which was tricky as it was all upside down at the moment. From the front passenger door where Pierre had dived out, if Tango Torres had wanted to cross to the weapons console, he'd most naturally walk...to the right of the laser.

And pass his legs through the beam! Good! He hoped it had hurt like hell.

"Not my blood. Or Rosa's. All I give a damn about."

Miranda didn't react, but Holly looked at him with sudden interest.

"Rosa?"

"Laser operator. I helped her get off the plane before I went to help the pilots. Only to witness their hijacking."

Holly's look said that he hadn't answered her question.

Well, to hell with her.

Miranda continued. "There's no failure of aircraft or pilot in either crash. I am an NTSB investigator, not a military criminal detective. I don't have the training for this."

"At this level, I don't think anyone does, Miranda." Holly's sympathy struck Pierre as not very helpful, however accurate.

"Therefore, we must go to your realm, Holly. What does your experience in the SASR make you conjecture?" Ha. That would teach Holly—turnabout was fair play.

But SASR? What the fuck? The pretty blonde had been

in the Australia Special Air Service Regiment? "Not an operator."

Her cool look told him that's exactly what she'd been.

Damn but that was seriously elite.

"My conjecture is that someone wants an AC-130J Ghostrider very badly."

"Only three of them out there so far," Pierre informed them. Then remembered where they were standing. "Two now."

"Yes, Eglin and Andrews," Miranda spoke up.

Which, again, was more than he knew.

But he did know that some general had wanted a Ghostrider. One that Rosa had promised to—no, "sworn allegiance to" she'd said (which was just crazy)—be a gunner for.

"Wait. What was that general's name you asked about earlier?"

"General Jorge Jesus Martinez."

"JJ for a nickname?"

Holly nodded carefully.

No way could he admit to knowing about that without incriminating Rosa.

Except he just had.

39

MIRANDA TRIED CALLING MIKE AS SOON AS THEY HAD CRAWLED out of the wrecked airplane and stood once again on the scorched stone pier of Avalon's harbor.

Mike didn't answer.

Jon answered on the first ring. "Hi, Miranda. I just wanted to apologize for pushing you to bring your team over to the military. That was unfair and I should have known to tell my boss 'No' without even asking. Something Auntie Elizabeth has just pointed out most emphatically."

"I have no idea what you're talking about. I can't reach Mike." Then she remembered, but since the answer was "No" she hadn't seen any point in dwelling on the offer.

"I was afraid that you'd be angry about—"

"Angry that I can't reach Mike? Why would that be? I need to speak with him. Is he on another call?"

"No, he's on another *flight*. He and Jeremy."

Miranda looked at the phone for a moment. Jon's name

was across the top of the display. But he was supposed to be
—"I thought you were going to protect Jeremy."

"He's fine. They're on a training flight of the Ghostrider.
Jeremy was like a kid in a candy store he was so excited."

Miranda almost handed the phone to Holly, like when
Drake was being all caught up in being the Chairman of the
Joint Chiefs.

No.

She had to learn to handle some of these things herself or
her entire brain would be outsourced to her team and she'd
have nothing left of her own. She did set it to speaker though.

"And you're not with them?" She had to make sure that
she had this right.

Holly looked at her strangely. She'd missed the
beginning of the conversation.

"Right."

"Who *are* you with?"

"Aunt...General Gray."

"Hand the phone to her." Then she recalled Mike's
training, "Please?"

There was a long pause as the phone changed hands.

"Hello, Miranda."

"I presume by the fact that Jon called you 'Aunt' that you
are now married to Drake?" Holly spoke up before she
could. "Congratulations!"

"He's being a little premature. We're engaged as of last
night."

"Doesn't matter! It's about time Drake scooped you up.
Go, General Gray! Whoo! Whoo! Whoo!" Holly made an
arm cranking like she was running an old printing press

which didn't seem relevant, unless she was imitating printing wedding announcements.

"Thanks, Holly. I just—"

"I can't reach Mike." Miranda tried to never cut anyone off, but they always seemed to think it was okay to cut her off. Maybe just this once. "I understand that he's on a training flight on an AC-130J Ghostrider."

"Yes. We were at Andrews inspecting the new modifications when a training crew boarded to fly some runs out over VACAPES Test Range. They invited Jeremy to go with them."

Miranda closed her eyes for a moment to block out Holly's expression as her skin went sheet white. She did her best to summon her patience before speaking.

"We're at the crash of the Ghostrider in Avalon Harbor. We have reason to believe that General JJ Martinez had a crew attempt to hijack that plane. Two pilots died in the attempt."

No one interrupted her.

"There are two other Ghostriders."

"Yes," Lizzy responded. "We warned Eglin to beef up the security around theirs."

"What about the one at Andrews?"

"At Andrews? It's the most secure air base in the country. We weren't more than a few hundred meters from Air Force One."

Miranda couldn't find the words.

Holly spoke up, though her voice sounded tight and strained. "Secure enough to stop a three-star general from leading a crew to steal a plane?"

"Oh shit!" Lizzy gasped.

"He's not answering his phone. Can you trace it?"

"Please hold."

Pierre was pacing the long stone pier, clearly troubled by something.

"It's still at Andrews. So is Jeremy's," Lizzy returned to the line.

"Well, that's a relief."

"No, because the plane isn't. I've got someone rushing to the phones' location. Hang on."

The next five minutes were perhaps the longest in Miranda's life.

40

LIZZY HAD MIRANDA ON ONE LINE, A CAPTAIN ON THE GROUND at Andrews on another, and the NSA contact who'd traced the phone on the third.

"Both numbers you gave me appear to be in airplane mode," the NSA contact reported. "We can follow a phone in that mode unless it is actually powered off. It simply means that the user can't send or receive."

"That's not encouraging."

"Best I've got."

"I found them," the captain at Andrews reported. "Actually I found three. Two together and a third that caught my headlights another twenty or so meters along the taxiway. Wouldn't have spotted it if they hadn't just mowed."

Back to the NSA, "Can you tell me who the third phone belongs to? It's presently co-located with the other two."

But she already knew!

Why was it only now that she remembered the shadow

of a small woman moving to the Ghostrider's sensor tech station? That had to be—

There was a sharp rattle of keys. "A Colonel Vicki Cortez. US Air Force issued the phone."

It was like a bad movie. The undead were coming back to haunt her.

If she'd listened more to Taz rather than tossing her out of the office.

If she'd mentioned that meeting to Drake.

If she'd paid attention to the crew climbing aboard the Ghostrider.

If…

General Elizabeth Gray tried to imagine any worse possible news than half of Miranda's team being swept up by Colonel Taz Cortez.

But she couldn't.

41

"SHOOTING A CIVILIAN WOULD NOT BE MY FIRST CHOICE." TAZ waited for Mike's smile to fade.

But it didn't. "No, really. What kind of game are you playing? Is this some sort of wargame scenario thing?"

She slammed the side of the gun across his face.

He dropped to the deck in a heap, clutching his cheek. His cry of surprise galvanized Jeremy, so she flicked off the safety and placed it against Jeremy's temple.

"Don't."

He froze while Mike groaned.

"Besides, I didn't hit him that hard."

"Shit! It feels as if you did."

She nudged his hip with a foot to roll him onto his back. "I find that sometimes it's easier this way."

"Easier?" Mike kept pulling his hands away to check for blood. There was only one small cut that would stop bleeding soon—the rest was just scrapes and scratches.

Though his eye would probably turn an impressive black-and-blue.

"When you're built like me, very few people take you seriously. As both a woman and an officer, I find that a little irritating."

Mike eased up slowly until he was sitting with his back against the hull and his knees up in front of him. "Yeah, I kind of get that now."

She shifted her aim back to Mike, but shifted her angle. If she had to shoot him, she didn't want the round punching through the hull or some other critical system behind him. Mike's body didn't look heavy enough to stop even the 9 mm ball rounds in her Beretta M9 sidearm.

"I'm going to talk, and you're going to listen."

"We're not going to the VACAPES for a training flight?" Jeremy blinked at her in surprise. He still hadn't caught on to what was happening.

"That would be a 'no,' buddy," Mike said softly, then hissed sharply as he placed a palm over his eye.

Taz sighed. Sergeant Rosa Cruz had signed up for this. Tango and Gutz had understood the risks. As had Major Danny Gonzalez from the Colorado flight, now at the controls of this plane, and his pilot, the missing-presumed-dead Lieutenant Colonel Luis Hernandez. There'd been no ping at all off his phone, and his "escape" motorcycle was still parked in Aspen hours after the crash.

These civilians knew nothing. Had agreed to nothing.

The only civilians she ever dealt with were defense contractors seeking the stamp of the general's approval. JJ Martinez's approval was the gold standard of Air Force requisitions and everyone up and down the line knew it. Part of her job had been assuring that it stayed golden. If he did authorize it, it had to perform.

He'd often sent her into meetings, not to find out anything technical, but rather to ferret out if they were telling the truth. Civilians and officers alike had learned, some the hard way, that lying to her didn't work...at all.

But, Mike and Jeremy weren't that kind of civilian.

"What are you?"

"Go to hell."

She knelt down in front of him.

"Look at me."

He shook his head no, then cursed and hissed again.

She flicked her safety back on, but it made a loud and satisfying metallic click even over the deep rumble of the engines.

He looked up at her, his left eye blinking hard.

"Stop that."

His gaze steadied.

"No blood in the eye. Any double vision?" When he shook his head no, she rolled her eyes. "You'll be fine. Now answer the question, what are you?"

"We're crash investigators for the NTSB," Mike growled. She understood that attitude better than all of his Mr. Smooth. "We've been on your trail since Colorado. I'm assuming that you're Colonel Vicki Cortez."

"Taz. Short for Taser. How did you know?"

"I'm the one who found your body double. Let's just say that you aren't real tall, especially in the military. Where did your body-doubles come from?"

"Mortuary fire in Tijuana." The owners had been only

too glad to dispose of the bodies—even the undamaged ones. They'd probably pocketed all the money for the cremations and given wood ash to the grieving families. "How long did it take you to figure out?"

"That the crash was fake? An hour or so."

They had planned for it to buy them a minimum of three days, well past the end of the present mission.

"You wouldn't look so surprised if you knew our boss," Mike's smile was coming back. If she was holding a Taser rather than an M9, she'd be sorely tempted to use it.

"She's amazing!" Jeremy joined the conversation. "I'll bet she's already figured out what happened in Catalina. She already had the last person off the plane with her."

Taz hadn't stuck around long enough to find out that anyone had made it off.

"Weapons officer. Said the pilots didn't make it."

Damn it! That should have been checked. Reacquiring Tech Sergeant Rosa Cruz would have been far less risky than trusting to her ability to coerce these two into performing.

Taz considered, sighed, then sat down in the sensor tech's seat.

The deck leveled as they reached their cruising altitude. Under ten thousand feet so that they wouldn't arouse the suspicions of overeager air traffic controllers. Because this was a military flight, not a commercial one, the engine's roar was so loud that she was stuck leaning forward to be able to talk to the two of them. All the lighting was nighttime red, except for the lights on the control stations themselves. Those were high-tech green or brilliantly multi-colored displays.

She hadn't fired her sidearm outside of minimum

practice range time. Had never seen war, except when the general had toured forward operations—a rare event. General Jorge Jesus Martinez was a Pentagon general, not some field man. He'd flown C-130s all the way back in Desert Storm and not much since, other than his personal jet.

I like the ability to make surprise inspections. He rarely took staff with him, other than herself. Another very unusual action for a three-star usually surrounded by an entire cast.

He trusted her.

He *depended* on her to make everything right in his world.

And now she had to coerce two civilians...

She holstered her weapon.

Taz knew Mike's type all too well. Everything was a joke. Or, better yet, a game. A chance for one-upmanship. "Being" was more important than "doing." It was the first time she'd pistol-whipped anyone, and Mike had deserved it less than most. She was definitely losing it.

Jeremy was something else entirely. She'd learned how to use his type, but never understood them. Like the rare warrior-pilots, he bore a stark commitment to truth over career. Only a rare few, like JJ, carried the warrior with him up to the heights of command without being corrupted.

Just like the Pentagon, all of the defense contractors had the same dichotomy. She'd learned to start with the doer-nerds, garner as much "truth" as she could, and *only then* meet with the Mikes of the world.

Taz had never tried to change the mind of the warrior caste before.

When all else fails, try the truth?

She ignored Mike, still sitting on the floor and patting his eye gently, and focused all of her attention on Jeremy.

"We need your help."

42

Pierre tried to remember how he'd ended up in this position, but couldn't quite put it together.

One moment he'd been standing just to the west side of the wrecked Ghostrider airplane he'd been flying in this morning. The evening sun fast approaching the high hills to the back of Avalon Harbor hid the worst of the devastation along the waterfront.

The next moment, his back was pinned against the hull. A very big combat blade from Holly's leg sheath was up against his throat—point digging painfully into his skin. Not poised to slice across, rather set to be jammed straight into his brain and end him. He could just manage to see the distinctive metal ring at the hilt that would slip over a rifle muzzle to make it a bayonet. A seven-inch M9. Straight to the brain indeed.

Her other hand wasn't at his throat or pinning one of his arms.

Instead it was clenched around his balls so tightly that if

he so much as coughed, or even tried to uncross his eyes at the searing pain, she'd crush them.

"Tell us everything you know about General JJ. Now." Her voice was dead calm, but there was no question that he was eye-to-eye with death—hers had turned to steel blue far harder than the steel of the knife at his throat. The setting sun directly behind her lit her blonde hair with fire.

He glanced at Miranda. She stood four paces back, still holding her phone, and just watching the situation. Her head was tipped slightly to the side. No help there.

"Back off." Pierre knew it was a mistake even as he said it. He'd moved his jaw too much and could now feel a hot trickle of blood slipping down his neck. "Please?" he whispered.

She eased the knife back about three millimeters, and her ironclad grip on his balls by about three grams. It wasn't good, but it was better than nothing.

"I wasn't part of it." It was hard to speak without moving his jaw.

"Part of what?"

Not daring to speak, he rolled his eyes toward the remains of the Ghostrider behind him.

"You know more?"

He nodded with just his eyes.

"And you've been keeping your mouth shut because?"

"Rosa," he managed to whisper.

And he'd just betrayed that trust.

But hadn't she done the same thing? Betrayed his and the Air Force's trust in her?

No question, he was definitely in hell.

He wanted to bang his head against the metal hull

behind him—but there was a knife at his throat. Then he heard the cold, slick sound of it disappearing back into its sheath.

He opened one eye carefully.

"Know that look in the mirror all too well, mate. Worse than a hornet in a bottle. So angry you want to choke yourself dead."

Pierre tested a breath to see if it was safe, but her hand was gone from his crotch as well. "Never seen anyone move that fast."

"Good thing I'm not in a bad mood. Start talking or I will be."

He edged away from the vise jaws of the lethal blonde and the dead plane. At the edge of the quay, he simply stood and stared out over the water. The sun was just disappearing into the central hills of the island, the last of the long shadows slicing across the scorched harbor.

The two women moved up to either side of him.

"I don't know much. Tech Sergeant Rosa...Rosa Cruz...is, was—I guess—the best damn laser operator in the US Air Force. Christ but that woman taught me so much about my own job. Absolutely incredible."

"And seriously hot," Holly said it flat.

"You have no idea. Brains, body, skills—the whole goddamn package. Just sexy as hell!" Then he twisted to look at her. She'd trapped him even more neatly than he'd trapped himself.

"You're gone on her."

"I am?" He supposed that was a stupid question. *Yeah, or you would have turned her right in rather than risking your career and your freedom.*

"What does Tech Sergeant Cruz have to do with the crash?" Miranda leaned forward to ask around him.

He grimaced. "There wasn't anything wrong with the plane; it was a hijacking. Gunners jumped out. I got Rosa into a chute and pushed her out."

Maybe, just maybe, she'd been looking for an out? Maybe she hadn't put on a parachute just to deceive him, to get him off the plane thinking she'd follow? Was her subconscious trying to protect her?

Little late to be thinking that. It was as if his brain was only now coming back online.

"Then I went to help the pilots. That's when I figured out it was a hijacking. They were both in on it, but there was a fight and one shot the other."

"What were they fighting over?" Holly asked. "Hold it! One jet jock shooting another? With the size of their egos? Musta been over some hot Sheila. Oh, your Rosa girlfriend."

"Not girlfriend." Maybe if he just threw himself off the pier... Not worth the effort; probably no convenient sharks to eat him alive and get him out of hell.

"Ooo! You like the tricky ones, don't you?"

He sighed and nodded.

He could feel Miranda waiting. All she cared about was the plane.

"As I mentioned," he turned to her, "I figured out that they were hijacking an AC-130J Ghostrider gunship. Didn't sound like a good idea to me. Before I escaped, I busted that piece out of the laser and turned it on. Pilot tried to shoot me —twice. I got lucky once, he flat missed the second. That blood stain on the deck, guess I scorched him some as a bonus."

Miranda was taking notes.

He sighed, still unsure which side to choose. "If you could leave this last fact out of your report, that'd be... I dunno anymore. Maybe pretend I didn't say this, but Rosa Cruz was also in on it. Would have been if I hadn't shoved her off the plane."

Miranda stared down at her notebook with her pen poised. "I'm not very good at pretending things."

Perfect. Just fucking perfect.

43

Pierre Jones looked distinctly unhappy every time Rosa was mentioned.

Miranda glanced over her notes to try and understand why. She'd recorded tiny emoji pictograms next to each of her notes. Checking her guesses with Mike after interviews had proved very useful.

The only time Pierre had smiled was when he'd said Rosa Cruz was "sexy as hell."

And when Holly said that he was gone on Rosa, she'd drawn a "surprised" symbol of a round mouth.

Miranda had to wonder if Major Jon Swift found *her* to be "sexy as hell"? She looked down at herself and found it hard to imagine. But he had said he enjoyed being with her and seeing her in various states of dress and undress. Perhaps he did.

"Rosa didn't say much," Pierre continued. "At least not about the plane. Just that General JJ Martinez needed a Ghostrider and she'd..." he swallowed hard "...*agreed* to help him. At least until I threw her off the plane while I still thought it was crashing."

"You've spoken to her since the crash?" Miranda's pen was still hesitating over the page regarding a note about Rosa's involvement in the hijacking.

"Sure, she's over in the VA hospital," he pointed toward the shore. "Dislocated shoulder and observation for mild hypothermia."

"We need to talk to her," Miranda needed more information if she was going to decide about whether or not the note was relevant to the investigation.

And maybe she could help them find Jeremy and Mike.

Yes, that was the priority. "We need to find her now."

"ASAP it is," Holly raced out to the road.

Miranda and Pierre followed just in time to see her step out in front of a Jeep, making it screech all four tires to avoid running her over. After a few intense moments, during which Holly kept her hand on her big knife, she waved them over.

Miranda and Pierre settled in the back of the Jeep for the long ride up to the airport. The driver looked very unhappy, but didn't say a word when Holly climbed into the passenger seat and thumped her knife in its sheath on the dash.

Good. She needed to think without distractions. Chatty cab drivers caused her significant issues when traveling.

She would treat the problem in layers. With no crash, she'd have to treat it just like a missing plane. No grid search was relevant, because the plane wasn't down.

She knew Point of Origin: Andrews Air Force Base.

Lizzy said that Andrews reported a tracked departure to the southwest at a heading of 235 degrees before losing contact. Lizzy was trying to thread together their flight pattern, but they'd turned off all tracking, staying down in the clutter of civilian, general aviation airspace. There were tens of thousands of that class of flights every day over the continental US.

No, they wouldn't have turned off *all* tracking, or they'd cause an alarm at any tracking station's radar as they flew over.

She sent a text to Lizzy, *They're squawking 1200.*

Of course! And a thumbs up emoji.

All general aviation flights, not using air traffic control's flight following service, would have their transponder set to send the 1200 code that would be sent every time the tracking radar swept over their plane. The Ghostrider would look just like any civilian plane to the nation's traffic control electronics, but they *would* be tracked.

Still, threading that path across hundreds or thousands of miles was going to be a very hard task and couldn't be counted on.

Instead, she must resort to interviews.

Pierre claimed he knew nothing else. Should she believe him? Though Miranda knew she was a poor judge of such things, Mike always said to trust her gut. All her gut was telling her was that the hand peach pie she'd eaten atop Snowmass Mountain had been a long time ago.

She'd withhold judgment until they interviewed Rosa Cruz.

Miranda was never very good at those.

"I wish Mike was here."

"Me too," Holly's voice was barely a whisper. "Miss the annoying bugger."

44

Miranda's inner calm was shredding.

Thirty minutes to the airport—in the Jeep that had turned out not to be a taxi after all—fifteen miles from Avalon at the far end of Santa Catalina Island. The flight to the mainland had taken under five minutes. Taxiing to the terminal at Santa Monica Airport had taken five more...and the four miles to the hospital took twenty through evening rush-hour traffic. Sixty minutes in transit.

And her calm wasn't shredding just at the fringes.

Ninety-seven minutes since the departure of the Ghostrider from Andrews Air Force Base with Jeremy and Mike aboard. Cruise speed of four hundred miles per hour equaled six hundred and forty-seven miles, not accounting for lower ground speed during climb-out to cruising altitude.

If they'd roughly held their heading, they could be over Paducah, Kentucky, Waynesboro, Tennessee, or

Birmingham, Alabama. If not? Northern Maine, southern Georgia, or the middle of the Atlantic Gulfstream current.

The external brain that had become embodied in her team was being stretched beyond even what her actual brain usually felt like.

Finally at the hospital, they discovered that Rosa's room was empty.

Before Holly could pull her knife on the entire nurses' station, Pierre proved that he understood military bureaucracies. He pulled out his military ID, told them he was her squad leader, and they'd better find her stat.

Tech Sergeant Rosa Cruz was in the process of checking out and should be down in the lobby.

Holly sprinted for the stairs and beat their elevator to the lobby.

She'd cornered a very pretty Mexican woman dressed in military fatigues and wearing a left arm sling that was commensurate with a recently dislocated shoulder.

Holly had her backed into a small potted palm. Her knife wasn't out, but her palm rested on the hilt.

"This her?" Holly snarled at Pierre.

"That's her. Hi, Rosa."

"Um... Hi, Pierre. Are you okay?"

"Never better."

Miranda understood how to interpret a smile and a frown, even a grimace. But Pierre's current expression of a half-smile and half-frown didn't make sense. Not even with the eye roll that she typically took to mean sarcasm. It's like his emotions were all mixed up.

Oh, his emotions *were* all mixed up. That actually made

sense. She took a moment to draw a careful emoji in her notebook with annotations for the different elements.

"You left a little abruptly and...I was worried," Rosa spoke softly.

Holly edged her a little deeper into the tree.

Rosa turned on her. "If you don't back off, lady, I'll—"

"No," Pierre cut her off. "You won't. Trust me." He rubbed at his throat where Holly had pricked him with her knife.

"Holly," Miranda spoke softly and that seemed to snap her out of warrior-mode and back into Holly-mode.

"Right. Sorry. We need to know everything about what you were supposed to do on the Ghostrider. General JJ's plans, his base of operations, everything. And we need it now."

Instead of looking at Holly, Rosa's attention snapped over to Pierre.

"I thought you weren't going to say anything." And that was very definitely a deep frown with no accompanying eye roll. Definitely anger. Or was it hurt? Even diagrams didn't help with emotions.

"You should talk to these folks. *We* can help *them.* They aren't Air Force. These two are with the NTSB. And your General JJ—"

"Or Taz Cortez," Holly snarled.

"Or Colonel Cortez," he agreed, "just kidnapped the other half of their team. About ninety minutes ago."

"A hundred and thirteen," Miranda sighed. Seven hundred and fifty-three miles. St. Louis, Missouri. Orlando, Florida...

45

They were passing north of Little Rock, Arkansas, on their way to meet a refueling KC-130 out of Fort Worth, Texas.

Taz explained the logic. "The pilots of the Marine Aerial Refueler Transport Squadron were only too happy to have an excuse to practice a midair refueling. They're also the least likely to report it to the Air Force except as a cross-service invoice for flight cost and fuel rendered. That could take months to wend its way through accounting."

She couldn't tell if Mike was paying attention to anything, or just zoned out with his back against the hull.

"Are the accounting systems really so archaic that no one would notice? And what about when they do find it, won't the Marines get in trouble for not questioning why they were called up in the middle of the night to do this?" Jeremy, however, was the ultimate litmus test of right and wrong.

"It will get signed off along with the other couple dozen refuelings that are probably going on just tonight all around the country. All of the information will be there, but it will be essentially untraceable."

Jeremy frowned unhappily.

Taz really needed to come to the point.

She'd delayed them with food—which was a woeful dinner at its best. Because of the speed of the operation to extract the second Ghostrider from Andrews, she hadn't had a chance to check or amend their food supplies.

The prior crew had left MREs, crackers (not Bretons or even Triscuits, but Ritz, which were all about the salt), and a half-used case of spray-can cheddar cheese (for which they should be court-martialed).

Mike had followed her lead in selecting the Lemon Pepper Tuna MRE. As Meals-Ready-to-Eat went, it was one of the best for pretending it was real food.

Jeremy on the other hand dove for one of the new MRE flavors, Pepperoni Pizza Slice. It also had Italian bread sticks with cheddar and jalapeno cheese spread (that should have been left in the can), cookies, and a marginal excuse for a cherry-blueberry cobbler. The chocolate protein drink powder was about the only redeeming element. Jeremy burned through two of everything and was eyeing a third.

"What the hell? One of those will feed a soldier with full kit on an infiltration hike."

"Jeremy and pizza. He's almost bad as Holly, except she'll eat anything."

"And probably looks it."

Jeremy went for the third slice, dumping the flameless heater in the outer bag. Just as he had twice before, on the verge of pouring in the water to activate it and slipping the sealed pizza slice bag in after it, he stopped. It could heat the pizza to almost palatable in under ten minutes. Instead he sliced open the inner bag and ate it cold, just like the first two.

"No. No, she's not a bit heavy." Mike stared over at the C-130's bulkhead. "She's hyper, chaotic, and a retired special operations warrior." His words slowed along with his thoughts.

"Easy to see what you're thinking of."

He blinked at her in surprise. "What? Holly? Are you crazy?"

"She'd kill him," Jeremy concurred with a full mouth.

"So, care to tell us why we're here?" Mike went for the subject change.

Taz sighed. She liked these two—not that such things had ever stopped her before. But she really didn't know how to sell them on what was about to happen; to get their willing participation.

"She wants us to fight a war for her general."

Taz could only gape at Jeremy as he continued to chew. He was absolutely right.

46

"THAT'S RIGHT, YOUNG MAN." JJ HAD NEVER SEEN TAZ hesitate about an assignment before. He'd come to check how she was doing with the civilians, but become fascinated by watching the dynamic. He'd been able to hear enough over the engines' steady thrum to follow what was happening from the shadows around the side of the control station. "What else have you concluded?"

"You must be Drake's friend, JJ." Jeremy held out a hand, then looked at it, wiped it on his pants, and held it out again.

His hands were almost as soft as a clerk's...and still slightly greasy from the pizza.

He saw Taz bristle, but he signaled her to stand down. "If you're a friend of Drake's, you're welcome to call me JJ."

Mike Munroe's self-introduction was more respectful. "A friend might be a strong word, sir, but he likes our boss a great deal, so we all get 'Drake' privileges by association. Sort of." His grimace spoke volumes he couldn't read. But he could read his handshake. It proved that he was even less used to real work.

JJ glanced at his own hands and wondered who was calling the kettle black. Three-star generals had an entourage to do everything from driving cars to pouring coffee. Most were climbers, hoping for a ride on a three-star's coattails. The last few weeks, with his pending retirement, they'd become relentless in seeking a last-minute favor. Few, like Taz, were useful. Too damn young to be given a star— too young to be a full colonel, but she'd earned it. Deserved the star more than most in the Pentagon.

"Your boss?" JJ was curious. He'd always been JJ, but Drake's stiff spine allowed only a very select few to have that privilege.

"Miranda Chase."

He glanced at Taz, whose memory was a steel trap for each detail of everyone who flowed past him. Stumped, she shook her head.

"Interesting. Colonel Taz Cortez remembers everyone."

Jeremy finished his pizza and started crunching loudly on his Italian breadsticks. "If you haven't dealt with plane crashes, then you wouldn't know about her. She's the best crash investigator the NTSB has ever had. Drake calls us in on all the really tricky ones. It only took her about an hour to figure out that your AC-130H crash was a fake."

"Jeremy!" Mike admonished him, but the boy was on a roll.

"And I'll bet she's solved the Catalina crash already."

That was information he'd like to possess. That crash was causing an inordinate amount of trouble, including their present situation of desperately needing Jeremy's aid.

However, JJ was not about to open up communications to anyone at this time. There wasn't a single military person on this flight or at his operating base who wouldn't be court-martialed the moment they were caught.

"She was talking to the weapons officer and she doesn't do interviews until she already knows what's happened. That's the last step in her investigation process," Mike agreed.

"But that doesn't make sense," Taz cut in while JJ was thinking how much he'd like to throttle Rosa Cruz for betraying them. "If she told your boss about this, why didn't she stop our flight?"

"He," Mike spoke up. "Miranda was with a *male* weapons officer."

"Oh." Taz glanced up but she shook her head. Not one of theirs.

"And she's probably trying to stop you right now. So, who are you about to have an illegal war with?" Jeremy asked as he dipped another breadstick into the cheese spread. He patted the control console like a favorite pet. "I mean, this baby specializes in area denial. You want to take out a tightly clustered group of weapons or people with extreme prejudice. You're also banking that they don't have the fighter jets to take you on, because as dangerous as the Ghostrider is, it's big, slow, and does its best work below ten thousand feet. Or do you have a couple of escort jets of your own?"

Mike was watching his companion intently. So, this was all the young investigator's conjecture.

JJ considered. Taz's nod concurred with his own thoughts that frankness seemed appropriate.

"We're going after people who have wronged every single person on this plane." And JJ could feel the fury deep in his gut as he did every time. That had been his leverage for recruiting each member of this team for his final mission.

Jeremy nodded, then leaned forward enough to pull on a hat that had been between his shoulders and the seat back. It was brilliantly garish, even in the dim combat lighting.

"Put it on, Mike. The Three Amigos! Well, the Two Amigos." Jeremy began popping cookies into his mouth.

"Why?" But Mike did as he was told.

"Because we're going to Mexico."

"And our chances of ever coming back?" Mike asked the astute question.

Jeremy looked at him blankly for a long moment, then choked on his cookies, and ended up coughing crumbs in every direction as Mike pounded on his back.

47

"Mexico?"

Rosa nodded, "But that's all I know. I think only Tang—" She made a strangling sound.

Miranda decided it was a good thing they were still in the hospital, seated at one of the VA hospital Patriot Café's tables. If Rosa needed a doctor—

But she cleared her throat, though she was far paler than a moment before, then continued, "I think only *one* of the pilots on the Ghostrider that crashed in Avalon knew where we were supposed to go."

"But you had agreed to leave the Air Force to do this. Whatever *this* was!" Despite sitting in a quiet back corner booth with an untouched milkshake in front of her, Holly seemed poised for battle. There was no hint at all of her Strine accent.

"I grew up in a super-close family. But my aunt and uncle died while trying to cross the border. They were seasonal pickers and went home each winter. One year the cartels kidnapped their daughter to force them to be drug mules. None of them survived."

Miranda finally saw the pattern and wondered why it had taken her so long. "Rosa Cruz, Mark Torres, Ron Gutierrez, Taz Cortez, JJ Martinez, Luis Hernandez, Danny—"

"Luis?" Rosa leaned forward and Pierre flinched.

She turned to him. "No, he was just a friend. His mother got sold into the sex-trafficking trade when she crossed the border. He was a good man."

"Well, now he's a dead man." Miranda continued.

Rosa spun back to face her.

"It appears his parachute failed after setting up the crash in Colorado." She pulled out her phone and called Jon.

He answered immediately.

"Are you still with Lizzy?"

"Yes. Miranda. I'm so sorry—"

"You said that already. There's no point in repeating it. Everyone JJ recruited appears to be Mexican. Or perhaps from Latin America. It would seem that every single person he recruited had a reason to hate some particular group or groups in Mexico. Traffickers and the like. Find out who."

"Wait. General Martinez is using a stolen Ghostrider to declare war on Mexico?"

"Our government managed to alienate the Mexican government enough that they've turned down our subsequent offer to send military assistance against the cartels. Drake said that JJ was an extreme patriot. It is therefore simple logic that JJ decided he'd had enough of politics and was going to defend his country."

"*Against all enemies, foreign and domestic.*" Pierre said it softly.

Rosa nodded. "His exact words."

Jon must have overheard. "The USAF officer's oath. Shit! I'm on it."

"The problem we have is how to stop him."

"Find him and shoot him down!" Pierre snarled.

Holly almost attacked him across the table. Probably would have if Miranda wasn't in the way.

Miranda placed a hand on Holly's arm and could feel it shaking. "That won't work, Pierre. Mike and Jeremy are on board."

"Then how the hell do we stop them? They're going to murder people and start a war."

There was a long tense silence.

"What we need," Rosa finally broke the silence, "is the third Ghostrider from Eglin. The laser doesn't have to be used on full power. It can also dazzle their plane's optics. If we're quick, we could damage any ability to deliver on a target without damaging the aircraft."

At that, Holly smiled.

If Miranda were to label her look with an emoji, it would have a devil's horns and tail.

"Now that's aces!"

48

"I'VE WATCHED MY PEOPLE," JJ THUMPED HIS CHEST HARD enough to hurt and it felt good. "I've watched them be decimated for too long by the drugs and the traffickers who see hardship and pain as opportunity. I've stood by as my own country has marginalized and attacked those in greatest need while allowing the users to thrive beyond reason. Mexico fights, but it is powerless." JJ had spent his whole career combating that desperate dichotomy.

"But won't they defend themselves?" Mike asked from where he sat on the deck.

"The government has three fighter jets, total."

"Northrop F-5s," Jeremy nodded. "They purchased them in 1982. But it's a 1950s design. Mexico is almost two-thirds the size of the contiguous US and they rely on about a hundred helicopters—most light utility—for air coverage. The idea was that they would depend on their closest neighbor, us, if there was ever a serious military conflict. But we're no help when that conflict is internal."

"Precisely." JJ now knew how to deal with Jeremy. Exactly the same way he dealt with Drake—integrity to integrity. "The DEA had the intel and the NRO turned that into targeting, but no one was willing to leverage that information. Taz has convinced them to share it with me. I have the primary operations center of every leading cartel lord and trafficker across the whole north of Mexico. Tomorrow night I'm going to lead a single strike down the entire length of the border."

"And you need a laser operator." For once, Jeremy was completely serious.

"Yes. Can you do it, son?"

"I...*can,*" he said carefully.

"*Will* you?"

JJ saw that both Mike and Taz were holding their breaths —Mike in worry and Taz in hope. Jeremy didn't look like the strong-willed type. But he suspected that inner core of right or wrong, once chosen, would be unflappable under any threat.

Jeremy stared down at the remains of his cherry-blueberry cobbler for a long time. "I just don't know. I have to think about what Miranda would say."

"I'll take the honest answer...for now." JJ held out his hand.

When Jeremy shook it, his hand didn't feel so soft anymore.

49

"You need *what?*" Lizzy stared at the phone. Thank God it was on a secure line.

"I said that I need the third Ghostrider. I need it fully armed and fueled and forward-stationed near the Mexican border for an illegal black-ops mission. I need a crew that is absolutely trustworthy."

"No! Whatever you're thinking, Miranda, just...no!"

"Hold please," and she was gone.

"What the hell?" Lizzy looked across her desk at Jon.

"I have no idea," he looked just as surprised as she felt. "But what Miranda said earlier is checking out. I have about half of the reports back. So far, every single person on our 'Death List' from the first crash had some awful experience with Mexican cartels. Sisters dying of overdoses. Fathers murdered by hitmen in cartel wars. Sex trafficking of cousins. These are a lot of very angry people who are also very skilled US Air Force officers. Only that technical sergeant, Rosa Cruz, is an enlisted. She's also noted as the

Number One laser operator on the Ghostrider in the entire Air Force."

"I don't—"

The call beeped back to life.

"Lizzy, I have Roy on the line here."

It took her a moment to think about that, then both she and Jon bolted to their feet.

Miranda was the only person Lizzy knew, other than the First Lady, who called the President of the United States by his first name. She was also one of the few people he was likely to take a direct call from without any question.

"Mr. President," Holly spoke up with a thick Strine accent. "One of your three-stars, General JJ Martinez, has decided to throw himself an extra-special retirement party. You know, shrimp on the barbie, a couple of shandies—"

"Shandies?" the President asked.

Lizzy knew that Holly enjoyed bucking authority, but this was the President. Well, not *her* President, being Australian, but still *the* President. But that didn't seem to stop her.

"Beer with lemonade. Really fine if it's a top drop brew and fresh-squeezed lemonade. He's also invited a shady lot of top-rank Latino officers and is holding it aboard a stolen AC-130J Ghostrider gunship to make it a real-and-proper piss-up."

"What was that last?"

"A 'piss-up' is a party, a good one, that—"

"No, the Ghostrider?" His tone was dark and dangerous.

But Jon was smiling at her. Lizzy knew that it might be "just the way Holly was" but...damn!

Miranda answered. "We have evidence that indicates

America's War on Drugs is about to be significantly escalated. The most likely time frame would be tomorrow night, because JJ is fast running out of darkness. Had he been able to retain the first Ghostrider gunship he attempted to hijack—"

"The *what?* Drake! What the hell is going on out there?"

Lizzy hadn't known that Drake was with the President.

"I don't know, sir. I've been here with you working on the Iran-Saudi mess."

Should she have called Drake earlier? But everything had seemed so normal that...

Except it hadn't been.

It was only Miranda's eternal calm—emotionless reactions?—that had made it seem normal. The AC-130H Spectre crash in Aspen had somehow naturally segued into the investigation of the AC-130J Ghostrider crash on Catalina Island. And that in turn leading to the inspection and subsequent hijacking of the second Ghostrider at Andrews Air Force Base which...

Lizzy decided that she'd be lucky if she wasn't in lock-up for her fiftieth birthday rather than getting married.

She loved being the head of the NRO, the being-a-general part *generally* sucked. But that wasn't going to stop her now.

"Sir, I have been working closely with the team for every step of this on-going..."

"Investigation?" Jon whispered when she hesitated. "Calamity? Crisis?"

"...issue. In the last five minutes, it has grossly increased in complexity and we—" she'd have to talk to Miranda about forcing her hand without asking first, not that it would do any good, "—felt that it was time to bring you both into the loop."

Holly quickly brought Drake and the President up-to-date.

"As I alluded to earlier," Miranda continued, "if weapons specialists Master Sergeant Pierre Jones and Tech Sergeant Rosa Cruz here hadn't stopped the hijacking of that first Ghostrider, JJ's war might have already begun."

There were two gasps of surprise in the background, but Miranda didn't slow down long enough for Lizzy to make any sense of them.

"But as JJ's best opportunity is under cover of darkness, I would estimate that he will..."

"Cozy up in his lair," Holly offered.

"...wait out the day?" Miranda countered. "We expect the attack on Mexican cartels and others will begin tomorrow night shortly after sunset. I need to get the third AC-130J Ghostrider, presently at Eglin, ready to counter those actions."

"Just send in some goddamn Raptors and take him out. I'll find a way to apologize to the Mexican President for spreading debris all over his landscape."

"No, Roy. That won't do at all."

Lizzy could only stare at the phone.

Jon, however, was positively grinning with delight. Clearly, Miranda could do no wrong in his eyes.

Lizzy gazed at the poster that Thorsen had gotten hung in record time, as if he'd already had it waiting. She'd flown that F-16 Viper into the early days of the Iraq War. She turned to the speaker phone.

"I must concur, Mr. President. Major Jon Swift assures

me that Cruz and Jones—" and Miranda had better be right about them "—can effectively disable the other stolen Ghostrider without taking it down. And, more importantly, not killing the innocents from Miranda's team who were kidnapped by General Martinez."

Jon looked at her in surprise because he'd said no such thing.

"In for a penny, in for a pound, nephew," she whispered to him.

He grimaced, but accepted his role with a shrug.

There was a long silence. Lizzy missed Mike and Jeremy. One of them would have something funny to say right now to break the tension—no matter how inappropriate.

"Do it!" the President snapped out. "But have our two best F-22 Raptor pilots shadowing their every move from just across the border. I want them loaded for bear and with permission to fire the instant your ploy fails. You better be goddamn right about this, General Gray."

"Sir, yes sir!"

"Well done, Drake," Roy Cole continued off to the side, then cut the connection.

Drake? *Drake!* Lizzy stared at her phone in disbelief. *What the hell had he done so well?*

For better or worse, this had been her and Miranda's operation.

And *Drake* was going to get the credit for it from the President?

She was going to ram her ring right down his goddamn throat!

50

Taz watched Mike and Jeremy sitting away from the others over the afternoon meal. Nothing exciting, MREs served under the open-sided camo canopy draped over the stolen Ghostrider.

The team waited in a lost valley baking under the scorching sun of central Baja. In small groups, they sat on the dusty ground or perched on ammo cans, all hoping for even the slightest cooling breeze. They'd slept through the morning, but the evening cool still lay hours away.

When she'd first traveled here, she'd been driving. Fifty kilometers away, the nearest town, El Rosario, was a nothing place. Seventeen hundred people perched close by the Pacific, halfway down Mexico's Baja Peninsula.

El Rosario was known for only two things.

It was traditionally the first rest stop in the six-day off-road rally race called the Baja 1000.

And it was the home of Mama Espinoza's restaurant.

Mama E. herself had died recently at the age of 109, but the kids had kept it going.

It was classic Mexico, except for the food being even better than usual. Since the 1930s, Mama E. had served meals in her home's dining room. It had taken off in the '60s, when it became the first checkpoint of the Baja 1000. And Mama E. had never looked back.

The house was now entirely restaurant. Painted brilliant red outside, with a half dozen long tables covered in plastic red-and-white checked tablecloths inside, it looked homey. Every wall was covered with photos of fifty years of racing. Mementos were everywhere, making it part museum as well. Racers had brought their motorcycles there to be blessed by Mama E. herself before the big races.

Taz could have moved in, if duty hadn't called. However, she remembered the burrito trio: crab, garlic shrimp, and local lobster. She could definitely go through another set of those right now.

As she'd done all of her life, she shrugged off what couldn't be and felt no regret. Her mother had taught her that. *Take care of the now.* Mama's answer to everything. Taz had made herself an *expert* in dealing with the now.

Bin Laden took out the Twin Towers and a whole side of the Pentagon? Didn't matter. That was now the past.

What action could she take in the moment? Do that. While everyone else was moaning or being enraged, she'd been calculating. She'd seen a fellow spirit in then-Colonel Jorge Jesus Martinez and made sure that she came to his notice. A choice she'd never regretted.

And she still didn't. Even now, fifty kilometers from Mama Espinoza's restaurant, she was still just as ready.

In a few hours they'd all be aloft on the final mission.

The only hesitation she felt were their unwilling passengers.

Mike and Jeremy were...easy together.

Civilians in a moment of quiet, enjoying each other's company despite the strangeness all around them. They laughed at something, as if it was the most normal thing to do. Every time Mike laughed, he covered his impressive black eye and made "Ooo! Ooo! Ooo!" sounds that always made Jeremy laugh harder. Perhaps he did it *because* Jeremy laughed each time.

Laughter hadn't been part of her upbringing. Her life in Mexico had been hard. And she certainly hadn't laughed since they left.

Papa had been a drug runner, a mule, who'd stolen the money from his own cartel for them to make the crossing. It had cost him his life.

Though Papa's money was enough for the demanded price by a competing cartel's cross-border trafficker, it hadn't been enough for the coyote man guiding them. Almost to the border, he'd demanded a bonus payment of Taz's eleven-year-old virginity. He'd collected it with his big hunting knife to Taz's throat while her mother had looked on silently.

Mama hadn't made a sound the whole time, not even as she helped Taz rinse her own blood off her legs. She'd only said two words about that moment—ever.

Once safely over the border, once they were clutching the identity papers of a recently deceased-but-unreported American mother and daughter—making her forever after Vicki Cruz—Mama had driven a hard knee into the coyote man's crotch. As he'd lain writhing on the ground, she'd handed Taz the man's big knife that she'd extracted from his sheath.

"He's yours."

Taz had cut off his dick, choked off his scream by ramming it down his throat, then slid the blade up into his heart. She'd held it there, twisting it deeper and deeper as *his* blood had streamed over her hands.

Mama had taken his share of their money back, and they'd disappeared into the morass that was Lincoln Park, San Diego.

Taz had taken his knife.

Mike's "Ooo! Ooo! Ooo!" and Jeremy's laugh snapped her back to the present.

Three hours to sunset.

Four hours to first possible takeoff.

Taz was on her feet before she knew what she was doing. She walked up to Jeremy, cutting Mike off mid-sentence.

"Come with me." When they both started to rise, she turned to Mike. "You stay."

Mike opened his mouth to protest. He was Jeremy's protector and took that role very seriously despite his being just a civilian.

"Don't worry. Just stay." She didn't know why, but it seemed...important.

Mike eased back onto his seat on a medkit can carefully. He'd been into it for some aspirin and salve for his blackening eye. After a moment, he smiled as if he knew things she didn't. He tucked something in Jeremy's back pocket even as Jeremy started to follow. Then he winked at her—and winced. But he didn't make any "Ooo! Ooo! Ooo!" noises.

She led Jeremy away from the plane and the camouflage canopy. A quick climb up the face of the western slope, they arrived at a place she'd discovered when initially scouting the area for suitability. If they survived the first night, they'd return here and then fly additional sorties for as long as they lasted. No one, not even JJ, had spoken of it, but none of them expected there to be a second chance.

In the now.

Taz's specialty.

Together, she and Jeremy stood on a shelf of rock notched into the cliff like a cave with no roof but the sky. It offered a sweeping view of this valley lost in the middle of Baja's mountains. The peaks to the west shadowed them from the blaze of the late afternoon sun.

If she didn't look too closely, the camo covering disappeared into the background. A step closer to the cliff and it was completely out of sight.

The easy roll of the desert floor stretched brown to the far hills. The river, dry in this season—in most seasons—was marked by a stripe of withered brush just waiting for its brief moment to flourish when the rare flash flood swept by.

"This is an amazing ecosystem," Jeremy stood beside her. "You wouldn't think that someplace so barren could harbor life. But there are snakes—which would totally freak out Mike so don't tell him—jackrabbits, lizards, and the occasional kit fox. Even in this place—"

"Why did I bring you here?" Taz cut him off.

"If you don't know, then I certainly don't."

Serving at the general's command, she'd given all of herself to the "now" with no other thought allowed.

The now.

Then she knew exactly what she wanted.

She pulled his t-shirt out of where it was neatly tucked into his pants. Once she peeled it off over his head, he just looked at her wild-eyed.

He was slender, but fit. Not built like some soldier. No battle wounds. Except—

She traced her finger along a scar on his shoulder.

Jeremy looked down at it. "My sister. I was fourteen, she was thirteen, and I teased her about something. She finally got so angry that she threw a hammer at me. The claw caught me there and I needed five stitches."

"What were you teasing her about?"

Jeremy blushed brightly. His brief glance at her chest and then the doubling of the blush on his fair skin answered that.

"Late bloomer?"

He nodded fiercely. "And we're Vietnamese. She never got very—" then he looked down at her chest again and lost his words.

"I wasn't."

He nodded fiercely again, then shook his head, then realized he was still staring down at her chest. His blush surged once more.

"It's okay to look." She peeled her own t-shirt and sports bra.

Jeremy glanced down, looked at her face, inspected the sky, and then checked her out again before stammering out, "Uh, those are...um...nice ones. Not that I've seen a lot. But, you know, they look really nice on you. I mean..."

She let him keep stumbling along as she undid his pants, finally kneeling to remove his sneakers as well when he seemed too shocked to help. Taz had them both naked while Jeremy was still trying to describe how he had so little to compare her breasts to in real life, other than a graduation present from someone named Nancy that he described in some detail, though he'd certainly seen breasts in movies, of course, but that was different and...

Taz wondered what Mike's smile had meant as he'd slipped something into Jeremy's pocket—he had been into the medkit. She retrieved Jeremy's pants from the ground long enough to unearth the twin foil packets. Mike was a good friend and more perceptive than she'd like.

When she held them up before Jeremy's eyes, his verbal wanderings finally stumbled to a halt. His arousal was very prominent.

At a gentle push on the center of his chest, he practically fell. A step back, then his knees appeared to give out and he sat down abruptly on the pile of their clothes. Another small nudge against his chest and he lay on them.

She peeled open a packet, sheathed him, and knelt over his hips.

"You're so beautiful," he managed in a whisper.

That stopped her. "You just like seeing a woman's breasts for the second time in your life."

In answer, he raised a hand and slipped his fingers into her hair. She hadn't remembered loosening it from its normal severe bun.

Jeremy toyed with it for a long moment before resting his hand on the side of her face and brushing a thumb along her check. "You feel amazing."

"You think *that* feels good?" Taz slid her hips down on him.

51

Lieutenant General Jorge Martinez stood on the hard sand surface beneath the burning Mexican sun, but he didn't feel the heat. It had taken him years, but the time had finally arrived and nothing else mattered.

"*Former* three-star general of the US Air Force," he told the parched desert.

He wished it could make him feel good...or bad. Something.

But all he felt was anger.

Not at the Air Force. He'd loved the Academy, his thirty-five years of service, and his part of making it the greatest fighting force in the world. They were more effective than the rest of the world's air forces combined.

No. There was nothing wrong with the tool. The problem was with the politicians who couldn't be trusted to wield a butter knife without fucking it up.

Desert Storm, where they'd been sent in to kick Saddam's ass—but only out of Kuwait. They should have taken him out in 1991, not 2003. Then once they'd finally gone in, the official Rules of Engagement had so tied their hands in Iraq and Afghanistan that they'd barely been able to act.

Known Prime Target in sights? Not even any risk of collateral civilian damage? Nope! Still need clearance from the politicos back in DC.

Taliban's and al-Qaeda's only ROE was *kill*. Fuckers didn't even care *who* so long as it got the job done. *That's* what America's Rules Of Engagement *should* have been.

Taz had picked a fine spot. With his wife Consuela gone, Taz was the only person he truly trusted and he'd been right to do so.

This small valley in the center of the Baja California lay just south of the Sierra de San Pedro Mártir—the highest mountains of the entire peninsula. Despite the narrowness of the peninsula, just a hundred kilometers wide here, it was easy to get lost in these mountains. The nearest road that deserved a name lay thirty kilometers away. The nearest town even farther.

The valley, his valley, had just one dirt track leading through it sideways. To the west Taz had dropped a cliff on it, and to the east she'd blown a switchback off the face of a steep pass. Now the only way in and out was by air or scrambling scree on foot.

The woman was amazing. Not Consuela, but amazing.

Consuela had stuck with him through the Academy and followed him around the globe as he'd flown the old AC-130H gunships. He'd taken them into Panama and flown for Bush I into Kuwait against Saddam.

For nine years, the Spectre and Consuela Martinez had

been the core of his life. Nine short years before she was knifed by a couple of coked-up yuppie punks needing the two hundred bucks she'd just gotten from the ATM for their next fix of Mexican nose candy. She'd lived just long enough to make sure they got life in prison.

When they were released on good behavior a mere six years later, his life had shifted paths. First he'd made sure they both died in pain far worse than Consuela's, fully aware of why.

Then he'd started building.

If the American justice system was so broken, he'd fix it himself.

A year later he'd found his fury embodied in a ridiculously petite Airman First Class Vicki Cortez.

When the rules of engagement no longer made sense, it was time to make new rules.

It was the one thing he'd never been able to convince Drake of.

52

Taz braced her palms against Jeremy's chest as the final shudders slammed through her.

Sweet Jesus but she'd needed this.

After he'd flailed uncertainly for a bit, she'd placed one of his hands on a breast and the other on her ass. He'd gotten the idea soon enough after that.

When she went to get off him, he didn't let go.

Instead, he shifted his hand from her breast and pulled her down to lie on him.

"Oh," he sighed in her ear when she finally gave in and lay against him. "This feels amazing, too. You're so hard and soft. It's just amazing. No, I already said that, but it is. I mean, you are. I can feel every muscle as strong as bone, but your skin is incredibly soft and smooth. Better than the leather on a custom SyberJet SJ30. And where your, uh, chest is on mine feels all soft and cushiony and—"

"Silence works, too."

He was quiet for about five seconds. "I was never very good at that." He tentatively slipped his arms around her back and waist, then squeezed her hard against him.

Again she tried to push off, but he kept holding her.

"Not yet. Please. This is too amazing...uh... incredible...good?"

Taz finally let herself simply lie against him.

As he cataloged—aloud—each sensation, she realized that was part of how he was processing the experience, storing it for future memory, so she let him go on. She had always taken Mama's lesson of silence as guidance—until it was mastered. Now there was no way that what happened inside her could possibly ever *reach* the outside world.

Never show them even a hint of weakness, had been another of Mama's favorite admonitions.

And she hadn't.

Not once.

Not when Mama had walked into a grocery store during a gang heist and been shot for her mistake.

And not to the Air Force recruiter who'd spoken at her school's Career Day. After his presentation, she'd simply walked up to him and said, "Where do I sign?" When he'd asked why the Air Force, she'd just repeated her request. He'd pointed; she'd signed. It was the farthest place she could imagine from where she was.

Oddly, each thing that Jeremy cataloged, right down to the cooling of their evaporating sweat and the offsetting warmth where their skin was in contact, made the sex more, rather than less real.

More important.

She finally let herself lay her ear on his chest and listen to his slowing heart and the soft rumble of his words as he stroked her hair and back.

This.

This must be what being alive felt like.

53

"I—"

"No! And not you either," Lizzy aimed a finger at Holly's chest.

"I *have* to be on that flight." Miranda could feel a pain welling up in her chest but unable to find any other way out.

"No. You don't. Are you a weapons specialist? A pilot?" Lizzy jabbed a finger toward the Ghostrider freshly landed from Eglin Air Force Base and now looming behind them on the Lackland Air Force Base tarmac in San Antonio, Texas. "That's a plane of war, going on a mission of war. The flight you need to be on is home to the Pacific Northwest. I'll make sure you get constant updates."

Miranda couldn't lose another person. Especially not her team. They were the only ones who really knew her. They were her—

Holly slid an arm around her shoulders and held her tightly in a sideways hug. It was all that kept her knees from going out beneath her.

"Get her out of here." Lizzy's words were soft but hurt just as much as if she'd shouted them.

Holly turned her toward the small Air Force C-21 Learjet that had taken them from Seattle to Aspen, then Catalina, LA, and finally here.

At the steps she turned and looked.

But it wasn't the Ghostrider from Eglin that she saw. Or the KC-130 aerial tanker that would be ready to meet up and refuel the Ghostrider if necessary. Not even the pair of stealth Black Hawk search-and-rescue helos from the 160th Night Stalkers.

No, all she could see was the pair of F-22 Raptors. Just sixty-two feet long and forty-four feet from wingtip to wingtip, they were Mach 2+ capable stealth fighters. They would never show up on Mexican air traffic control radars. They could outrun, out maneuver, and outgun Mexico's aging F-5 fighters.

And they could definitely kill an AC-130J Ghostrider— *Jeremy and Mike's Ghostrider*— before it could possibly know they were there.

Miranda could feel herself closing down as Holly strapped her into her seat.

The strong acceleration as the pilots took off and punched for altitude made her world crash in about her.

Helpless.

Like her parents strapped down in the second row of their doomed 747. They were so far away that it seemed she barely remembered them.

Couldn't find them.

It was the end.

All out of her control.

There was nothing but the image of the Ghostrider, the two Raptors, and the KC-130 tanker.

She had to trust Rosa's and Pierre's promises to bring them home safe. But how could she do that if she wasn't there to make sure?

That was her job.

To investigate, verify, and report.

Except her job *wasn't* to fight.

Even if she wanted to, she didn't know how. All she could do was huddle in her seat like excess baggage.

Now it was out of her hands.

Ghostrider.

Raptor.

KC-130.

KC-130?

Why did she keep thinking about the KC-130 tanker? The Ghostrider could fly five hours and thirty-two hundred kilometers on a single load of fuel.

From Lackland Air Force Base they could fly the length *and* breadth of Mexico on a single tanking.

Fuel burn rates in cruise versus combat performance varied less on a C-130 than most other combat aircraft. A fighter jet burned an immense amount of fuel on afterburner or during turning combat. A C-130 Hercules was much more a steady-state aircraft with little variation of fuel burn rates except those based on altitude and payload changes. Even during an AC-130 gunship's banking flight as it circled over a target to bring its weapons to bear on a single point below, its fuel consumption varied very little.

She ran multiple battle scenarios in her head. The results were actually fascinating. She'd never thought to graph fuel consumption of non-jet military aircraft over different scenarios. Its combat radius varied from its "ferry range" of straight-and-level flight by only...

Straight-and-level flight...

From Andrews Air Force Base...

"Turn the plane around! We need to turn the plane around!"

Holly jolted in her seat. She took one look at Miranda, nodded her head, and unbelted to head to the cockpit.

Even as she did so, one of the pilots reached back and closed the access door. It locked with a loud click. A moment later he was on the PA.

"I'm sorry, ma'am. But we're under strict orders to return you to where we found you. We're less than an hour out."

An hour to Tacoma?

"Sorry, ma'am. General Gray's orders." And the microphone clicked off.

Holly eyed the door for a long moment, then sat across from her.

"An hour to Tacoma?" Miranda blinked out the window and indeed saw Elko, Nevada rolling by below them. "What happened?"

Holly glanced at her watch. "You've been pretty out of it for the last two and a quarter hours."

How had she lost—

"What's up, Miranda?"

"Fuel. It's all about the fuel. I've got to tell Lizzy. We've got to turn the plane around."

Holly smiled and pointed at the plane's secure phone.

54

Lizzy figured she was being an idiot. She wasn't following her own advice, but she had to see it through. Boarding the Ghostrider at Lackland AFB had felt right, even though she had no purpose aboard.

Pierre sat at the laser console with Rosa, still wearing her sling, hovering in the sole weapons observer seat close behind him. The normal operator had been off-base on authorized leave when they'd called for the plane. Unable to reach him, Miranda had put Rosa and Pierre forward as the best team for the job. *They* were needed.

However, as the Ghostrider took off from Lackland at sunset, she and Jon were both aboard in the cockpit's observer seats. And they *weren't* needed. At least not in the air.

"Not a weapons specialist? Not a pilot? At least I'm a pilot," Jon teased her.

"Flying a giant cargo van like a C-5 Galaxy doesn't count.

And don't forget that I flew F-16 Vipers for almost as long as you've even been *in* the Air Force."

"Don't know if that even counts, Auntie General Gray. A squidgy little fighter jet? Who cares about those? I mean, good God, they only have like one engine? How do they even get aloft? You need at least four. From the C-130 all the way to the C-5, any decent plane has four. Besides, without us cargo guys, you jet jocks wouldn't have any place to go to."

She appreciated what he was trying to do, lighten the mood for even a moment. But it wasn't working. At this point she just wanted something, anything, to show up so that she could "switch to guns" and shoot it out of the sky.

Her phone rang—she'd patched it into the Ghostrider's system.

Miranda.

She almost didn't answer it.

"It's only been about twenty minutes since we took off, Miranda. We aren't even out of Lackland airspace yet."

Miranda didn't even acknowledge that and plunged right in. "The Ghostrider is an area-denial specialist weapon—for extremely small areas. If you were going to hit the cartels and traffickers, and really hit them hard, where would you strike? Mexicali, Nogales, and Ciudad Juárez right along the border from Tijuana to the western tip of Texas. The exact targets would come from the Drug Enforcement Administration or maybe inside your own NRO. Drug lords' homes, arsenals, and processing and shipping plants."

"Makes sense. I'd need to—"

"They can't afford to waste fuel," Miranda was still on a roll. "They would plan to either start at Texas and sweep west or start in the west and sweep east."

"We already know tha—"

"Yes," Miranda insisted. "But from Andrews Air Force Base to Mexico—"

"Holy shit! They would have burned all of their fuel in transit!" Lizzy couldn't believe she hadn't seen that. Jon was right, it had been too long since she'd flown. The combat range of her F-16 had been only three hundred miles—a tenth of its ferry radius. Fuel was a constant calculation and a major tradeoff between reach and the ability to climb, turn, and fight. It was at the forefront of every pilot's brain.

"Precisely. Though I've never understood that phrase. *Is there such a thing as blessed excrement?* Never mind. I can almost guarantee that they refueled last night. Probably over Texas."

"By a Marine KC-130 out of Fort Worth, just like ours."

Was this what it felt like inside Miranda's head? This smooth flow so fast but so right?

Then Lizzy remembered the feeling from another time. It was like flying with the very best pilots—that instant when it was a privilege and honor to be flying together.

"We'll get right on it. We'll know something of their heading once we confirm where they were refueled."

Jon already had the pilots calling down to the KC-130 tanker. Yes, that would be the fastest way to get an answer.

He gave her a thumbs up. Faster than she'd expected.

"Same pilots," Jon spoke as he listened over his intercom headset. "Over Roswell, New Mexico... About two a.m., which is right for the flight time from Andrews... Short-notice Air Force flight... Full fuel load."

She relayed the information to Miranda.

"They're starting from the west," Miranda declared it as

fact. "I'm guessing that they're somewhere in Sonora or Baja. Probably Baja as it is relatively unpopulated and therefore easy to hide in. Also, they could cover the whole range from Tijuana to Ciudad Juárez in a single pass out and back. It's under a thousand miles round trip. They can cover that twice on the fuel they'd already have aboard. They probably planned on ducking back across the border and calling up the Marines again if they needed a refuel for additional sorties."

Lizzy called out to Jon. "I don't care who you have to bribe, lie to, or shoot. Get us permission to circle over the Sea of Cortez."

"You mean the Gulf of California?" He smiled at her and he finally made her smile back.

"Shut up, you young pup. I was brought up properly." Her fifth-grade schoolteacher had been very traditional about his use of geography names and she'd always done the same. She also knew of its earliest Western name, the Vermillion Sea, though he'd be disappointed that she didn't recall the original native name. "Just make sure that we're way high, so that we look like an airliner."

A thousand miles from San Antonio to Baja. It was already sunset here. It would be sunset there in just over an hour, but it was two hours of flying time away.

Shit! They were going to be late.

Next she called Captain Thorsen back in DC.

"Get me imaging of Baja and west Sonora in Mexico. I don't care what satellite time you need to grab or whose program you have to bump, just do it. They'll be aloft at local sunset. I want to know if so much as a bug takes off without a flight plan."

He snorted a laugh, "I think you overestimate our satellites. How about bigger than a robin?"

"Fine. A robin."

Jon looked at her strangely.

"Then, very quietly, find out who Colonel Vicki Taz Cortez got to. Could be DEA, but it could be us. It would have been after her meeting with me about two weeks ago."

"I've got it on the calendar, ma'am." And he was gone.

If there was a leak in her NRO, she was going to plug it but good—with a round from the Ghostrider's M102 howitzer if necessary.

55

"We have to get moving. It will be sunset here soon."

"Okay." Jeremy stood and offered her a hand to her feet.

She felt surprisingly self-conscious as she dressed. Another thing that had never been an issue for her.

When she was done, Jeremy pulled her back against his chest and simply hugged her, resting his cheek on her hair. Definitely not something she was used to.

"I've decided what I'm willing to do."

She pushed back enough to look up at him. She and JJ had conferred while Mike and Jeremy slept. He'd accepted her recommendation to allow Jeremy to decide for himself, at least at first.

"I don't shoot people."

She'd known that. Inside she'd known that. But she also knew that JJ wouldn't sanction that.

"However, I have no compunction about shooting arsenals or vehicles."

Taz sighed. It was reasonable. It was right for Jeremy.

But that wasn't enough either.

"I know that expression. It's how Miranda looks when a solution isn't right yet."

Taz nodded reluctantly.

"Okay," Jeremy looked at the sky, but kept holding her close. "The laser is tricky. But I can teach you to run the howitzer. How to target, aim, and fire. I can't make you a brilliant gunner in one day. I never fired one myself anyway, but I can help you with how to read the sensor data and the basics of how to read the control systems."

"How do you know all that?"

"It's controlled by a computer. I'm good with those. If I tried to fire an actual gun, I'd probably shoot myself."

She nodded. *That* she could sell to the general.

Jeremy looked down at her. "You can really kill people?"

"Yes."

"Wow. Um...okay. You didn't even hesitate. I've got nothing in my life that tells me how you can say that. Um... nope. Not a thing. That's either really strong or really scary. Maybe scary and strong both. That sounds right. I just—"

Taz wondered what his life had been that he could ask such a question. She pictured the gun battles that used to rake through her Iztapalapa neighborhood of Mexico City. The starvation, the garbage, not even safe water. Finding her father just moments after his execution. The coyote man and the other rapists of the San Diego gangs. Her mother never said how many times she was attacked. Taz only knew of three and she'd dealt with them all for Mama, permanently.

Jeremy pulled her in tight one last time.

She really, really didn't understand people like him.

56

JJ DIDN'T KNOW WHETHER TO BE AMUSED...OR WORRIED.

Taz had informed him of the deal that Jeremy was willing to make. She had also made it clear, without so many words, that JJ would accept it at face value.

Taz was now on someone else's side. Perhaps not Jeremy's, but perhaps her own. And as she was the most dangerous weapon he'd ever wielded, far more dangerous than an AC-130 gunship, he suspected caution was the best course of action.

Colonel Vicki Taser Cortez, the ultimate in self-guided weaponry.

They waited for full dark before they pulled aloft, turning northeast.

He wondered if he'd be back to see the dawn.

57

LIZZY HAD GIVEN UP LOOKING; WHENEVER HER PHONE RANG, she just answered.

Miranda had just unloaded another line of reasoned thinking on her, laying out likely targets, angles of attack.

I only had a chance to study the laser on the Ghostrider at Lackland for a few minutes. I wish I'd had more time. But it will work for both defensive and attack scenarios. The pilots may not have thought this through, but with the AC-130J Ghostrider's maneuverability they...

She'd hated to do it, but she'd unloaded that call onto the copilot. The fact that, from her seat close behind the pilots, she could see him scribbling frantic notes was either interesting or very unnerving.

If Miranda was still tied up with the pilots, then maybe Thorsen had some satellite data for—

"Hey, honey. You free for a late dinner?"

"Drake. Hi. Not really."

"Busy day?"

"You mean other than gunships falling out of the sky?"

"Right, sorry. I spaced it." Drake did sound exhausted. "Busy day here. Think we got the cork back in the bottle. We'll have to wait to see what happens in Yemen and Iraq over the next forty-eight hours to be sure."

"Good. I'm glad you got that fixed. Even just temporarily."

"Sure you're not up for something? I could grab some Italian or a pizza and come by your office?"

"Pizza is Italian. Besides—"

"Yes," Jon did a fist pump as he got off his phone. "We're cleared into Mexico."

"You're *what?*" Drake roared over the phone.

"Uh, we're cleared into Mexican airspace."

"As a cargo transport with emergency supplies," Jon called out cheerfully over the engines' steady roar.

"As a *what?*"

"Drake. Just calm down. You know the Ghostrider from Eglin that the President authorized to go after JJ?"

"Ye-es." It was a low, drawn-out sound.

"Well, the observer seat is quite comfortable."

"Lizzy, are you out of your goddamn mind?" Again the bull's roar.

"Drake—"

"You turn that goddamn plane around and—"

"General Drake Nason! Shut up or I'll stuff this ring right down your throat."

Jon stared at her wide-eyed as if *she* was the one who'd lost her mind.

Drake was suddenly much meeker. "You wouldn't do that, would you? Give it back I mean. You wouldn't really—"

"You're goddamn tempting me! This is *my* operation, apparently because *you* were too busy with the goddamn Saudis and had to fucking blow off Miranda this morning when she called for help in finding JJ. Did you know that because his clearance was still active and had no alerts attached to it, he just strolled through the front gate at Andrews Air Force Base to steal that second Ghostrider?"

He was wise enough to answer her with silence.

"Well, she's cracked it wide open and I'm dealing with it. And if the President keeps giving *you* all the goddamn credit for *our* goddamn work, then you can *both* go to hell and neither of you is ever getting my vote again. And I'll tell Miranda to do the same."

"My, but you *are* a jet jockey. All this time and I didn't know you had a mouth like that on you, Lizzy. Besides, I'm not elected; I'm appointed, then consented to by the Senate."

"Go to fucking hell and die, Drake."

"Yeah, about that. Don't be dying out there. I want you back."

"Fat chance!" But she regretted the words as soon as she said them.

There was a long silence.

Long enough for her review her other words. She agreed with most of them. But she could feel the ring on her finger. So unfamiliar, so new, and so perfect that she never wanted to take it off again.

"That thing you said," Drake spoke softly.

"Which one?"

"The one about me taking credit for your work? You know I'd never do that, right?"

"I goddamn *heard* you! Right at the end of our last

conversation. Roy saying, 'Well done, Drake.' " Lizzy did her best to lower her voice like President Cole's.

Drake burst out laughing.

She'd have hung up on him if she could have unclenched her hand enough to do so.

"He was congratulating me on falling for a woman with enough balls to go out and get things done, and damn the consequences because it was the right thing to do."

"...Oh."

"That's all you have to say? 'Oh.'?" Drake's chuckle was low and sexy.

"Um...yes." Not what she'd expected.

"Are you going to keep the ring?" Now he was teasing her.

"Yes," was all she could manage. She clenched her left fist tightly and held it up against her heart.

"Okay. You know that the point of being a general is that you no longer need to go out in the field yourself."

"Tell that to Patton."

"That's a little different. You're the Director of the NRO, not the commander of the Third Army."

"Or General JJ Martinez."

Again that silence stretched before Drake spoke again, "Yeah, about that. Be damned careful. He's an exceptionally tough man to kill. Many people have tried, both metaphorically and a few literally. He's the kind of guy who makes Patton look like a pussycat."

"I'm not out to kill him."

"General Gray, please take this as advice from the Chairman of the Joint Chiefs of Staff: you'd better *start* preparing yourself for that eventuality. You've made yourself the commanding officer on the scene, and it's an order you may have to give."

She couldn't breathe past the sudden tightness in her chest.

Drake waited several long beats before speaking again. "You need anything?"

"A miracle."

"I'll get to work on that. I love you, Lizzy. Come back safe."

"I love you too, Drake."

Lizzy hung up the phone and just held on to it as she tried to make sense of everything that was going on.

"You okay, General Gray?" Jon leaned close enough to rest a hand on her arm.

"I have no idea."

"Did Uncle Drake, the guy who can't even hug my mother, his sister, when he visits, actually say, 'I love you'?"

She glanced over at him. "He did."

"In as many words?"

Lizzy could only nod.

"I'll be damned." Jon leaned back and whistled in surprise. "I think you just got your miracle, General Gray."

58

"THEY'RE ALOFT." AT LIZZY'S REQUEST, HOLLY WAS HANDLING the phone calls after Miranda's long talk with the copilot.

He and Miranda had talked about tactics, specifically the implications of design capabilities versus real-world limitations.

The pilots had been deeply trained in air-to-ground combat and air-to-air scenarios, but never against another AC-130J Ghostrider. It simply hadn't been a consideration.

She and the copilot had taken most of the Ghostrider's flight between El Paso, Texas, and Nogales, Sonora, to work out the essential considerations. They'd signed off as her flight began its descent into Joint Base Lewis-McChord in Tacoma, Washington.

He had asked if they could meet later to work through more of the permutations.

She'd agreed.

Neither of them had mentioned that there might not be a later.

Miranda knew it was out of her hands. She'd done everything she could think of.

"Don't think about it," Holly anticipated her thoughts.

She stared at Holly. "How?"

She shrugged. "Don't ask me; I don't know Christmas from Bourke Street. Just...don't."

"I have Mike and Jeremy on one plane and Jon with Lizzy on the other. Their present closing speed is seven hundred knots—eight hundred miles an hour. There is no scenario that I can simulate where this ends well."

Holly looked grim, then listened to the phone for a moment.

"First contact will be in about thirty minutes, just after we land."

59

"Coming up on the first target. We're just southeast of Mexicali. The compound of Hector Vasquez," the pilot announced over the Ghostrider's intercom.

It was a mission near and dear to Taz's heart.

Vasquez was the one who'd taken their money and chosen the coyote man to take them safely over the border. How many women, who hadn't had the premium for the legitimate papers, had simply been sold into the sex trade after he'd enjoyed a bit of rape?

Jeremy had showed her how and she had the night-vision image up on the targeting monitor.

"The armory is here and the garage is here," she showed Jeremy his targets. She set a cursor on the screen between their stations that showed an infrared view of Vasquez's compound. Then she shifted to the second location.

"Got them. You ready?" Jeremy had drilled her diligently on aiming and firing the M102 howitzer from the moment they were aboard. Mike had even helped when

Jeremy became too technical and she'd needed a translation.

"As ready as you can make me." She slewed the targeting for the howitzer to Vasquez's private compound and hoped the circular balcony marked the master bedroom.

She glanced at JJ, "I'd still like the order to proceed, sir."

"Granted, Colonel Cortez. Weapons free. Fire at will."

To Jeremy's credit, he didn't hesitate. He lit the armory. The beam would be invisible from the ground, but their instruments displayed a brilliant green-white blaze on the roof of the armory.

She fired the howitzer at the same moment. The big round traveled at twice the speed of sound—four seconds from their current altitude.

Their gun crew required ten seconds to reload the howitzer, so all she could do was wait and watch.

The corner of the hacienda disappeared in a ball of white. She moved her cursor to highlight the next corner of the hacienda. Her indicator turned green but she didn't fire.

The computer will compensate for most scenarios, Jeremy had told her. *Windage, air speed, and so on. But if you can wait until the target remains steady in your crosshairs for at least two or three seconds, then the chances of the projectile flying true increase drastically.*

Just as she hit the Fire button, Jeremy's laser must have finally burned through the armory roof.

The entire compound disappeared beneath the blinding glare on their screens.

"What just happened?" It looked as if everything had blown up.

"Screen overload. It will compensate in a few moments,

but right now the CCD and the computer are simply overwhelmed with photon impact which is—"

"Did it blow up the whole compound?" JJ was leaning in over her shoulder.

"No, see." Jeremy pointed. "The bloom is going away. So...now we can see what happened when the armory exploded. Though the brightness of the fire is continuing to mask the extent of the actual damage."

A second flash of brightness, even bigger than the first, smeared across the screen so suddenly that she slammed back into her seat and JJ stumbled back.

"What did you do, Jeremy?"

"A laser isn't like a shell. There's no aim, fire, wait. Though there are problems of atmospheric blooming and energy usage from sustained firing, but we're well within the performance envelopes of this weapon in the current environmental conditions. So, I can simply re-aim the beam. I didn't want to expend energy burning through the garage roof, but I then spotted the fuel dump. Fifty-five-gallon drums aren't designed to withstand hundred-and-fifty-kilowatt lasers. Ka-Pow! Bang! Boom!" He waved his hands in the air as he made exploding sounds.

Mike spoke up. "Just like a little kid, Jeremy. Jeffrey would approve." They didn't laugh, but they clearly enjoyed the shared memory.

Taz turned away, unable to watch. It hurt. She didn't know why, but it did.

People were racing across the compound in every direction.

A lone vehicle roared out of the compound. By its look it was a very fast sports car, not some mere SUV.

"Hit it, Jeremy!"

He shook his head. "No. I don't shoot people. That's the deal."

"How do I do it? That's got to be Hector Vasquez. He loves his supercars. He's *got* to go down." She tried to aim the howitzer but it only had a very small range that must be aligned off the right wing. And Jeremy had told her that moving targets required techniques he didn't have time to teach her.

Jeremy watched her closely as the vehicle bounced violently over the rough road but kept gaining speed.

"He's *got* to, Jeremy. There aren't many worse people in the world."

For a long second he looked in her eyes, then reached out and took her hand. Rather than squeezing it with some unwanted but expected sympathy, he moved it to the laser's joystick. "Get a feel for tracking the vehicle. It's moving fast, so you'll need to keep it steady in the crosshairs for longer than you'd think."

At first she was veering side-to-side. Finally she had a feel for how to keep it steady in the crosshairs, reasonably.

Jeremy tapped in a quick series of settings, called in a correction to the cockpit, then pointed at a red Fire button.

He sat back to watch her carefully. His face totally unreadable. She glanced at Mike, who noticed the change as well.

She wanted Jeremy to think well of her.

But she wanted Vasquez dead. So much of the pain in her life—and Mama's—had been his doing.

Why had a man who headed a cartel, a violent

competitor of the one her father worked for, helped them out at all?

And then she knew what other price Mama had paid to Hector Vasquez for their safe passage.

Taz punched and held the Fire button.

His vehicle glowed brightly in the infrared as the supercar heated. It swerved left and right but she kept the beam steady. Finally, perhaps in desperation to escape or perhaps while dying of heat stroke, it swerved too far and rolled.

When it came to rest upside down, she held her aim on the car.

A second later there was the massive bloom of an explosion as the gas tank ruptured.

Jeremy had to tug a little to get her finger off the Fire button.

Together they watched Vasquez burn.

JJ rested his hand on her shoulder and squeezed it in sympathy. He knew what this kill meant to her. Perhaps had even made it first on his list to ensure that it was done before whatever shitstorm was coming their way landed.

"Ready for the next target," JJ said over the headset.

The plane turned away.

Taz watched the fire for as long as it was in sight, and for a while after.

60

"I HAVE A HARD TRACK ON THEM THAT I'M FEEDING TO YOUR pilots," Thorsen informed her. "Three targets down. Two in Mexicali. One halfway to Nogales. They've turned mostly toward you again, probably heading for number four."

"How close?" Lizzy knew that they should have anticipated this better. Or sent the Raptors that could have been there, cleaned house, and gone all the way back to Lackland by now. A Super Hercules at four hundred miles an hour just didn't compare with an F-22 ticking along at fifteen hundred.

She was banking everything on their own ability to stop JJ's Ghostrider without either killing them or being killed.

"Under a hundred miles. And, General?"

"Yes, Thorsen?"

"I've got your mole. Colonel Cortez used the oldest trick in the book."

"Sex?"

"Sex? The Taser? No way. Can't even imagine that. She

used the second oldest trick then. Money. O'Neil, one of former Director Patrick's favorite colonels."

"Have him arrested on my authorization. Strip everything. His files, his bank accounts, his goddamn Rolodex."

"They use phone contacts now."

"I don't care. Down to the dirt. And make sure that it's all documented and well-publicized. Do it by the book; I want a full court-martial, Captain Thorsen."

"Already done," he sounded very pleased. "All on your authorization, General."

Lizzy considered if she should be pissed or pleased at his taking liberty with her authority. She had to think about three seconds. "Thank you, *Major* Thorsen. And I expect your promotion recommendation letter drafted and on my desk by the time I get back. And Thorsen?"

"Thank you, ma'am. Yes ma'am?"

"If I don't make it back from this, you have my authorization to sign it on my behalf."

His voice was dead serious when he finally replied. "Not a chance I'll need to do that, ma'am. It will be there —unsigned."

61

Rosa stood behind Pierre's seat. For the last two hours in transit she'd drilled him in every advanced technique she knew.

Every challenge, every scenario, even ones that she'd barely survived, he found a way through. It wasn't always pretty, but his solutions worked and his accuracy was exceptional. Speed was the only place she could still outperform him.

They were discussing implications of the far corners of temperature-humidity-air density diagrams—high altitude arctic-cold achingly dry, and low-jungle monsoon—when General Gray came back to their station.

"Is he ready?"

"Yes ma'am."

"I wanted to thank you both. I know that facing a renegade American unit is not within your typical mandate."

"It's our country and our honor, ma'am," Pierre answered with a straight face.

Rosa tried to echo him. But she couldn't. She remembered when the truth of her treason came out. The fear churning so hard in her gut that she was afraid she'd miscarry her six-week-old child right here on the cargo deck.

Pierre had told her secret to the NTSB agents, who had then vouched for her surety. It was wrong. It was all so wrong. What she'd done... What she was still hiding. And she knew she'd involved a good man in her own subterfuge.

"I..." She wet her lips, hung on to the back of Pierre's chair with her one good hand, and tried again. "I need to—"

"No, Rosa," Pierre was on his feet and in her face. "No, you don't need to do this."

"Yes, Pierre, I do." She brushed a hand over his cheek and then pushed him back into his chair.

The general was smiling. "It will have to be something pretty spectacular to surprise me today."

Pierre hung his head. Rosa wanted to rest her hand on his shoulder for strength. But he was the innocent party in all this.

"I'm supposed to be the HEL-A laser operator for General Martinez. Not Miranda's team member."

The general just nodded. "Anything else?"

Rosa didn't know what to say to that. She'd agreed to break her oath of service and commit treason. Only a kiss and Pierre leveraging her out a plane's door had kept her from her sworn task.

"We found your name on the 'Death List' of the initial crash. Since then you've fully cooperated—but that's not why I'm trusting you. Nor is it the man almost weeping with relief under your hand."

He hadn't been worried about her being sent down for this; he'd been terrified.

"You care about me that much?"

He nodded without looking up.

"And my child?"

This time he turned to look at her. "You think I'd hold a useless shit of a father against a kid?"

No. No, she didn't. She looked back at General Gray. "Then why?"

"Okay, the baby counts as a surprise," the general shrugged it off. "As to why? Miranda Chase recommended you—I heard both of you gasp in surprise in the background. It didn't take much to figure out why. You both assumed you were going down. Damn well should. But you have no idea how hard it is to impress Miranda. She doesn't know it, but she's the best judge of character ever born."

"She is...interesting," Rosa managed.

"That she is," the general almost laughed. Then she sobered. "I do have a suggestion as an Air Force officer that would make *me* more comfortable with the dropping of this matter."

Rosa braced herself.

"It's clear that you're an exceptional trainer. You may wish to consider a transfer request from combat duty to a training corps. Your child might appreciate that as well."

Before Rosa could even begin to think of how to thank her, the general looked at her watch.

"We're five minutes to intercept. Please try not to kill..." The general had a puzzled look for a moment, then smiled radiantly.

"Please try not to kill my maid of honor's teammates."

62

"CROSSING AIRCRAFT. HEADING TWO-THREE-FIVE AT FLIGHT Level Two-eight-zero."

At the pilot's announcement, Taz looked up at the ceiling of the C-130, then felt foolish. First, there were no windows there. Second, they would already be gone by as the flight was heading southwest to their own east. Third, two-eight-zero was twenty-eight thousand feet. Their own plane was almost four miles lower at eight thousand feet.

It was the third crossing flight of the night. Not important.

Except that Jeremy was also looking at their plane's ceiling with a puzzled look on his face.

"What?" She didn't know why she was whispering.

Jeremy shook his head.

"*What?*"

He glanced up again. Then over at Mike.

Mike sat in the corner where the hull met the aft bulkhead of the weapons control space. On the other side of the, only marginally, sound-insulating wall stood the rack of thirty-three pound, three-foot-long shells for the howitzer. At each target, the pounding thumps from the big gun had seemed to slam into him. He became somehow smaller with each round fired.

She then studied Jeremy. He too looked tired and his nerves stretched thin. She'd stopped taking over the laser controls. If someone got away from her howitzer now, they got to live. But she made damn sure their operation was blasted to hell.

"What is it, Jeremy?" His eyes had once again traveled upward. "Something about that plane."

He turned to look at her. His gaze was rock steady, but his eyes were so sad. They weren't the eyes of the young man who'd made love to her in a desert cloister. They were of a grown man haunted. She had done this to him—twisted him into helping her kill people.

These were bad men and this was a war that General Martinez had fought for years with no one listening to him.

Then she glanced aloft herself.

Something about that flight.

"What's southwest of here?" His whisper barely reached her ears and they certainly didn't reach JJ in the observer's chair that Mike had abandoned to him an hour ago.

"From here there's..." Sonora and Baja. But was there even a single airport big enough for a high-flying plane? Beyond that was...nothing. Hawaii was north of west from here. Australia and New Zealand were a world away. And weren't passenger jets usually up in the high thirty-thousands, not twenty-eight? It was—

"They're here?"

Jeremy nodded.

"Can we—" She glanced to the laser console, then hated herself for it.

"I. Will. Not. Shoot at Americans."

Taz stared hard at the console. She tried to remember the good and the evil she'd done.

Putting down rapist dogs didn't even count. Tonight she'd killed many more, and felt no regrets.

But she'd also wrecked the careers of men who'd blocked the general's agenda, with the absolute confidence that the general knew what was right. That JJ led the Clear and True Way, whatever that was.

While such a path was welcome to use up people like her and the general, it should never use up people like Jeremy or Mike, or what was its purpose? Not even the Rosa Cruzes of the world should have been caught under its grinding wheel.

"What can we do?"

Jeremy didn't shrug. Didn't evade. "He'll never surrender. Nor any of the other officers. You've all gone too far to turn back. I can only think of one thing to do."

"What's that?"

Jeremy brushed a hand over her cheek before smiling sadly.

"Nothing."

63

JJ KNEW WHAT WAS HAPPENING AS SOON AS THE PILOT announced the errant flight over the intercom.

They'd be circling down to come in on his starboard side, away from the weapons. And from on high, because his weapons couldn't be brought to bear on them—the laser and howitzer were built to fire down, possibly horizontal, but not up.

He recalled Jeremy's earlier explanation to Taz of the possibilities of engaging in inverted flight. But he didn't need to overhear Jeremy and Taz's conversation to know the conclusion of it.

There was only one option left.

Pushing to his feet, he stepped up beside Taz.

She looked up at him warily.

All these years, she'd trusted him. Done his bidding without question, without hesitation. Had she been less loyal, would they have ended up in this same place? He expected that he would have, at least—though perhaps with even less success to show for it. Three major cartel headquarters had gone down hard tonight.

Now, the clear caution in her eyes, the wary loss of that trust. It cut almost as deeply as the loss of his Consuela.

After all these years of her living up to his standards, he realized that it was time he lived up to hers.

"Time to next target?"

She looked at the console and then back to him. "Six minutes." She said it too softly to hear, but he could read it on her lips.

And he could see in the expressionlessness of her face that she understood his intent.

The other aircraft was going to do whatever it did.

Unhindered.

Unattacked.

Their own operation would end as it had begun, only attacking the scum along the Mexican border who thrived on America's weakness.

He nodded and turned away.

Starting at the rear of the aircraft, he made a point of stopping and checking in with each man. Three he'd flown with. Two others he'd personally recommended to the Academy back in the day. And two more had worked with him on advanced designs of this very aircraft.

That's where he'd gotten the idea.

Somehow, the military had found out what he was doing before his work was done. Before it was barely begun. Now he could only hope that someone would learn from his example. Though he knew that they wouldn't. Instead, he'd be excoriated on the altar of what was ethically and politically permissible—and he'd gone way over that line.

He finished his brief tour at the cockpit and thumped each pilot on the shoulder. Then he gripped their seat backs as they turned steeply left above what would be their final target in Nogales—their final target ever.

The pilots banked over until the port wing centered and remained aimed at a major Sinaloa cartel mansion as they circled high above it. The leaders were meeting there tonight.

In aiming the weapons downward, the plane behind and above him would know that his Ghostrider wasn't positioned to fire at them.

Opening up the intercom, he announced plane-wide, "Weapons free."

64

PIERRE STARED AT THE DISPLAY IN DISBELIEF.

"I don't get it. He has to know you're there," Holly's voice sounded over the open intercom. Holly and Miranda were in a secure room at Joint Base Lewis-McChord in Washington State.

General Gray and Rosa stood close beside his chair. Major Jon Swift remained with the pilots.

The stolen Ghostrider was shredding a mansion on the outskirts of Nogales as if they were alone in the sky without a worry in the world.

"Think, Holly," Miranda's voice sounded over their headsets. "You already know. General Martinez is so like you."

"A man of honor," General Elizabeth Gray whispered.

For once, Holly had no snappy reply.

Pierre had feared that he wouldn't be good enough, no matter how well Rosa said he was doing. That somehow he'd screw up. Then JJ's stolen plane would kill them, and it would all be his fault.

But they weren't going to fight back.

That meant they were going to live. The only challenge now was to cripple but not kill the other plane.

"Damn," Rosa said softly. "Their laser operator is awfully good. Look at the precision of those hits. All against physical rather than human targets."

"That would be our Jeremy," Holly announced happily.

"Where did he train?" Pierre asked as he prepared his weapons for the attack.

General Gray answered. "The first time he ever sat at a console was at Andrews Air Force Base. By the time we exited the plane, perhaps twenty minutes later, he was demonstrating the challenges of inverted firing tactics."

Pierre glanced up at Rosa. She hadn't shown him any of those. By her look, she'd never thought to try one.

He supposed it was always good to know when to be a little humbled. Her look of chagrin said the same. It had been a very humbling day in many ways—Rosa the greatest among those.

"How long until you're in firing range, Master Sergeant?"

He turned to General Gray. "We're just there now, ma'am."

She took a deep breath, stared hard at her bright blue ring for a moment.

The future. There was going to be a future.

In that case, he'd have to get Rosa a nice ring. But not Air Force blue. Nor would any stone match her dark eyes; so he'd make it a diamond to shine light in them. And then they'd find a way to serve *way* below the radar.

"Master Sergeant," the general's voice was steady when she looked up from her ring. "Fire at will."

With the stolen Ghostrider's port wing pointed steeply down at the targeted mansion, the sensor ball on the left side of their fuselage was aimed nearly straight down. He instructed the pilots to make a high-speed dive and zoom-climb pass, dipping only momentarily low enough to target only the highly sensitive sensor array.

He narrowed the beam as tightly as possible.

At the bottom of the dive, he fired.

65

THEIR SCREENS FUZZED FOR ONE LONG SECOND, THEN BLANKED all at once. Only the sight camera on the howitzer's barrel remained operative. A far less effective system.

"Continue firing," JJ called over the intercom.

Taz did the best she could with the crippled system.

"Release bombs."

Jeremy had trained her how to pre-align those so that she wouldn't have to think about them during an attack, just release them.

She checked that the pilot was still maintaining his pylon turn so that the port wing was aimed at the center of the target.

He was.

Taz knew it was their last drop, so she didn't attempt to conserve anything. She released everything that remained. Sixteen bombs—four thousand pounds of explosives—launched off the tail. The mansion had covered more than an acre.

More by luck than design, all of the bombs landed inside the compound walls. Everything was obliterated.

She continued firing the big howitzer into the devastation as fast as the crew could load it. It was their last target—ever.

"One last round," the gun crew called.

"Thank you, everyone. Due north, please." JJ announced over the intercom.

"Why north?" Jeremy asked quickly as the deck leveled.

"He's taking you back home to the US. And removing this plane from potential capture by any foreign agency. Even an ally like Mexico. The border isn't far."

When the light went green, she aimed at the trailing fire. Just before she punched the Fire button to send the final round down into the conflagration where it could make no possible difference, the screen flared and blanked.

"What the—" Taz tried to stop the motion of her finger, but didn't quite manage it.

66

"MASSIVE EXPLOSION ON THE PORT SIDE," PIERRE ANNOUNCED. "We have a massive explosion on the port side of the target Ghostrider."

"What the hell did you do?" Someone shouted at him. Holly?

"I fired the laser at the barrel of the M102 howitzer as we agreed. My goal was to take out the sight camera along the barrel."

"How hot would the barrel have become?" Miranda asked in the strangely analytical way that told him what had happened.

"They were already firing at the gun's maximum rate. If they fired a round into a hot barrel at the same moment I was heating it with the laser... The round must have exploded as it was leaving the breech."

"Flames now," Rosa pointed.

"Oh shit!" Pierre could only watch in horror. "They've got a real fire over there. A bad one."

67

"Go. Now!" Taz shoved the two parachutes she'd stashed into Jeremy's and Mike's arms. JJ had ordered that there be none aboard—burning the ships behind them, like her almost namesake Cortés had five hundred years ago to motivate the men. She'd kept two back, well hidden.

Mike dragged on his chute with the signs of previous, if not deep, experience. Jeremy fumbled at the straps until he was actually holding it upside down. Something as simple as donning a chute had no place in his genius world. Other than a brief moment on a mountainous Baja rock shelf, their worlds had no overlap. One glimpse of another way life could be.

"Where's yours?" Jeremy asked as she and Mike worked together to get Jeremy strapped in.

"I don't have one." She fisted the emergency release on the forward passenger door, then yanked the handle. It rolled upward on its tracks. The wind-and-propeller roar filled the cabin. It only served to fan the flames that were fast consuming the rear of the plane. None of the gun crew had survived the initial blast.

Even as she glanced down, the brightly lit US border passed below them. Safely north of the border. At least she wouldn't die in Mexico.

Jeremy grabbed both her arms as she double-checked his gear. "Come *with* me. We're both light. The parachute must be strong enough."

It was. A military chute could take a strapping Special Forces operator and a full kit weighing more than her hundred and five pounds with perfect safety.

"No."

"But—"

"A life in Leavenworth or some Mexican jail? Not for me."

"I know the Chairman of the Joint Chiefs. Miranda knows the President. We can get you a pardon."

Mike nodded to confirm the unlikely truth of that.

For a moment, just a moment, she blinked.

In that split instant she saw a different world. One that might have been. Back before she'd buried a knife in the coyote man's chest. Before she'd become who she was.

"Out and down to stay below the prop," she shouted at Mike. Seeing her decision, he offered a sad smile, then was gone.

She kissed Jeremy for that glimpse. Fast, as time was running, but hard so that he'd remember her.

"Pull this after you're clear," she shouted and put his hand on the ripcord handle.

"But—"

"I can't leave the general."

Jeremy reached into his pocket and pulled out something to hand to her.

She took it and then she shoved hard against the middle of his chest.

Jeremy tumbled out the door, down and backward into the slipstream—gone into the night.

She slapped the Door Close control before she could be tempted to dive after him.

The crippled AC-130J Ghostrider was twisting down through the sky. It wouldn't be long now.

In her hand she clutched an MRE bag. Inside were the three unused heaters from his prodigious consumption of pizza slices. There was also a lighter he'd scrounged from somewhere.

Three together. Add water. Flick a spark. And the hydrogen gas generated by three flameless heaters together would make an impressive one-shot flamethrower. Enough to permanently blind her, the general, or maybe both.

Jeremy had built a weapon out of nothing...but had chosen not to use it on her.

Taz clutched the bag to her chest and felt both ridiculous and—

She spotted General Martinez watching her intently.

"Was there anything you needed, sir?" Her throat was tight, but she managed to get out the words.

"No, Vicki. No. Not a thing. I just wanted to thank you for your service." And he saluted her crisply as the plane died beneath their feet.

She hadn't even known that he knew her first name.

68

Miranda barely recognized Mike and Jeremy as they disembarked from the C-21 Learjet that had returned them to Tacoma Narrows Airport.

Jon had waited until they'd been rescued and checked out medically. Then he'd brought them home himself.

She and Holly had been returned from JBLM only minutes before the others landed. Together they'd waited outside their hangar in the cool, rising-dawn light. Soon the sun would clear the towering Cascades, but for now the sky was shot with reds and golds. Even the icy beacon of the glaciers atop Mount Rainier weren't lit yet.

The air was still, the dead calm of sunrise so typical of the Pacific Northwest. Often dawn and dusk were the only truly calm times of day here.

Hearing what to expect was one thing, but seeing it was much worse.

Jeremy had a cast on his arm from a bad parachute landing. One side of Mike's face was all black and blue. The other side had been badly scraped as his parachute had dragged him over the rough ground.

The moment they deplaned, Holly threw herself at them and locked them both in a hard hug. Protests and complaints of pain made no difference.

Miranda made sure that her own welcomes were gentler. "I'm so very pleased to see you."

Mike touched her cheek, then rubbed his fingers together. "I feel the same, Miranda."

She brushed at her own cheeks, surprised to discover that they were wet.

They all laughed, briefly, but it died fast and felt awkward.

Jon flagged her from the cockpit of the little Learjet.

"Oh, I didn't realize he was staying." She hurried to unlock the hangar door.

"Duh!" Holly's voice sounded behind her.

When it slid open, the pine scent of the Northwest was replaced by the sharper smells of fresh paint and new leather. She squinted into the dim depths of the hangar. *Wonderful!*

Then she stepped aside and let the others enter first.

They were halfway across before anyone noticed the new wall, sectioning off the back of the hangar. Holly was first, as usual, "By crikey."

Jeremy and Mike both blinked in surprise, but couldn't seem to find any words at all. The door stood open. A small envelope hung beside an outer keypad, which would be the default combination for the new room's security system.

Jeremy and Mike crossed the threshold side by side and stumbled to a halt. Miranda tried going up on tiptoes to see over their shoulders, then tried looking between them to no avail.

Holly finally pushed the two boys far enough apart that she could step between them. Miranda followed through the brief gap.

"Well, I'll be stuffed, mate!" Holly amended her assessment.

The renovation crews had been working hard for the two days they'd been gone.

The back of the hangar now had two large windows facing the runway, and a third facing south over Puget Sound. The one-way glass barely dimmed the view. The golden dawn filled the visible sky and glinted off the ice-capped towers of the Olympic Mountains. Now, not only could she hear the distinctive sound of a Cessna 172's Lycoming four-cylinder engine and two-blade propeller lifting off the runway, she could see its happily blinking navigation lights. The two passengers were just visible in the front seats, silhouetted against the lightening sky.

The new-built room had been finished in soft pastels. She liked the distinction from her wood-finished home up on Spieden Island. She'd opted for a laminate floor with Douglas fir patterning to stand up to whatever abuses the future would bring, but she'd also selected several modern throw rugs.

With the views out the big windows, there was no need for art on the walls.

"This is *amazing!*" Jeremy had found his workbench. She'd doubled its size and added drawers below and cubbies above. The tool cabinets sat off to either side and she'd updated all of the equipment to a full digital test suite and a high-speed computer for modeling aerodynamics.

Mike ran his fingers over the top-of-the-line Breville Oracle home espresso machine and the matching Grind Control grinder-brewer as he inspected the kitchenette with a soft smile. Then, with a sigh of relief that Miranda was fairly sure was happy, he settled slowly into the vintage cordovan-leather Chesterfield wingback armchair she'd found for him.

Holly plunged into the oversized deep-cushioned armchair next to him and propped her boots on the stout teak coffee table. Her chair was centered directly across from the big-screen television that could run simulations from Jeremy's bench, or movies.

Her own teak rolltop desk sat just to the side of the big windows so that she could watch the planes while she was working.

She could feel Jon come up behind her after rolling the Air Force C-21 into the hangar. He slid his hands around her waist from behind and laced his fingers as she laid her hands over his.

"Pretty nice digs you have here," his whisper tickled her ear.

"Thank you."

She didn't yet know him well enough to get the right kind of chair for him. For now, he'd have to share one of the couches with either her or Jeremy.

69

Too exhausted to fly home, Miranda had opted to stay at the team's Gig Harbor house. Holly had insisted on sleeping out on the couch so that she and Jon could have the privacy of a bedroom.

Despite the harrowing two days and the long morning and afternoon just catching up with events, Miranda lay wide awake at midnight.

Jon slept soundly beside her.

He had gone to some trouble to prove that he liked her in her NTSB clothes, liked taking them off her before introducing her to several new experiences in the shower, and then finally liked helping her to slip on her nightgown. She no longer needed him to explain that each was good but different; he'd proven his point with precise demonstration and a most enjoyable thoroughness.

Though her body was very well sated, she was unable to stop the whirl of her thoughts. Slipping from his arms, she went into the bathroom and once more changed.

As she eased out through the bedroom's darkness, Jon spoke up softly.

"I thought it was the guy who was supposed to slip away in the middle of the night."

"They are? Why would they do that?"

Jon's voice was thick with sleep and a soft laugh. "To avoid attachment? Utter stupidity? As for me, I like the idea of waking up with you."

She was fairly sure that she was right in imagining his smile even though she couldn't see it.

"Where are you going? A walk in the moonlight? Do you want company?"

"I'm not sure. The moon set over an hour ago. And no."

"Well," she could hear him shift in the sheets. "That certainly puts me in my place."

"There's just something I have to see, I think. Goodbye, Jon."

"Hold it. Wait!" His shadow rose from the bed and stepped up close enough that she could feel his warmth, smell the curious scent of him that she couldn't put words to despite several attempts.

"Is that like a goodbye-goodbye or a goodbye-until-I-see-you-next-time goodbye?"

Another one of those words with situational meanings. She really wished she could rewrite the English language and eradicate them all permanently.

"Are you asking if we can have sex again in the future? Yes, Jon, I'd like that very much."

"No. I wasn't asking that."

"Oh," Miranda could feel herself wilt a little inside.

"I was..." Jon paused, then laughed. "Okay, yes, I'd love to have sex with you again. I also like you, Miranda, very much. I'd enjoy spending more time with you."

"Oh, okay then." She'd like that too. "I'm going to go now."

Without any more confusing words, he pulled her hard against his bare chest and held her tight. Her nose was slightly crushed against his breastbone, but the rest of it felt very nice and she let herself be held. After a moment, she realized that he would want to be held back so she slipped her arms around him. They stood that way for a long minute with his cheek on her hair and her nose smushed against his breastbone.

Now she knew what urge had driven her from the bed, and where she had to go.

70

Miranda wasn't sure where Holly had gone. Her sheets were still on the great room couch, but she was nowhere to be seen. She couldn't easily imagine her being in Mike's room, but his door was closed and Mike usually slept with it cracked open.

All the cars were still out front, so, however much Holly had declared it to be impossible, Mike's room was where she must be.

To get to the airport, Miranda borrowed Holly's Corvette —which was almost as fun as a jet—and was soon racing her F-86 Sabrejet east across the country at just below the speed of sound. She flew high, at 45,000 feet, and caught up with the sunrise shortly before descending into Washington, DC.

A taxi delivered her to CIA headquarters and the pass issued by Vice President Clark Winston, when he was still the director here, gained her admittance. She only ever visited two places at the CIA.

The first was the Memorial Wall. Rows of simple silver

stars, each smaller than her palm, were mounted on the white marble. Each represented an unnamed agent killed in the line of duty; one that could not be acknowledged in normal ways for security reasons.

Director Winston had pointed out which stars were her parents—dead on TWA 800. They'd been undercover to plan the earliest expansions of US drones for clandestine operations into the Middle East theater. Their acknowledged employment by the CIA would have caused problems with the Israelis and Arabs alike, so they'd received stars despite dying on a domestic disaster en route to that task.

She rubbed her fingertips along the edges of both stars, but couldn't feel her parents. She didn't know the CIA agents that her parents had been—a role she hadn't even known about until last year. They weren't here. Now that she understood that, she'd never have to visit this spot again.

The pass from Clark also permitted her entry into the central courtyard, a small parklike area that lay between the Old and New Headquarters Buildings. Most people hurried down the connecting corridors to either side that linked the two buildings and formed the east and west boundaries of the courtyard. Perhaps at lunchtime on a sunny day there would be people here.

Just past sunrise, the area was empty.

The courtyard had two broad paths, a fountain, and areas for comfortable seating.

But for her, the courtyard was dominated by the sculpture tucked out of the way in the northwest corner.

Miranda turned left and followed the broad path to Kryptos.

The enigmatic bronze sculpture held a significant role in her past. It stood eight feet high and sixteen long. It was in a horizontal S shape, like a rippled piece of paper stood on edge. Its entire surface was cut out in hand-sized letters through the thick bronze. Four panels, each of which contained a secret code.

She and her father had spent many happy hours attempting to unravel them. It was well after his death when the solution to the first three was published—the fourth remained unresolved. And there were rumors of a fifth, a codified encryption that would only be revealed after the first four panels were solved.

Miranda ran her hand over the surface. Her father had commissioned a three-foot-tall replica for their home garden on Spieden Island. It seemed that Sam Chase still hovered there every time she sat out by it to watch the birds flit about the feeders her mother had placed all around. It was always a place of peace for her.

Standing at the real Kryptos was different. Here their mutual visits had been separated by decades, but they had both stood right here. In an odd way, it made her feel more connected to him than in the garden where they'd sat together so many times.

There she'd been the child.

Here they'd both been adults.

But she couldn't place her mother. Their relationship had been so different from her and her father's. She loved her mother, she remembered that, but the connection was dissociated from her memorial star, from Kryptos, even from the garden at home, though she'd often tended it while

Miranda and her father had contemplated their copy of the sculpture.

No, her father was here...but not her mother. She was—

"What are *you* doing here?"

Miranda turned and had to look up.

Clarissa Reese, the Director of the CIA, stood five-foot-ten, without the high heels. She wore a sleek summer dress of white fabric that seemed to shine in the morning sunlight.

Aggressively white?

At Mike's advice, Miranda had been practicing associating emotion to color, and, though the dress itself wasn't severe, aggressively white seemed appropriate. It had a nicely fitted top and bell quarter-sleeves that emphasized Clarissa's strong shoulders and bust. Then, from a wide white belt at her trim waist, it belled out slightly down to her knees.

Her white-blonde hair, while still back in its typical long ponytail, was less aggressively (that word again) slicked back than usual. It was actually the softest look she'd ever seen on Clarissa.

"My father loved Kryptos. I needed to come visit it."

"Oh." Clarissa fell silent.

Together they watched the sun shift through the hundreds of holes that the letters formed.

"I come here sometimes to think and..." Clarissa trailed off in a way that Miranda now understood meant that she didn't want to finish the sentence.

Is that what she herself was doing here? Miranda wasn't sure. It didn't feel as if she was thinking more or harder in the presence of Kryptos than she did at other times. In fact, her thoughts felt quieter here that in most places. The final panel of Kryptos was far too complex to be solved by staring at it. And she had no other role here at the CIA.

"Perhaps…" And Miranda herself trailed off, the incompleteness of her own sentence curiously unsettling, yet strangely appropriate.

"Perhaps what?" Apparently incomplete thoughts bothered Clarissa as well. Miranda pulled out her notebook and noted down that it was possible there was some previously unconsidered degree of commonality between herself and Clarissa. But she'd think about that at another time.

"Perhaps…" Miranda considered after tucking her notebook away, "I come here to *feel* rather than to *think*."

Clarissa turned to look down at her but Miranda kept her eyes on the puzzle that was so much a part of her past.

"I can feel my father's presence in this place even though we never stood here together at the same time. Not even in the same millennium, as he died when I was thirteen in 1996."

"You miss him?"

"Terribly. I loved him very much."

The silence stretched so long that Miranda finally glanced at Clarissa, who seemed to be staring at nothing at all.

"You're very lucky," Clarissa finally whispered.

Was she? For thirteen wonderful years, she'd had parents who loved her. They weren't around much and never for long when they were. On assignment as CIA agents she now knew. Working together as a team, and leaving her to be mostly raised by Tante Daniels.

But the moments her father was home had shone so brightly that they overshadowed the rest.

Until his death.

Had she been lucky?

Holly's parents had disowned her. Mike never spoke of his as if he'd been born the day he joined her NTSB team. Jeremy's parents loved him, though they were also confused and disappointed by him.

Rosa's and Pierre's had both been very close.

What little Jeremy had said made it sound as if Taz's mother had been a very hard woman. Colonel Vicki Cortez's effect on Jeremy had been profound, but he wasn't speaking about it, which, she supposed, was the most surprising thing of all.

"Yes, I *was* lucky." Miranda turned but Clarissa was gone.

She turned back to Kryptos as a sparrow flitted to a landing inside the center letter of the eighth row of the second panel. A Q, which, when the panel was decrypted, was a D in the word BURIED.

"*Very* lucky," she told the sparrow before it chirped at her brightly and flew off.

71

FLIGHT TWA 800 HAD DEPARTED JFK AIRPORT AT 8:19 P.M. on July 17th, 1996, after a long, hot delay on the tarmac. At thirteen thousand seven hundred feet above the Atlantic Ocean, a stray spark in a mostly empty fuel tank had created a massive explosion in the sky that sliced the 747 in two.

In the largest and longest NTSB investigation in history, ninety-five percent of the debris was recovered from the depths of the continental shelf. The main fuselage was entirely reconstructed, one tiny piece at a time, until the investigators were able to trace the exact cause, and make numerous safety recommendations. Some of those safety measures would be implemented on every commercial airliner and military plane throughout the world. The death of her parents and the other two hundred and twenty-eight people aboard had gone on to save innumerable lives.

The critical eighty feet of the 747's main fuselage, a long, open-ended, twenty-one-foot-four-inch-diameter tube, had been installed in the NTSB Training Academy's lobby as a practical model for teaching students about such a complex investigation. Every piece that had been recovered was there: sections of the hull's skin, the bits and pieces of the fuel tank, decking, and seats. Even most of the Plexiglas windows and overhead bins had been recovered and placed correctly.

Miranda had barfed violently in the bathroom before every visit she'd had to make here during training.

Not this time.

This time she sat in the foremost recovered seat on the left-hand side, Row 8, Seat B, one in from the hull. The bright room lights shone in through the rounded windows, the two open ends of the fuselage section, and a thousand cracks in the plane's reconstructed skin: a mosaic of light.

Seven rows, an inch under thirty-four feet, ahead of where she sat had been her father's seat 2B. The first-class section had been blown off the front of the plane and had fallen eighty-three seconds down to the sea. Not relevant to the explosion itself, it had not been retained and put on display here.

Yet, he had sat there, all those years ago. Flying to his next mission with Mom beside him. Perhaps they'd even been discussing their plan for Miranda to follow them in a week after her horse-riding camp was done.

She shifted to the leftmost window seat, 8A, directly behind 2A.

And there she was.

Mom.

As if her ghost had just been waiting for Miranda to finally come to this exact place and ride with her for a moment.

Mom had been no taller than Miranda was now. They

had also shared a slender build, though her own eyes had come from Dad, and her face from some long-lost relative.

Miranda remembered Mom more clearly now. The quiet center to her father's drive. It was Mom, not Dad, who had sat with her for so many hours, teaching her the complex tasks of daily life. The clues regarding how to interpret people and situations. The strategies of how to unsnarl the onslaught of information that came at her in every waking moment.

She blinked in surprise.

Not *just* Mom.

Miranda had known that Tante Daniels hadn't started as her governess, only becoming so after her parents' deaths. Nor had she just been the babysitter whenever her parents traveled that Miranda always thought she was.

Tante Daniels had been her therapist.

From her and Mom, Miranda had slowly learned the skills that came so easily to other children: dressing, controlling emotions, even how to eat.

Though her mind had thrived under Dad's constant challenges, she never learned to do more than tolerate his effusive hugs. Or Tante Daniels' gentle ones.

But she could remember losing herself in Mom's.

The hypersensitivity of her youth had made a full hug intolerable.

For years she'd resisted all human contact. But Holly's hard grabs—calling them hugs was too gentle a word—and Jon's embraces of a lover had proven they could be good as well.

But when she had leaned sideways into Mom's one-armed hugs, that was when she'd felt the most secure. She'd forgotten about that, but in those moments was when the world had been...perfect.

Miranda closed her eyes and leaned ever so slightly to the side, just thirty-three feet and eleven inches behind seat 2A.

Mom's memory was here.

But...she wasn't.

Maybe Mom's and Dad's ghosts had finally flown elsewhere together.

Miranda sat up straight and looked ahead. Perhaps it was time for her own flight to begin.

AFTERWORD

If you enjoyed Ghostrider
please consider leaving a review.
They really help.

Keep reading for an exciting excerpt from:
Miranda Chase #5, Raider

A list of characters and aircraft may be found at:
https://mlbuchman.com/people-places-planes

A free bonus story/scene and a recipe from the book may be be
found at:
https://mlbuchman.com/fan-club-freebies

RAIDER (EXCERPT)

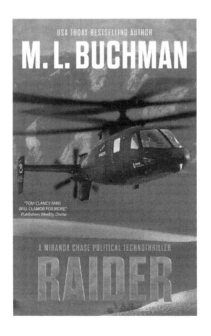

RAIDER (EXCERPT)
MIRANDA CHASE #5

Ankara, Turkey
Siberkume – Cyber Security Cluster
Subbasement #2

METIN STRUGGLED AGAINST THE COLLAPSING CODE RACING UP his computer screen.

The American satellite's onboard software was self-correcting—constantly checking its synchronization and alignment.

His right-hand computer screen showed the geographic shift he'd managed to induce in seven of the thirty-three satellites in this single system. It wasn't systemic but, exactly as required, it was very localized.

On his central screen, the American code he had decrypted was about to rotate. Every hour, the encryption routine scrambled itself. He'd had one hour to decrypt and infiltrate his own code before the door closed again, and he'd have had to start over from scratch.

It had taken fifty-seven minutes for his program on the left screen to crack that code. That had left him only a three-minute window to alter the data broadcast that the satellites beamed downward.

After three months of trying, his first successful hack had finally told him which path he'd needed to pursue. A week to break down and rebuild his code had taken out the element of chance that had let him crack it the first time.

It still wasn't an easy task, but he'd done it! In under the required hour and targeted the exact location called for in the new mission profile.

But, between sixty minutes and sixty minutes-and-one second, the window into the American's code imploded once more into encrypted gibberish.

Metin collapsed back into his chair, drained as if he'd been on the attack for sixty hours, not sixty minutes.

The noises around him came back slowly, the same way Gaye Su Akyol eased into her Anatolian rock videos.

Siberkume was humming tonight, though with a very different tune.

In the big room's half-light that made it easier to stay focused on the screens, there sounded the harsh rattle of keys, soft-murmured conversations, and quiet curses of code gone wrong. It washed back and forth across the twenty stations crammed into the concrete bunker like a familiar tide. The sharp snap of an opening Red Bull can sounded like a gunshot. He liked that the Americans—all it took was watching the many eSports players Red Bull sponsored to know he belonged—were running on the same fuel he was, but still he'd beaten them.

He snapped his own Red Bull because he definitely needed something to fight back the shakes from the sustained code dive.

Siberkume might not have the vast banks of hackers like the Russians or Chinese, but he was part of a lean, mean, fighting machine.

General Firat came striding up to his station like he owned the world. Since he ran Siberkume, he certainly owned Metin's world.

"I'm sorry, General. That was the best I could do this time." It was the Cyber Security Cluster's first real test of their abilities against a force like the Americans. *He* was the one who'd done it, but it was better to be cautious with the military. Their moods were more unpredictable than his sister's crazy cat.

"No, Metin. That was a very good start. Very good. You are *çacal*—'like the coyote'."

General Firat thumped him hard enough on the shoulder that his keyboarding would be ten percent below normal speed for at least an hour.

But "Metin the Coyote"?

He could get down with that. It was seriously high praise.

"I'll get the effective window wider, General. I don't know if I can beat the hourly reset. But now that I know how to get in, I can hone my code. I'll make it faster so we have more time." Though he had no idea how. He'd already streamlined it with every trick he knew to beat that one-hour limit.

Unless he could talk his way onto the Yildiz SVR supercomputer...

Wouldn't that be *hot shit?* (He loved American slang and ferreted it out whenever he could sneak online.)

"Yes, yes." Clearly the General hadn't understood a word of what he'd said about what could and couldn't be done.

Metin considered simplifying it, but he wasn't sure how. It didn't matter; General Firat didn't pause for a breath.

"Be ready. You have one week for the next level test. You are the very first one to make it through. Your skills have not gone unnoticed. Well done, *Çacal.* Bravo!" The general must mean it as he said the last loudly enough to be easily overheard by the ten closest programmers before striding off into the dim shadows of Siberkume.

Metin grinned across the aisle at Onur.

Onur groaned, but Metin didn't rub it in too much. Onur's sister Asli was the most lovely girl in the world, and his ability to visit with her, without appearing to visit with her, depended largely on Onur's continuing friendship.

But to rub it in a little, he rolled back his shoulders and pushed out his chest like Blackpink's Rosé being so nice and just a little nasty. They'd watched all of the group's K-pop videos over a totally illegal VPN to YouTube. It was one of the luxuries of working at Siberkume: access to the outside world—if you didn't get caught.

I've so got the stuff.

Onur snorted and gave him an Obi-Wan Kenobi, *Yeah, right!* look. Onur didn't look anything like Ewan McGregor, even with the expression. Of course, he himself didn't look much like the superhot Rosé.

Raider (excerpt)

Available at fine retailers everywhere:
Raider
And don't forget that review. Thanks for reading.

ABOUT THE AUTHOR

USA Today and Amazon #1 Bestseller M. L. "Matt" Buchman started writing on a flight south from Japan to ride his bicycle across the Australian Outback. Just part of a solo around-the-world trip that ultimately launched his writing career.

From the very beginning, his powerful female heroines insisted on putting character first, *then* a great adventure. He's since written over 70 action-adventure thrillers and military romantic suspense novels. And more than 125 short stories, and a fast-growing pile of read-by-author audiobooks.

PW declares of his Miranda Chase action-adventure thrillers: "Tom Clancy fans open to a strong female lead will clamor for more." About his military romantic thrillers: "Like Robert Ludlum and Nora Roberts had a book baby."

His fans say: "I want more now...of everything!" That his characters are even more insistent than his fans is a hoot. He is also the founder and editor of *Thrill Ride – the Magazine.*

As a 30-year project manager with a geophysics degree who has designed and built houses, flown and jumped out of planes, and solo-sailed a 50' ketch, he is awed by what is possible. He and his wife presently live on the North Shore of Massachusetts. More at: www.mlbuchman.com.

Other works by M. L. Buchman: *(* - also in audio)*

Action-Adventure Thrillers

Dead Chef
One Chef!
Two Chef!

Miranda Chase
Drone*
Thunderbolt*
Condor*
Ghostrider*
Raider*
Chinook*
Havoc*
White Top*
Start the Chase*
Lightning*
Skibird*
Nightwatch*
Osprey*
Gryphon*

Science Fiction / Fantasy

Deities Anonymous
Cookbook from Hell: Reheated
Saviors 101

Contemporary Romance

Eagle Cove
Return to Eagle Cove
Recipe for Eagle Cove
Longing for Eagle Cove
Keepsake for Eagle Cove

Love Abroad
Heart of the Cotswolds: England
Path of Love: Cinque Terre, Italy

Where Dreams
Where Dreams are Born
Where Dreams Reside
Where Dreams Are of Christmas*
Where Dreams Unfold
Where Dreams Are Written
Where Dreams Continue

Non-Fiction

Strategies for Success
Managing Your Inner Artist/Writer
Estate Planning for Authors*
Character Voice
Narrate and Record Your Own
Audiobook*

Short Story Series by M. L. Buchman:

Action-Adventure Thrillers

Dead Chef

Miranda Chase Stories

Romantic Suspense

Antarctic Ice Fliers

US Coast Guard

Contemporary Romance

Eagle Cove

Other

Deities Anonymous (fantasy)

Single Titles

The Emily Beale Universe
(military romantic suspense)

The Night Stalkers
MAIN FLIGHT
The Night Is Mine
I Own the Dawn
Wait Until Dark
Take Over at Midnight
Light Up the Night
Bring On the Dusk
By Break of Day
Target of the Heart
Target Lock on Love
Target of Mine
Target of One's Own
NIGHT STALKERS HOLIDAYS
Daniel's Christmas*
Frank's Independence Day*
Peter's Christmas*
Christmas at Steel Beach
Zachary's Christmas*
Roy's Independence Day*
Damien's Christmas*
Christmas at Peleliu Cove

Henderson's Ranch
Nathan's Big Sky*
Big Sky, Loyal Heart*
Big Sky Dog Whisperer*
Tales of Henderson's Ranch*

Shadow Force: Psi
At the Slightest Sound*
At the Quietest Word*
At the Merest Glance*
At the Clearest Sensation*

White House Protection Force
Off the Leash*
On Your Mark*
In the Weeds*

Firehawks
Pure Heat
Full Blaze
Hot Point*
Flash of Fire*
Wild Fire
SMOKEJUMPERS
Wildfire at Dawn*
Wildfire at Larch Creek*
Wildfire on the Skagit*

Delta Force
Target Engaged*
Heart Strike*
Wild Justice*
Midnight Trust*

Emily Beale Universe Short Story Series

The Night Stalkers
The Night Stalkers Stories
The Night Stalkers CSAR
The Night Stalkers Wedding Stories
The Future Night Stalkers

Delta Force
Th Delta Force Shooters
The Delta Force Warriors

Firehawks
The Firehawks Lookouts
The Firehawks Hotshots
The Firebirds

White House Protection Force
Stories

Future Night Stalkers
Stories (Science Fiction)

SIGN UP FOR M. L. BUCHMAN'S NEWSLETTER TODAY

and receive:
Release News
Free Short Stories
a Free Book

Get your free book today. Do it now.
free-book.mlbuchman.com

Printed in Great Britain
by Amazon

32694720R00202